Utmost

Good

Faith

Utmost

Good

Faith

L M SHAKESPEARE

ST. MARTIN'S PRESS
NEW YORK

All characters in this publication are fictitious and any resemblance to real persons, living or dead, is purely coincidental.

Library of Congress Cataloging-in-Publication Data

Shakespeare, L. M.
     Utmost good faith.

     I. Title.
PR6069.H285U8   1989   823'.914   88-30571
ISBN 0-312-02665-X

First published in Great Britain by Macdonald & Co., Ltd.

First U.S. Edition

10 9 8 7 6 5 4 3 2 1

To my father, Dr John Ernest Thomas

Acknowledgments

I am particularly grateful to David Evers for his invaluable advice on background material. Similarly to Captain William and Mary Sitwell for their information on shipping and life at sea. Also to Mostyn Cole for his interest and for giving me a copy of Noel Mostert's *Supership*, John Wilkes (Lloyd's underwriter), Barbara Conway who wrote *The Piracy Business*, Paul Manousso for painting a mental landscape of Piraeus, and Trevor Mostyn, formerly of *MEED* (*Middle East Economic Digest*) and author of *UAE, A MEED Practical Guide*.

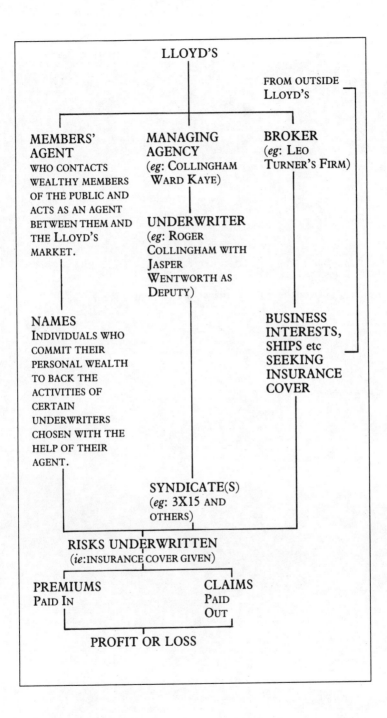

LLOYD'S

FROM OUTSIDE
LLOYD'S

MEMBERS'
AGENT
WHO CONTACTS
WEALTHY MEMBERS
OF THE PUBLIC AND
ACTS AS AN AGENT
BETWEEN THEM AND
THE LLOYD'S
MARKET.

MANAGING
AGENCY
(*eg*: COLLINGHAM
WARD KAYE)

BROKER
(*eg*: LEO
TURNER'S FIRM)

UNDERWRITER
(*eg*: ROGER
COLLINGHAM WITH
JASPER
WENTWORTH AS
DEPUTY)

NAMES
INDIVIDUALS WHO
COMMIT THEIR
PERSONAL WEALTH
TO BACK THE
ACTIVITIES OF
CERTAIN
UNDERWRITERS
CHOSEN WITH THE
HELP OF THEIR
AGENT.

BUSINESS
INTERESTS,
SHIPS etc
SEEKING
INSURANCE
COVER

SYNDICATE(S)
(*eg*: 3X15 AND
OTHERS)

RISKS UNDERWRITTEN
(*ie*:INSURANCE COVER GIVEN)

PREMIUMS
PAID IN

CLAIMS
PAID
OUT

PROFIT OR LOSS

'Touching the perils we are content to bear . . .'

Utmost

Good

Faith

Chapter 1

WITH ANOTHER CRASH the phone rang.

I took my time to pick it up.

Collingham's voice, as expected, snapped 'Sorry!' over the line.

Still drunk with rage he made it sound like a one syllable word. I couldn't say that I was angry myself, even though the glass of my office door which he had slammed behind him lay in pieces within easy view of where I was sitting. Cheerful I was not.

'Where are you phoning from?' I said.

'The station.'

'Stay in town for dinner?'

I could imagine him looking at his watch, thinking about Sylvie. In the end he said, 'Thanks Leo but – I'll go home. We'll talk again if you don't mind. I'm really sorry to take it out on you.'

'That's alright,' I said. 'What are brothers for?'

'Sodding bastard,' he said. He didn't mean me of course. Not then. The phone cut off and I put my end down in the empty room feeling worried but not half as worried as I should have been. I cleared up the office, locked what was left of the door and headed for a solitary dinner and an early night. As an afterthought I put the War Risk file in my briefcase and in the restaurant I propped it beside my plate, but I had no new ideas. At the time it didn't seem so important and the memory of the evening's outburst only served to take the edge off the taste of the wine and ruin the *boeuf en daube*. Collingham Ward Kaye was the biggest marine syndicate in Lloyd's: my half-brother, Roger Collingham, the leading underwriter on the box with arguably the best reputation in the Room at the time. I couldn't see it as a serious problem if he had temporarily lost his lead in one small area of his War Risk empire. It was honest competition. If he wanted it back he'd have to think of something new. I should never have suggested it.

I paid my bill and left. I walked back to my flat in Chelsea slightly out of tune with the week-ending *joie-de-vivre* of Friday night Londoners. No reason. The flat was empty of course. Out on the river the evening sun lay like golden oil on the water, too urban and too much like work. I should have been in Essex for the weekend if things hadn't gone wrong with Charlotte but that's another story. At all events, it did nothing for my morale. Nothing, either, for the muted feeling I had as if a war had started, or a storm, all the more disconcerting for the silence. Into this uneasy scene came the phone call and I took it with relief. It was my sister-in-law, Sylvie.

'Leo,' she said, and at the sound of her voice my heart as usual clattered against my ribs like a bottle rolling down a flight of stone steps, 'do I ring too late?'

'No,' I said, 'not at all. Anything happening?'

'Not exactly, but . . .' she hesitated. Collingham spoke in the background and she turned away from the phone. I waited. 'We were wondering – it's very late to ask you, but are you busy this weekend? Roger and I wish you would come down and stay. It looks like being fabulous weather and the races are on at Newbury.'

So I went to bed early because that was Friday pretty well sewn up, and Saturday would be another day.

Chapter 2

I DROVE OUT of London in the morning, and it was one of those days when May blossom and blue skies race along in tandem like balloons tied to the side of the car. Not at all the sort of atmosphere for worrying about Collingham's business, and at first I didn't. I thought of my beautiful French sister-in-law, Sylvie, instead; of her short delicate upper lip, sweet turn of phrase and clipped black hair that curled a little at the ends like the ruffled plumage of an exotic bird. If I were Roger I'd be far more worried about somebody poaching a bit of her than the marine business.

That brought me back to what Roger thought his worries were, and I turned off the motorway with a corresponding deceleration of enthusiasm. Roger – who everyone else called Collingham including me sometimes. Fifteen years older than me, tall, straight blond hair, big-boned but thin, and the hero of the weedy little infant his mother produced *en deuzième noces* to a Cambridge don called Alex Turner. I got less weedy as I grew up but the hero worship stuck. Roger Collingham was not only my half brother but also the best friend I ever had. He inherited the Managing Agency and Syndicates of Collingham Ward Kaye from his father and I learnt about the City and Lloyd's from the vantage point of an admiring school-boy. After university I went straight in like a homing pigeon, on the broking side.

Lloyd's is an extraordinary institution; much more an intellectual, esoteric game than a normal business. Insurance may be dull if your version of it is a shop on some high street filling in forms. Lloyd's itself is another matter, not unlike Hesse's *Glass Bead Game* where the intelligentsia of a nation invented a system of play that reflected all the intricacies of human life. From its beginning in a seventeenth century coffee shop where the original Lloyd dealt with the ships' captains, to the present day, it has been evolving and now, when the broker comes up to the underwriter's box in Lloyd's to buy cover for risks, whether it's a film star's legs or a rig in the North Sea, the permutations of that amazing system will come up with a figure. From tap dancing to shipping, the untamed laws of chance are put in harness. Each item of news, each event in the outside world, alters the pattern of the whole. For example, all the news of all the shipping in the world comes into Lloyd's. Lonely watchers at sea ports abroad scrutinising through binoculars the plimsol lines of loaded vessels leaving harbour send their reports to Lloyd's. A man who scratches another man's car on the crossroads fractionally effects the intricate fall of the dice between underwriters whose calculations must be adjusted to take the incident into account, and included in the permutations to beat Fate and win a profit at the end of the year. Whether it's a fire in a factory in America or a typhoon in the Far East or an industrial accident in India, there is a piece to be moved from one part of the board to another and a calculation to be made by the expert participators at the centre of the game.

I'm not an underwriter myself but a broker. With Roger's help I had now started my own firm. Since I got a good deal of marine business I broked to Collingham's most of the time, and we met every day, quite often lunched together. Up until now it had gone very smoothly, or so I'd thought. This then was the scene where Roger had his millions and I was coming up behind him with my half. There was nothing wrong with Monday mornings from our point of view and until the beginning of this story nothing wrong with Friday nights. I'd got my girl friends to take my mind off Sylvie. He'd got the real thing. But I didn't envy him. I fancied her perhaps too much, but I didn't want her. I wanted things to stay the way they were.

I reached the beginning of the mile long drive which led through the fields to Court House and turned in just in time to avoid being held up by Bob Skinner and his cows. The grounds were deserted. I drove slowly towards the house. No-one seemed to be about but the sun, browsing peacefully in the cow-meadow beyond the ha-ha and in the flower crammed walks and herbaceous borders of the garden. To my unsuspicious gaze at that moment the permanence of human satisfaction seemed impregnable.

I took my case out of the boot of the car and stood for just a moment looking up the bank of pitched flowers and birdsong that overhung the kitchen entrance like any other man who didn't know that Fate had his perfect life wired for demolition. As soon as I'd crossed the stone-flagged scullery floor and stood in the entrance to the kitchen I saw that the first charge had gone off some time ago.

The room was wrecked. Perhaps not every plate was smashed but it looked like it, and in the middle stood Sylvie, holding a mop, the strands of which were soaked in what I only hoped was red wine, not blood. After a moment's pause it was possible to reinterpret the scene as being the result of some sort of domestic upheaval rather than a bomb blast.

'Party?' I said, smiling.

'Oh Leo! You startled me. I didn't hear you.'

I was the one who was startled. 'Not surprising. You're busy.'

She tried to smile but didn't answer. I looked at the mess but politely; not, I hoped, with too much vulgar concern. I wished I could put my arms around her and stroke the ruffled feathers of her hair. She looked tired out and had been crying.

'Let me help,' I said. 'Bachelors are good at housework.'

I rolled up my sleeves and turned the tap on to the shards in the sink. I found two plates intact and washed them before she came up to me and put one hand on my shoulder.

'What is it?' I said. 'Have you been caught hiding your lovers in the cupboard again?'

She laughed, but only faintly, dropping her hand from my

shoulder and turning disconsolately to the main disaster area. I could still feel the touch of her hand after she had taken it away. I fished about for more fragments.

'How about pouring us both a drink?'

'Oh Leo. I'm so sorry! Of course. White wine? Chablis?'

'Lovely,' I said. 'Where shall I put these?'

'In the bin. There.'

It had been good china too. I dried my hands and took the bottle and corkscrew from her.

'So it's the business.'

'Yes. Of course.'

'Richard Brock?'

'That name!'

I poured out two glasses and handed her one.

'Who is he?' she said. 'What has he really done?'

'He's a marine underwriter who has successfully competed with Roger for a section of the War Risk market.'

'But . . .'

'I know.' I would have said more but we both heard a door open. Sylvie got up, her face shadowed immediately with apprehension. I picked up a cloth and said, 'Where's Grace? Is she on holiday?'

'Oh no. We can leave all this. She'll be here in twenty minutes. I just wanted . . .' She stopped short.

'Hello Leo,' Roger said from the doorway. 'What a mess.' He came a few steps into the room and looked with a mingled expression of embarrassment, defiance and misery at the carnage. I slung the drying up cloth over my shoulder and said facetiously, 'Hello sport. Did the Aussies lose the match then?'

His glance sharpened. For a moment I thought he was going to pin down my unintentionally inept joke about the sort of man who goes home and beats his wife when his side loses a match, but he just shrugged and said with a slight laugh, 'Looks like it.'

There was a pause.

'Well, I'll go upstairs and dump my case,' I said. I picked it up, and my glass, which I felt I needed. 'See you in a while.'

When I got to my room I opened the window, took a deep

breath and looked out. Nobody had tampered with the garden. On this side of the house Sylvie had had a French garden laid out with round and diagonal parterres filled with flowers and herbs that stretched right down to the river. On the left, between the house and the water, could be seen the broad bent back of Mr Chaffey as he trimmed a foot high box hedge with what was probably a pair of nail scissors. No wonder Roger got jumpy at the thought of his premium income being reduced. I couldn't resist a smile, but there was no comfort in it. I looked at him now as he appeared at the bedroom door.

'I'm sorry Leo,' he said, 'this business is getting me down.' He swept one hand through his hair and sat abruptly on the small armchair beside the window to fasten his shirt cuff. His fingers were trembling still and the binge, although it may have vented some anger, had done nothing for the depression.

'However,' he continued, 'I've got an idea.'

'You don't look very happy about it.'

'Well – it's risky.'

'I thought it might be,' I said. A companionable silence built up between us. Roger was in no hurry to explain further.

'The garden's looking nice,' I said eventually.

'Ah!'

When I glanced round at him he was just looking back from me to his own hands with a self-mocking smile. He got the inference. There was a lot to lose.

At that moment Sylvie called from downstairs and Roger got up with a groan at the effort it caused him.

'We're all going to the races with those friends of ours down the road. The Managing Agency's got a box. Did she mention it?'

He stood in front of the mirror trying to find an angle at which his reflection didn't look so much as if it had been slept in.

'Will that suit you?'

'Fine,' I said. 'Are we eating with them?'

'Fortunately yes. Well, let us go and enjoy ourselves.' And with that last sepulchral remark he ushered me out of the room.

15

'Down the road' was across twenty acres of rolling parkland, and 'lunch' the sort of summer entertainment at which English country houses excel. And yet I could see it wasn't doing Roger any good. He drank a great deal and when it was time to leave for the races he said he wasn't coming. Sylvie protested but he shook his head with a distracted frown.

'What do you think he can be working on?' she said sadly, watching him stride off across the grass.

'I wonder,' I said.

'It is some plan that he tells me he will have ready this evening and will explain to us at dinner.'

'Ah,' I said, 'then we have something to look forward to, don't we?' But I remembered to smile, so that my forebodings didn't ruin her afternoon.

By the time we returned home at around seven o'clock the possibility of normality had raised its tempting head again. The house was quiet and I followed Sylvie in companionable silence as she went through checking on the arrangements for dinner. The table in the dining room was laid for three; no extra company. A bowl of white lace-cap hydrangeas, cut very short, cast their deep and languid reflection in the polished wood of the table, and the open window framed, green and golden, the evening of English gardens; homing birds, long leggy sun and peace. Peace of a kind. But from the back of my mind the shadow of Roger's ill-ease re-emerged from where it had lurked all afternoon.

'Where is he do you think?'

'Darling, I don't know. Probably the library.'

'I'll go and see.'

'Dinner in half an hour,' she called after me as I went into the hall. The sun, warm on the polished floor, the scent of flowers exuded an atmosphere of security and hushed calm which began to make me nervous.

'Roger?'

The library was empty. I walked over to the open French windows. The breeze stirred a paper lying on the floor. I could see Roger some distance away, down by the water's edge.

16

Gudrun, who worked in the kitchen, crossed the grass on the other side with a small basket and went back to ground in the corner of my line of vision. I turned to look at the paper, bent to pick it up. About ten sheets lay beside it on the floor hidden by the upholstered side of the chair. I leafed through them. All calculations. Reinsurances, claims, premiums, and then reworked premiums, reinsurances, claims. It took me a while to orientate the figures, but then I reckoned I knew what it was about and that Roger had certainly been working hard.

I went upstairs to change my clothes and have a bath before dinner, turning over recent events in my mind. I had certainly been slow to realise the extent of Roger's growing frustration over Brock; but in the circumstances it was not surprising. I couldn't believe that Roger was actually financially threatened. His marine syndicate was thriving. The last closed year had brought the Names £8000 per 20,000 share. There were three hundred Names on the syndicate. I was on it myself. Roger's reputation was second to none in Lloyd's. I wrapped the bath towel round myself and walked back into the bedroom. That precisely was the trouble of course. Second to none. Roger could not take kindly to the idea of having his pre-eminence challenged.

Since the previous afternoon when he had disclosed the full extent of his resentment against Richard Brock, I had known perfectly well that this financial tea-cup had an emotional, home-brewed storm. He could say what he liked about the threat to his War Risk business. I knew better, and it was time I said so. I went downstairs with plenty of resolution and poured myself a stiff drink. I had no opportunity to speak to him before dinner however and, when it came to it, Roger's solution silenced even me. We had an excellent meal, talking a certain amount of shop but avoiding the crucial issue of Richard Brock. I didn't really want to produce my analysis of the situation in front of Sylvie and so I thankfully let the time go by until it was too late.

The food was delicious as usual; the wine marvellous. Sylvie, although she didn't really know much about Lloyd's, always showed enough interest to make talking between the three of us fun, even now in this obsessive time when Roger seemed temporarily to be unable to talk about anything else. But just when the cheese was put on the table and I was privately admiring the milk white curve of Sylvie's arm he said, 'Very well, my children,' and playtime was suddenly over. I didn't like what he had to say, even at that stage. There was, all at once, an edge to his voice, challenging, almost belligerent, cowed, that boded no good. I waited and so did Sylvie, her face pleased and expectant but with an overtone of theatrical management.

'As we know,' Roger began. It was going to be a speech. His audience smiled indulgently and settled back.

'I've been having a bad time. We've been having a bad time,' he corrected, looking at Sylvie with rather a long look not entirely uncomplicated. I realised he wasn't far from being drunk again.

'I have had to put up with seeing my business decimated, and I have done nothing. Now, however . . .' I braced myself. 'I am not any longer going to let the syndicate my father started and which he passed on to me – which has been the most prestigious in Lloyd's for a generation – be shuffled into second place by the underhand ways of some ruddy newcomer.'

So far so familiar. The newcomer referred to was Richard Brock of course. I tipped the blade of a knife with my finger as it lay on the polished table and it gleamed with reflected light.

As I had said, or meant to say to Sylvie, Richard Brock had not actually done anything underhand. He had had an idea and made a fortune out of it in five years. Just like a manufacturer bringing out a new product that suddenly everyone wants to buy, he had brought out a new package of protection for ships passing through the Straits of Hormuz into the Persian Gulf. Up until that moment this had been Roger's territory. The Gulf voyage was insured like any other against hull risk, war risk, whatever was required, and my brother had been the established lead underwriter on the market. But Brock realised that the geographical bottleneck of the Straits posed a unique threat to ships whose profitability absolutely depended on rapid loading and unloading and immediate unhampered exit back to the high seas. Of course in such an unstable area the ships could always be blown out of the water anyway and for this the hull risk cover applied and was broked all round the Room. But the risk of blocking and trapping – of being held in the Gulf through political reasons, diplomatic warfare or silting and refused exit through the Straits, so that trapped tankers would lose their revenue – that was where he had so cleverly cornered a new market for himself. He concentrated on that and he dictated the rates. And the banks, worried about their mortgages on tankers worth upwards of £10 million, insisted on the cover being bought. All this represented no real damage to Collingham's interests. Professional jealousy's an odd thing.

'You tell me,' said Roger fixing me with his eye, 'no, tell Sylvie. Remind Sylvie, what the terms of Brock's insurance are.'

'One hundred per cent repayment,' I said, 'of the total value of the ship if it remains trapped in the Gulf for twelve months. Partial payment commencing only after six months.'

'Right,' he said. 'Right.' He lowered his head and seemed to wait like an actor who knows the tension in the audience is growing. 'And the banks or other mortgage holders make the shipowners take it on at a premium of one percent. One percent of ten, fifteen million! Every single vessel – almost every single vessel that does that journey goes to him now. But on Monday he will lose the business because, as you suggested Leo, I've decided to make a move. I am going to undercut his market and the terms will be . . .' he paused histrionically. I knew of course that he had dreamed up something suicidal. 'One hundred percent repayment,' he said, 'after six months, commencing after three. I undercut Brock by 50%'

Sylvie looked from Roger to me, unsure whether this was good or bad news. Perhaps it would indeed have sounded quite innocuous if you didn't know the precision with which these rates were calculated; the absolute mega-crashes that could result from a key figure throwing up a window and taking a walk along the outside of the building. Brock's rates were already fixed too low, in order to keep competition at bay. But he'd been lucky and he'd built up his reserves for five years. To compete with this sort of reduction would expose Collingham's to utter disaster.

I said all this. I said it very tidily, careful to keep my voice level, hanging on for dear life to the assumption that Roger's professional ability to calculate risk would survive vanity or wounded pride or threatened ambition. But he kept quoting those figures from the library like some alchemist who'd discovered a new chemical in the dead of night. He couldn't wait to put a few drops of it on the bonfire of his personal fortunes.

'Surely,' I added, 'that ingenious reinsurance scheme you've devised is too expensive to take out now, and would find no takers at the first breath of adverse rumour.'

He just shook his head. 'I've told you, I've done a specific as well on my war account. For the first fifteen losses the reinsurances don't come in.'

'Fifteen! Will you double the premiums then?'

'Of course not.'

'You always said a good underwriter doesn't bank on Luck.'

'These are war rates,' he said grimly, referring not to the cover but to his private war with Brock. 'Are you with me or not?'

I knew the answer to that one whatever he decided to do. I'd have to reason with him later. Perhaps the Board of Collingham Ward Kaye would persuade him. The power, as lead underwriter and shareholder, was all his. Roger poured himself some wine and in the silence lifted his glass and smiled at both of us. I pushed mine fractionally in his direction and he refilled it.

'So you'll drink to it?' he said. His smile relaxed and some warmth came back into his eyes. I smiled back and raised my glass.

'Sylvie can tell them for us,' I said, 'that we owe a cock to Aesculapius.'

Chapter 3

On Monday it rained and from the long-dry pavements rose the unmistakably distilled smell of fish and the sea. I was back in the City near the Monument where my office is and where, until about seven years ago, Billingsgate Fish Market had also been. Its olfactory ghost haunted the neighbourhood and I don't think there was anyone local who didn't have a nostalgic liking for the smell of wet fish.

When I got up to my office the depressing reminder of Roger's outburst was the focus of Polly Rose's full attention.

'You're meant to be our clerk, Polly, not a cleaner. Get Anne to phone Tidy's.'

She looked surprised – as well she might. I usually spent the first quarter hour of Monday mornings discussing her weekend's harvest of emotional entanglements, not barking orders about broken glass. She said, 'Who did it?'

'Never mind.'

'I bet I can guess,' she said. 'I've got a nose for trouble brewing.'

'Great,' I said. 'So that means you know about those overdue claims from Badgetts. See to them.'

But I didn't really like it. It wasn't my style, and I sat down with the intention of getting back to normal as soon as I had my first cup of coffee.

Half an hour later my partner, David Wigan, came in and

the day's work began to settle down. The unobtrusive symphony of small sounds which I find so comforting played itself around us as we worked. Pigeons on the window-ledge cooing, Polly's chair scraping as she got up, the pleasantly industrious rustle of papers. At eleven I looked at my watch. It was almost time to go over to Lloyd's. David pushed back his chair. We enquired politely after each other's weekends, and he raised his eyebrows when I said I had spent mine with Roger and his wife. He had heard the beginnings of the row on Friday before leaving.

'More fireworks?'

'Nothing like what's to come I imagine.'

David shook his head. 'I don't know why he's got the Gulf so much up his nose. The War Risk market is big enough for everyone, especially now for heaven's sake. He should think of a new angle.'

I refrained from mentioning Roger Collingham's version of something new in the vain hope that it might not materialise.

'Something in the wind is there?' said David casually.

'Let's just hope it doesn't happen.'

'As bad as that!'

He leaned further back in his chair, his spectacles positively glinting, his fluffy blond hair already dishevelled. He was always a great one for scandal. I laughed grimly.

'You have no heart at all, you cad,' I said. 'You're the first naturally evolved case of a computerised circulation.'

He obviously took it as a compliment. I picked up my slip case.

'I'd better go,' I said. 'I'll meet you for lunch if you like. Myttons at 1.30.'

Even on that morning the brief walk along the pavement to Lloyd's building still retained some of its charm. Familiar faces, the general aura of being involved in an interesting market, and the sun had come out fitfully again and cast blinding rays into the wet patches on the road. As I walked along Lime Street the demolition men were at work on the old Lloyd's building on my left and gleefully let crash the finely carved stone capital of a column they had no intention of replacing. It hit the ground at a distance and the scrolled stonework flew off in fragments to join the rest of the rubble. I turned into the main entrance and through to the Underwriting Room.

A waiter had just finished delivering mail and was walking away from the booth next to mine as I approached it. The engraved brass plate with my name, Leo Turner, screwed on under the telephone still gave me satisfaction. I opened the drawer with my key and put some papers into it, picked up the mail and spent ten minutes going through it for anything unexpected or urgent. There didn't seem to be anything unusual in the atmosphere of the boxes as I surveyed the Room. I turned back and put the rest of the mail in the drawer, locked it and pocketed the key. I was hoping to be able to pass by Roger's box for the moment without being noticed, as several brokers were standing waiting to talk to him already.

His box consists of four benches with their high backs like pews drawn in a hollow square with tables before each. I dealt mainly with Roger's underwriter for Hull Risk when Roger himself didn't need me or I had nothing special to offer. This was not to be the case this morning, however, because he saw me as I began to make my way across the floor and beckoned. I stopped and walked back.

'Hello,' I said. 'Thanks very much for the weekend. I was going to come back later when the queue had gone.'

Roger glanced at the waiting broker and made a friendly gesture to him implying he'd have to wait. The man nodded and stood, unhurried, with his slipcase under his arm. I took out three slips for credit risks which Roger's syndicate also underwrote. Why didn't he content himself with that for the time being, I thought to myself, as we discussed the business and he made his calculations. He put the last stamp on and hung it back on the rack.

'Have you got anything else there for me?' I knew very well what he wanted and I knew very well that he was aware that I would have, as I usually did have, a ship or two going into the Gulf; vessels whose Hull Risk was already written.

'I have two here,' I said. 'VLCC's going into the Gulf on the 14th and 15th respectively.'

'Let me see. Have they been led off yet?'

I handed them to him. Both, in the normal course of events, would have ended up with Richard Brock.

'Roger,' I started to remonstrate, but he was already picking up his pen.

'I'll lead off,' he said. 'You know the terms. Presumably you'll accept.' He knew very well that, as a broker, I couldn't do other than secure the best quote for a client. As a brother, however, I was damned if I would. I put my hand out and took the corner of the slip but he was too fast for me. He brought his rather large solid hand down flat on the sheet and held it to the desk. It made a noise and one or two faces turned briefly and then back again. The waiting broker became frankly attentive.

'Sorry Roger. I'll have to think about it,' I said, but the expression on his face as he looked up at me made me change my mind. It wasn't any use. I took my hand away and straightened up slightly. Roger got to work again with his pen. Fourteen days' cover. At one percent. Three months and the stamp.

'There you are,' he handed them to me and I took them, I suppose very glumly because he patted my arm impatiently and said in a friendly but dismissive tone, 'Leo, stop reacting as if I hadn't given you the best deal on the market. And don't worry, OK.'

He turned from me with a glance at the waiting broker who stepped forward and sat down beside him on the bench. I went off in the direction of Stadham, an underwriter who would add his lines to the Hull Risk I had on hand and was relieved to have to wait for a while so that I could collect my thoughts.

The morning's business was beginning to warm up. Centuries ago when Lloyd's was a coffee shop frequented by sea captains and shipowners, the waiters handed messages around the room and the messengers are still called waiters although they no longer bring you coffee. I could have done with a drink myself at that moment. I was gazing abstractedly at the silver-backs of the files on Stadham's box when there was a sudden and noticeable increase in the tempo of activity and a ripple of excitement through the hall. With apprehension I saw several brokers converge eagerly on Roger's box; and on the periphery of their unusually heightened field of activity, other figures, caught like animals in the headlights of a car, faces lifted towards one point, their bodies still and wary.

The four other underwriters in Collingham's were included in this reaction although they must have been warned. In the four sides of the box which formed the square their business came momentarily to a halt and I took in the calm stoic expression of Jasper Wentworth, the senior deputy underwriter, who was nearest to me. The ripple of the reaction had spread beyond the point at which the cause of it had been observed in the first place, and on the periphery of the Room first one man and then another stopped suddenly in the middle of something he was doing, and could be seen asking his neighbours what was going on, or listening carefully with staccato glances towards the focal point of interest. Needless to say Stadham was also included. The slip he had been working on lay unattended while he and the broker stood up, looking towards Collingham. At once Stadham remembered me and said, 'D'you know what's going on? '

It was no good my pretending not to, as I was known to work closely with Roger. I did my best to force a confident smile.

'It must be the new quote on blocking and trapping causing a bit of a stir,' I said.

He asked immediately, 'What is the quote?'

I'd never particularly noticed before what a bad complexion the man had. His skin had a waxen look as if he never went out into clean air; the sort of hue that some people's ears have.

'Straits of Hormuz into Persian Gulf,' I said. 'One hundred percent, fourteen days journey, with a three month clause.'

'Three months!' he repeated after me softly with a lingering look towards Collingham as he said it.

'Quite,' I said brusquely.

Stadham and the broker turned back at last and completed their business. I sat down in the other man's place as soon as he left and arranged cover on two of my slips. By the time I was on the move again some people were on their way to lunch but the still heightened atmosphere was prolonging the morning's business. I found myself passing Richard Brock's box just as he was standing up putting his pen into his inside pocket and looking across the floor with a frown.

'Leo.'

I came to a stop without a word and for a second he said nothing more. He is a much smaller man than my brother – small boned, tightly knit, dark wavy hair and glasses in steel frames. He lowered his hand slowly and sunk it in his trouser pocket still looking depressed. I nodded.

'Is it true?' he said without any conviction. He knew it was.

'Look here,' he said. 'Can't you stop him?'

'Why should I?'

'Not to save 3X15 that's for sure,' he said, quoting his own syndicate number. 'You know that perfectly well. He'll ruin himself.'

'Not if he's lucky,' I said.

He gave me a hard look accompanied by a three second silence. I bit back my excuses.

'Have it your own way,' he said in the end, and added curtly, 'Nobody gets that lucky.'

Chapter 4

BY THE END of the week Roger had recovered his market exactly as he had apparently intended and I was beginning to wonder why on earth I had ever liked my job. It was like watching your best friend give a champagne party in the middle of a mine field. Each morning when it was time to go round Lloyd's I looked at my watch with apprehension. I was obliged to take all the broking I had to do on ships entering the Gulf to Collinghams, since it was more than my reputation was worth to suggest my clients should not take advantage of his terms. This meant seeing Roger every day and personally witnessing over and over again, like a recurring nightmare, that suicidal sequence with the old Waterman's fountain pen and the rubber stamp.

When I could I lunched with him or got him to stay in town for dinner but our conversations got me nowhere. He no longer wanted to talk about the new cover except from the point of view of a daily bulletin on the mortification of Richard Brock. Reinsurances, roll over funds, facultative reinsurance, any hedge betting device, the views of his fellow directors on Collingham Ward Kaye, all were topics brushed aside with unfamiliar impatience and a tetchy snap in the look of his eye which was completely new to me. I also noticed how much he drank; but my influence was at a low ebb. Whereas he had always treated me flatteringly as an equal, now, when I no longer was one, he treated me as an annoying schoolboy, and said, 'Leo, for God's sake go on holiday. You need a break.'

So I decided to take his advice since he wouldn't take mine and leave him to it.

It was with this very point in mind that I bumped into Spitty in Mincing Lane one day just coming out of Lucullus: Stavros Spitsodopoulos, called Spitty by his friends. There is nothing like the powerful aura of a handsome, rich Greek shipowner after a good lunch. The surrounding buildings reverberated with his happy laugh as he crushed my hand in appreciation of the joke, and I decided on the spot to go to Greece. I could do with a dose of those flashing gold teeth and roaring laughs and radiant brutal zest for life. And I knew other Greeks also shared these qualities even if they didn't have a share of Spitty's vast wealth.

I went back to the office turning the idea over in my mind and found Polly eating one of her health lunches at her desk. Since she looked a typical example of healthy American youth, with always shining straight brown hair, flawless skin, neat perfect hands and huge unfocussed eyes behind enormous spectacles I presumed it must be doing her some good.

She had long ago forgiven me my outburst about the door and our relationship was back to normal; which is to say that until she was good and ready to go back home and run the American market single handed, which was obviously what she had in mind, she was by far the most efficient clerk I'd ever had. She spent an amazing amount of her spare time rooting around in our files and asking questions in pursuit of what she called her qualifications.

'You can't fool me Polly,' I said.

'What exactly?'

'The flawless fresh breakfast cereal type you make yourself out to be. I know you're secretly eating broken glass.'

She frowned suddenly, as if seriously trying to make something out.

However, my mind was on other things. I had two friends who lived in Greece and had at various times invited me to stay when I could. The trouble was I couldn't phone because they weren't wired up for it. The best I could do would be to send a telegram asking them to contact me at an hotel in Piraeus, from which I could get a boat to the islands. Now that I'd got the idea I wanted to be off before the weekend.

'Do you happen to know a good hotel in Piraeus, Polly?' I said.

'Piraeus! Who's going there?'

'I am,' I said.

'Why?'

'Well – no reason,' I said, slightly surprised, 'except I'm going to take a holiday. That's all.'

'Oh, holiday,' she said. 'Holiday!' She put both hands flat on the desk, drawing the word out as only Americans can, as if for some reason it was a joke at her own expense, and swinging her hair in a circle.

'You look pleased at the idea.'

'Yes,' she said. 'You need one.' But there was no doubt that she was changing tack somewhere in her mind. I wondered why, and I could think of one or two quite pleasing explanations.

'Come over here,' I said, 'and write the name down for me. I suppose it's unpronounceable.'

She came and wrote it down in Greek. Her hair tickled my face and she smelt of something halfway between soap and aromatic wood burning.

'What's that?'

'My aunt's hotel. You asked me to write the name. It belongs to my father's sister.'

'Is she Greek?'

'Of course.'

'But . . .'

'You know we Americans! Omelettes to a man!'

'Ah!' I looked at her again. 'You take after your mother,' I said.

'Shall I make the reservation for you.'

'Yes please. I like surprises.'

She gave me a jaunty look and started dialling without looking up any figures. She spoke fluent Greek of course. I just assumed that at some point during the exuberant phone call that followed my room got booked.

When David came in he received the news with unflattering enthusiasm. 'You need a break,' he said, 'and while you're there try this.' He dashed off a note on a piece of paper like a doctor making out a prescription. The resulting scrawl was almost as indecipherable.

'Very good restaurant.'

'What is it?'

'The Odenthos,' he spelled out, 'O D E N . . . it's by the sea in Piraeus. Have you been there before?' I shook my head. 'Very jolly place but a bit like Butlins by the Thalassa. Restaurants packed along the water's edge, a lot of singing. But if you actually want to eat good food in a quiet place unknown to tourists get a table at the Odenthos downstairs, remember downstairs. Greeks only, but they won't actually refuse to take you. It's the best.' I thanked him and put the paper carefully in my wallet.

The following evening I telephoned the house and Sylvie answered the phone.

'Holiday?' she said. 'Oh Leo!'

Torn between irritation and dismay I launched into an explanation of how I was quite unable to help or hinder Roger in the course he was set on. But she was talking about herself and I knew it. I found the idea of her being unhappy suddenly so painful that I was annoyed with her.

'But you don't understand Leo,' she said. 'Roger . . .'

'What is it?'

'Well . . .'

'Please Sylvie. I can't hear what you're saying.'

Her voice choked.

'Is he drinking too much?'

'Yes!'

I hated to hear her cry. 'He's not getting angry with you is he?'

'No. Yes. No.' She paused. 'Not violent, but strange.'

'How strange?'

'Oh . . .' She gave up. 'I can't explain Leo.'

'Not answering when you speak to him? Strung up? Or worse?' I had no idea what a nervous breakdown really was but perhaps Roger was heading for one. I would be, if I had taken Fate on with an eyeball to eyeball challenge like his rates. 'Listen,' I said, not giving her a chance to answer, 'there's nothing we can do for the moment. It will probably wear off when he's had enough of showing everyone how he can cut Brock down to size. And provided nothing drastic happens in the shipping world he's got time to come back to his senses.'

'Yes,' she said.

'You just hang on and don't take too much notice. I'll only be away for a fortnight.'

'Yes,' she said. 'But . . .'

I didn't answer.

'Are you still there?'

I said 'Yes' just to keep the conversation going but I was sizing up my role in a possible crisis between Roger and Sylvie. At normal times I occasionally poured oil on troubled waters. But as Sylvie pointed out, Roger was not in a normal frame of mind. Like the war rates, our triangular relationship was in precarious balance. Seen in imagination through his eyes I caught at once the suspicious flash of too much feeling if I should try to protect Sylvie at this moment. There was and always had been in my brotherly feelings for her such a poignant edge. In this case it would show. 'Roger won't listen to me at the moment. He distances himself,' I said.

'Yes. That is how he is with me. But worse.'

'It's not really you,' I said. 'It's nothing to do with altered feelings towards you.'

'Are you sure?'

'Yes. I'm sure.'

'Two weeks.'

'That's right,' I said. 'I'll be back, and if things aren't better by then we'll get together and work something out. Alright?'

'Alright,' she echoed, her voice bleak, solitary and unconvinced, appealing to me over the line like a child stranded in a tree that it couldn't climb down from.

'Goodbye Leo. I won't see you unless I come up to town in the morning.'

I hung up feeling like a coward and went off to pack.

I gathered clothes together and realised I'd need to do some last minute shopping. Also my hair had become too long. The only person who was any good at cutting it was Sylvie. It is black and straight and hairdressers make it look too tidy. I picked up the scissors and chopped one or two bits off experimentally. There would, I thought at the time, be no opportunity to see Sylvie before leaving.

When she turned up at the flat the next morning, the first thing she said was, 'Good heavens Leo, you've been cutting your own hair. I rang the office and they said you were at home. Can I make coffee?'

I wasn't really surprised to see her. 'I was just about to do it myself,' I said. 'It will be far better if you make it.' She went into the kitchen and I followed her. She knew where everything was. I sat down and carried on polishing the shoes I had put out.

'How are you?'

She just tipped her chin and said, referring to our conversation on the phone, 'I was silly. Forget it, Leo.'

I felt uneasy. She certainly looked fine. Not at all despondent, as she had sounded.

'When is your flight?'

'Evening plane. Six o'clock.'

'It will be much too hot there at this time of year, you know that, don't you.'

There was a spiteful edge to her voice which made me laugh.

'It's certainly too hot for me here right now. A bit of common or garden 140 degrees will be quite welcome. What have you been up to anyway? You look quite guilty.'

She blushed and spilt some coffee. I'd hit the nail on the head of course, but I didn't know it and she didn't think she was going to have to tell me. 'I've brought you some suntan oil and mosquito spray.'

'I can see you're hoping I'll have a terrible time,' I said with a laugh.

When the bell rang at the front door I got to my feet with a glance at my watch thinking it was probably the milkman trying to get paid.

'Don't move,' I said. 'I'll be back in a minute.' I went into the bedroom to pick up my cheque book and got there just as the bell rang again. It was Roger. He shouldered his way past me without speaking and at once saw his wife through the open kitchen door.

'I thought I'd find you here,' he said. She looked pale enough to faint but her voice sounded so normal and calm, if a little cold, as she replied to him, that I decided it must be my imagination.

'Have some coffee,' she said. 'I thought you were going straight to your office.'

'Why didn't you say you were coming here?'

'I didn't plan to.'

I listened and watched both fascinated and horrified. One or other of them was always dropping in on me when in London.

'What made you change your mind then, may I ask?'

Roger had still not so much as acknowledged my presence.

'What made you change your mind?' Roger asked again. Sylvie's lip trembled and she turned unsteadily towards the window.

'Does it matter?' I said. 'I can't understand. What's the fuss?'

Roger turned on me. For a second the expression on his face wavered but the unaccustomed hatred flowed back in a wave of malice.

'You snake in the grass,' he spat at me.

'What do you mean?'

'My wife!' he said, going one better and flinging out a finger first at her and then at me. 'My wife!'

'What on earth are you trying to say, you suicide malin!' she gasped, spinning round in the window with a sudden flash of sun setting fire to the feathers of her hair. I watched it burn in fascination, like the fireless flame that gave eternal youth to that woman in the book by Rider Haggard. Then Roger hit me and the lights went out.

I woke with Sylvie holding a wet cloth against my forehead. Roger wasn't there. The door was open. Presumably he had gone through it. Sylvie said, 'If I help you Leo, can you sit in this chair?'

I crawled to my feet and slumped two steps across the room. She handed me a glass and I swallowed. It was neat whisky. Before doing me a lot of harm it gave me an unwelcome moment of lucidity. I suppressed a groan as the implications of the recent scene began to filter through.

I said, without looking at Sylvie, 'What happened?'

'He hit you.'

I could have given her a sarcastic reply, but I wasn't up to it. 'Why?'

'He thinks we are having an affair.'

'Why?'

I looked at her now, and I could see she thought at first I hadn't heard. Then she said, 'Because I told him so.'

I drank another mouthful of the whisky although I knew I shouldn't. I wanted to say, 'You've told a lie which will be all the harder to repudiate because it could so easily have been true,' but I found that I couldn't remember how sentences were assembled. The wrong words struggled to the surface of my mind in the wrong order. I could remember how to say banana for some odd reason. At that moment the whole race of women, with all their twists and turns, their passions, sufferings, complications and excruciating graces and intensities seemed expendable to me. I never wanted to have anything more to do with one single one of them. And as a first step in that direction I passed out.

When I eventually woke I was lying on my bed, without any idea of how I got there. I looked at my watch. It was three o'clock. My head ached. As I later discovered, I had had concussion. I still hadn't recovered completely, but my mind was clear and my first impulse was to catch that plane. I heard a sound in the kitchen and I called out.

'Sylvie!'

'She's gone,' a voice called back, and the next minute Polly appeared in the doorway.

'Polly Rose! What are you doing here?'

'Looking after you.'

'But what's going on? How did you get here?'

'By taxi.'

I lay back again with a groan. The inside of my skull was

still resentful of the way it had been treated. Not up to jokes.

'Your sister-in-law phoned the office. She said you'd had an accident.'

'You carried me into this bed?'

'No. The doctor did it. I mopped up the sick.'

'God!' Dim fragmentary images of memory stirred in what was left of my mind.

I'm sorry Polly. Thanks. You shouldn't have been bothered,' I said.

She probably made a face but I had my eyes closed.

She said, 'You'll feel better when you've had something to eat. I'll get the soup.'

'There isn't any.'

'There is now.'

She disappeared and came back with a tray. I sat up under protest and swallowed some. It tasted wonderful. I swallowed some more.

'She had to go,' Polly volunteered. 'Her husband rang up.'

'Oh.'

I finished the soup. The return of physical comfort combined with the hideous ravages wreaked on my emotional life confused me. I looked up through a mist of sentimentality at Polly's huge spectacles bent maternally on the subject of the wounded hero drinking her soup. It made me laugh. She blinked and tilted her head sideways.

'I've made a fish pie,' she said. 'Want some?'

I didn't argue this time.

'You're a sensational cook Polly,' I said when I'd eaten it. 'Now I'm going to see if I can stand up.'

'Why? Oh, I guess you want to go to the bathroom?'

'That, and I've got a plane to catch.'

She stood at a distance and watched me doubtfully like a child, catching the delicate little pink corner of her lower lip between all-American perfect little white teeth as I tried to drag myself upright. I couldn't make it.

'Whisky?' she said.

'Good God no. I hate the stuff. I wouldn't keep it in the flat if I thought the place was going to be infested with women trying to pour it down my throat.'

'Sorry.'

I took another breath and stood up. 'Leave me to it,' I said. 'It hurts but I'll live.'

That was for sure. I had only fifty-fifty success. I could pee but I damn well couldn't pack. It was unlikely that Roger should have kicked me after knocking me down, but something had certainly got in amongst my ribs and my spine. Presumably the kitchen furniture. I slumped on the chair by the bed and called softly, 'Polly!'

She came back from the kitchen wiping her hands on her skirt. The sight of her was very soothing, and not only because she was pretty. I suspected the steam had clouded her spectacles when she bumped into the frame of the doorway and bent myopically towards me saying, 'Oh you poor thing. You do look washed up!'

'Thanks,' I replied. 'I was going to ask you if you'd come away with me.'

'What do you mean?'

'Look, I'm meant to be going on holiday and if I had reasons to want to get away before, I've got twice as many now.'

'Uh ha. But you're too sick.'

'That's how I feel. I need some help, but my God I'd still like to get away from here. How about you coming?'

'But . . .'

'I'll pay.'

'It's crazy.' However, I could tell she liked the idea.

'I'm booked into your aunt's hotel aren't I?'

'Sure, but how about the office?'

'Business trip.'

I was running out of energy even for conversation.

'Gee, only an Englishman would think of taking me along just to carry his suitcases,' she said as if to herself, with a spiteful little smile. 'And it's not a business trip. You're going on holiday.'

'You never know,' I said, 'business may crop up.'

Sometimes in retrospect my own psychic powers take my breath away.

Chapter
5

ONCE IN PIRAEUS I remembered Sylvie's words. Too hot by half. Athens was like an overheated oven with the door open. In Piraeus what might have been a cooling sea breeze came off the darkened water and was swallowed whole by a seething mass of Greeks and tourists. For a man trying to recover from concussion it was the last straw.

'Is it OK?' Polly asked.

'The bed's fine,' I said.

I was wondering if it was meant to be just for me or for both of us, since at the moment she was making the arrangements. Polly's presence was delectably soothing by reason of her neat hygienic American prettiness. But at the same time the dragging sick aftermath of my morning's adventure weighted my body down like the boa constrictor's top hat – my imagination was dulled and heavy.

'My room's across the landing,' she said, reading my mind. 'Come on to the balcony.'

From there I looked down on to the road that ran between the hotel and the sea. Three cars with horns blaring hacked a swathe through the night life. I took the aspirin she gave me and a strong drink and sat down again on the bed. She closed the balcony shutters and opened the window on the other side. Blessed quietness; even some cool air.

'Will you be alright now?'

I nodded, but carefully.

'Sleep well then. God bless.'

I smiled gratefully at her. Even if it was only American night-speak for 'Have a good day' it sounded like good advice to me and I hoped He was listening.

When I eventually woke the next day my body was improved; my mind not much. Dreams receded more slowly than usual, like a backwash of thick oil that clung to the rocks of normal life. Distorted reflections of Sylvie and Roger haunted my shaving mirror. And Polly. Polly standing in the middle of a space: quiet, neat, delectable and secretive. Secretive? I paused and searched the unwholesome shadow of my dream. I needed something to eat, to telephone London. And I needed some peace of the kind that's difficult to get hold of.

I set off in search of the first item on my list.

The small concrete landing off which opened two rooms, my own and the one opposite, topped a straight flight of concrete stairs to the hotel foyer. Not five star. Down there the reception counter was a slab of the favoured material furnished with inept mosaics and number of superficially rich-looking trappings belied by other pieces of equally gaudy looking bric-a-brac. My jaded senses recoiled from the chairs with multi-coloured bootlace plastic webbing, and I thought of the Parthenon with astonishment. There was another flight of stairs on the other side of the reception counter, presumably leading to the bulk of the accommodation as there were fifty hooks on the room board. There was also a glass door to a large, empty dining room and another, at the bottom of the main stairs, leading to a bar. No-one and no food. I looked at my watch for the first time. It was four p.m. The only other opening was an arch behind the reception counter. I approached it cautiously and parted the floppy curtain of plastic strings. A broad white-washed passageway turned the corner just beyond it and I went in. I could hear the voices of several women. At the very moment when I realised that one of the voices was familiar, I came in sight of the kitchen and there was Polly with two huge women clothed in black and a thin adolescent girl leaning on the table with her elbows. Polly had a white plate in one hand held high in a demonstrative way and, speaking rapid Greek, she was dropping items from the plate into a black cauldron. The older of the two women was stirring the contents and they were both shouting exuberantly after Polly; I halted foolishly and grinned.

'Why hello there,' said Polly, placidly hooking a lock of her hair behind one ear with a spare finger. 'How's the head?'

I sat down on a chair rushed forward by one of the women, jumped up again to shake her hand, sat down again.

'Cooking lesson,' Polly said across the gunfire of unintelligible greetings. 'This is my Aunt Electra Christopolou.' The old woman, hearing her name, rushed forward again with a flash of gold teeth and shook my hand for the second time. 'And this is Iphigenia Pilato and her daughter Effie.'

I shook hands with them all.

'He wants something to eat, poor lamb,' said Polly. I hadn't had a chance to say a word. '*Hriasite fieto.*'

Iphigenia and Electra responded to the simultaneous translation with unbridled enthusiasm, addressing their remarks as much to me as to Polly, regardless of my incomprehension.

'My aunt likes you,' Polly translated. 'She says you're handsome and am I going to marry you?'

'If that's bacon and eggs you're about to fry,' I said, 'tell her yes.'

They beat their skirts and flashed their gold teeth in laughter. I started on the white bread, yoghourt, honey and coffee that they put in front of me.

'I looked in on you while you were sleeping,' Polly said, 'But I didn't want to disturb you.'

'Maybe that's why I dreamt about you then.'

'What was I doing?'

'You were up to no good.'

'Oh?'

I looked ravenously at her back view as she dawdled over the bacon and eggs.

'How's that?'

'I don't know. I can't really remember. Are they ready yet?' She checked up on me over her shoulder.

'Here it comes. Sunny side up. Is that what you wanted?'

She sat down on the other side of the table.

'Perfect,' I said. 'Thank you, Polly. You look as delectable as your breakfast. If I was less hungry I wouldn't know which to eat first.'

'What a cheek,' she said absent mindedly. 'I'm *à la carte*. There's a telegram for you.'

'Who from?'

'Did you say your friends lived in Poros?'

'Yes.'

'That's it then.'

'Good.' I refilled my coffee cup. 'Let's go along to the reservation office and book places on the next boat. This is Saturday isn't it? Maybe Monday? Tuesday?'

'Sure.'

The kitchen, never quiet in the first place, was becoming increasingly and flamboyantly frenetic in preparation for dinner. We said our goodbyes and escaped via the entrance lobby, picking up the telegram in passing.

'They're expecting me,' I said, 'that's OK.'

'How about me though?'

'Fine,' I said confidently. 'You'll like them.'

She didn't argue. It was already getting dark. The sun would soon go down but it had left plenty of heat stored in the stones and buildings to keep everyone at melting point until the next day. We turned left out of the hotel entrance. On one side of the road souvenir shops, more hotels, restaurants, offices, cafés; on the other the sea. The road itself, partly cobbled where the tarmac had worn off, was a sweaty mass of tourists and traffic. On the other side, heavy mooring posts at intervals marked the edge of the pavement except when a restaurant opposite had built a seating area out over the water. Already an overpowering smell of meat and fish roasting in the open combined with multicoloured lights and passionate loud Greek music to tout for the evening trade.

'Where can I make a phone call from when I get back?' I said.

'Local?'

'No. London.'

'I'll ask Electra to let you use theirs. The other's in the lobby. Watch out.'

I dodged a waiter with a loaded tray on his way to the waterfront and he dodged a car. Polly laughed. She didn't laugh all that often. She joked and wisecracked with the same cool demeanour as she read the papers, but the thought of me being run over had obviously touched a chord.

'How about a quiet dinner in the Odenthos later on,' I said, putting my hand through her arm.

'Oh. I'm sorry. I promised Electra I'd eat with them. Do you mind?'

'No.'

'You're invited too.'

I didn't feel up to a noisy evening with an extended Greek family, none of whom spoke English. 'Maybe I'll skip it tonight,' I shouted over the music from the restaurant we were passing, 'as long as they won't be offended.'

'Oh no,' she said. 'I'll explain.'

I thought about Polly later as I made my way to the Odenthos. In spite of an unsatisfactory attempt at telephoning Roger and Sylvie and a superficially more successful call to David at his home which resulted in having my head bitten off for removing Polly, it was her delicate image that occupied my mind.

I found my way to the restaurant after a few false starts and insisted on a table downstairs. I was given a place almost out of sight at the bottom of the steps, but I didn't want to push my luck. Neither was I particularly hungry. I planned on a quiet dinner and an early night. Unless. A muted background of music from the convivial floor above was the only obvious tourist intrusion, apart from myself. The menu was all in Greek; no translation. I ordered by pointing out a few things and waited to see what would happen. Waited, that is, with a very limited idea of what to expect. If I had been served shark on toast I couldn't have been more surprised at what I got. The food was alright but the entertainment was catastrophic.

It started quietly with Stavros Spitsodopoulos. He appeared on the stairs with three companions, all men, and as soon as I realised that there was a good chance he wouldn't see me I kept my head down and hoped for the best. The room was dimly lit and my table was in an excellent position to be unnoticed since anyone coming down the stairs would tend to look ahead into the main body of the room rather than round to the left where I sat slightly in the shadow. I wasn't in the mood for a chance encounter with business acquaintances from London.

Stavros and his party, to my relief, carried straight on, and I had lost sight of them until I heard, very close, the voice of Spitty speaking with the waiter and then the scraping of chairs. It seemed that after walking into the middle of the room they had come back to the table hidden from mine by a mock partition built to disguise some sort of an air vent, which ran from floor to ceiling and stuck out just beyond the width of the table. While they ordered I lit a cigarette and wondered what to do. I had just decided on keeping quiet when Stavros' voice said, 'We will speak English. There's no danger of being overheard here.'

What on earth for I thought irritably. Absurdity seemed to be the new direction of my personal life. If I got up they would see me. And if I left without eating there would be the waiter to deal with. At that point I had no desire to eavesdrop on their conversation. An unknown American voice said emphatically, 'Thank you,' in response and I put my hand on the arm of the chair to stand up. I'd have to walk around the partition, play out the scene of bonhomous chance encounter as if I was back on the pavement of Lime Street, and then what? While I thought it out one of them proposed a toast. To Lloyd's. It was not only the subject of the toast but the manner of it that made me change my mind and relax back into my seat. I wanted to share the joke that gave rise to such a murmur of appreciative laughter. I began to listen with the guilty concentration of a trapped schoolboy, but with the next remark I abandoned all idea of trying to extricate myself. The American said, 'Are you sure the new syndicate will be able to meet our claim?' And I heard Stavros reply as clearly as if he was sitting at my own table, 'Collingham Ward Kaye's not a new syndicate, Kinneston. How many times do I have to tell you.'

'There's been talk of instability,' Kinneston muttered stubbornly and another voice cut in, 'A hundred and twenty million's a lot of money.'

I agreed with him, whoever he was. No syndicate, even Roger's, could pay out a hundred and twenty million and stay in business.

The waiter must have come to their table because the conversation was suspended as food was ordered. But they came back to it. The discussion was more general and I missed some of it, but whatever deal they were working on they had started out with Brock in mind and ended up with Collingham. That could only mean one thing: blocking and trapping. It meant Ultra Large Crude Carriers (ULCCs) and it meant the Straits of Hormuz and the Gulf. However, a group of shipowners anxious about legitimate business in the escalating political chaos of the Persian Gulf was no concern of mine.

'My friends,' Spitty suddenly broke out, 'why are we fidgeting on the brink of our good fortune like a nervous group of old ladies?' There was a reluctant murmur of laughter. He lowered his voice but I could still just hear.

'We start with a problem; to close the Straits to shipping for twelve months. Difficult. Much can happen in a year. But . . .'

The pause was long, histrionic even, but no one broke the silence. As for me, I hung upon his lips. In a stage whisper he continued:

'A miracle happens. Just in time, this – benefactor – ' a pause for appreciation 'makes everything easier for us. The rates are cut in half. Six months.' He had finished. He had carried his audience with him. I was wrong. One of them still grumbled something I didn't hear and Stavros gave the flat reply, 'Lloyd's Central Fund is there to back all claims.'

'I thought they wouldn't pay out.'

'Not to Names. You've got it wrong, Stefanidis. To the insured there has never been a failure – '

At this point the impulse to fling back my chair and stride around the partition momentarily made my blood boil. But I held my peace, prompted by a cold fury and determination to hear whatever else they had to tell me. In the ensuing quarter of an hour I was able to piece together the fact that they had fourteen ships between them. Twelve were due to pass the Straits between the ninth and thirteenth of August. The last two, arriving simultaneously on the fifteenth would block it and bring shipping to a standstill. I even had the names of the two ships: the *Chios* and the *Aenaftis*. I noted them down grimly on the margin of my newspaper. Just let them go on talking a bit longer about the method to be used to keep the Straits closed to shipping for the necessary length of time to validate their claims and I could go straight back to London and hand their whole conspiracy over to the underwriter. That is, to Collingham and his board.

Some fool of a tourist upstairs started a terrible noise of singing along with the music, which had been only faint before. A number of voices joined in and I could feel the muscles behind my eyes rigid with tension as I willed them to stop. By the time the disturbance died down I had missed an essential link in the debate behind me. There was talk of a Contractor, and at first I couldn't make out the context, until I realised that they must have commissioned a professional criminal to orchestrate the necessary events. This was the man they referred to as the Contractor. A chair scraped. I thought they were getting up but it was a false alarm.

One man said, 'We must know the name of the Contractor.' Spitsodopoulos said, 'no.' Several of them spoke together. But like a good chairman Spitty finally subdued them. 'Saldi! Gentlemen.'

I thought I'd recognised his voice. That was Andrea Saldi, so I could identify two more ships when I got back to London. He muttered something in Greek. The American said, 'Speak English, please.' There was an abrupt pause and I heard the waiter talking and the sound of plates being distributed or gathered up; I had lost track of which. As for myself, I was fortunately getting the usual treatment for a single foreign interloper and the waiter ignored my table. When the interruptions were over, Spitty got going in a low rapid tone that I had to strain to hear. It was a resumé, a statement that was maddeningly recited like a priest hurrying through the liturgy, of which I caught only phrases and occasional sentences. The ships, the essential coordination of their timetables, and the closing of the Straits with repeated reference to the Contractor. This was the crux of the argument and it struck me as very reasonable from my side of the partition. Two ships sunk in the Straits were not alone sufficient to close it. Additional pressure – political? financial? – was needed. The Contractor would organise it but he would only make his contract with the one principle – Spitsodopoulos – given a free hand, presumably a very sizeable fee and no disclosure.

'Too right!' I thought, scathingly reviewing the careless assumptions that had led to this discussion in the imagined security of a public place. But inconvenient – like Stefanidis and Kinnerton and the other two I should have liked to know the missing name.

'I assure you,' Stavros broke in again, 'he has a reputation,' and his voice changed conveying to me, by the tone, his familiar sudden leonine smile, 'that ensures success.' He seemed to have won agreement. 'We have twelve ships trapped inside the Gulf, two sunk, six months later we have our hundred per cent, the Contractor gets his second payment. Finished.'

That's what I would be if they saw me there. The waiter had certainly been a long time and any minute now he might actually come again to my table. I looked for the Gents – the other side of the room. A side door – there wasn't one. And at that moment Polly appeared. She stood at the top of the stairs. A party of four were on their way out. She started to come down, looking for me. She saw me. As they crowded past she raised her hand and was about to wave. I held my fingers against my lips like a kid playing grandmother's footsteps who had just discovered that the wolf is real. She paused. I frantically shook my head, and when I next looked up she was walking collectedly towards me. I scribbled on my paper with frantic haste and held it towards her. I had written 'Don't speak a word of English'. There wasn't time for more. She sat down with a scattering of remarks in Greek. 'Oh God,' I thought, 'don't let her speak Greek with an American accent.' The waiter came. She ordered coffee.

'What did you say?' I wrote and handed her the pen.

'I ordered coffee.'

'When he comes,' I wrote, 'ask for the bill. In Greek. Only Greek.' I added, 'Do you speak Greek with an American accent?'

She laughed. There was a scraping of chairs behind my back. I stiffened. Stavros might see me yet. I leaned over and grabbed Polly's hand and pulled her towards me across the table. I got close enough to put an arm around her shoulder and bury my face in her hair. Stavros and his party emerged and made towards the exit. I crouched in the dark silky mass, breathing in the scent of herbs and soap.

After a longish pause she said in English, 'They've gone. You can come out.' And I sat up.

'What do people usually say to you when you save their lives?' I said, straightening myself up. 'From your performance so far I presume it's something you do about once a week.' She laughed.

'So what have you done to Stavros Spitsodopoulos that he should be after you?'

'It's what he's planning to do to me,' I said, gratefully taking the coffee the waiter had just brought, 'or rather, Collingham.' The coffee was thick and sweet the way the Turks taught the Greeks to make it.

'Does he know you, incidentally? Will he have recognised you?'

'I doubt it,' she said. 'I've seen him in Lloyd's when he's been in the Room on his associates' ticket but we've never met. Besides, Greek men don't take any notice of women, except in the proper place.'

'That's a novel view which must go down well with your father's folks,' I said.

She sat back and pressed her lips neatly together. 'What's been going on anyway?'

I told her. Stavros and three other men, all ship owners with expensive surplus Ultra Large Crude Carriers not paying their way on a falling market, planning to offload their losses onto Lloyd's by an ingenious exploitation of the blocking and trapping insurance. And so on.

'Oh come on!' she said. 'You're joking.'

I shook my head.

She stared at me in disbelief. 'Fourteen ships?'

'ULCCs.'

'They're upwards of ten million each.'

'Exactly.'

'But why. Why do it?'

'A lot of tanker owners are losing money. Not enough charter. It's been going on for a long time.'

'Of course! God what a scheme! They'll never make it.'

'You're right. They won't.'

She gave me a startled look.

'Blocking and trapping,' I said. 'Remember?'

She nodded slowly. Caught her lip in that characteristic gesture and mouthed rather than said the name, 'Collingham!?'

'But they're not doing it alone.'

'Of course,' she said.

'They've got a local man I think. An acknowledged expert of some kind.'

'Oh.'

I looked at her sharply. 'You know your way around here pretty well, don't you? '

'So so.'

Disingenuousness, very faint, like the scent of a flower several fields away, pricked at my senses. 'Come on,' I said, 'this is fraud. It will ruin the syndicate and take Names down with it. And who knows what catastrophic manoeuvre will be used to close the Straits!'

'Honestly, Leo,' she said, raising her eyes and looking straight at me, clear now, as if she'd made up her mind about something. 'I'll help you in any way I can.'

I didn't trust her, somehow. But I was going to need her. Perhaps. And inappropriately I felt sharply for the first time the real attraction of her little mouth and the white perfect teeth. I remembered the smell of her hair and neck as well as that distant frisson of deception. Perhaps I like lying women.

She smiled. 'It's a lot of money.'

'That's right,' I said. 'A hundred and twenty million. Come on. We're going home.'

Chapter
6

IT RAINED AT Heathrow. From Greece, where the air was twenty-two carat from the ground up, we flew in blissful ignorance above the cloud ceiling until the moment came to drop. Blissful ignorance of the impending weather that is. Spitty's plans had put an end to my general peace of mind. And whatever mental energy I had to spare was hooked on the poisoned bait of Polly's delectable physical presence beside me and her dubious connections. Out of the corner of my eye I watched her pretty hand on the arm-rest. It was white and very slightly plump with tapering fingers and neat perfect nails unvarnished: a few simple rings – nothing special. The same effortless perfection of long straight brown hair, complexion of English purity, huge eyes, long lashes, neat rosy mouth neither large nor small, and perfect teeth seemed to sum up her face with that sort of delectable self-sufficient detachment which children have and also, not infrequently, Americans. I was reminded of *Twelfth Night*; 'Item two lips, indifferent red. Item two grey eyes with lids to them. Item one neck, one chin . . .'

She said, 'Mind your own business.'

I laughed. It was irresistible to touch the white hand and feel the charge that ran from it like a delicious version of electricity. I said, 'Whose business are you minding?' and wondered if she blushed because of the question or the contact. She didn't take her hand away.

There was a crash as the stewardess wheeled her trolley into the side of my chair. She bent, scrutinised the wheel, adjusted something, and turned helpfully. She said in tones of automatic charm, 'Sorry about that. Would you like something to drink? Madam? Sir?'

Polly ordered apple juice and I ordered gin and tonic but I was thinking.

'Tell me,' I said again when the trolley had passed on, 'Whose business are you minding?'

She shot a child-like glance of naked calculation out of the corner of her eye and said, 'Yours of course.'

I took no notice. 'You're half Greek. Piraeus is the centre for marine fraud. You came . . .'

'It's nothing to do with that,' she broke in. 'Oh my God, you're going to be mad at me!'

She gulped down her apple juice as if it was neat gin.

'Go on.'

'I'm doing research.'

'You mean in addition to your job with us in London?'

'For an American corporation. On European broking.'

'I see.'

'I didn't want to approach the subject head on, because if I did I'd get all the hand-outs; the brochures.'

I could see her point.

'So I took the job with your firm to give me a base. I earn my keep don't I?'

I had to agree. She did. She was good. But. I turned my glass round in my hand. In our office she had a better chance of being in the know: a small set-up, David always keen on City gossip, one person handling various types of business. In a bigger firm she would have been restricted to one field.

'I should have realised that a Harvard business graduate with a first class degree could get a better job than clerking stroke broking for a small firm.'

'Oh my God, I feel terrible.'

'So you damn well should.'

She didn't look though as if she was feeling that terrible to me. Perhaps I was getting suspicious but I could swear that there was just a lick of satisfaction in her anxious eyes. Perhaps embarrassment about a London disclosure was preferable to one about Greece and a shipping conspiracy.

'I want to see what you've written.'

'I haven't written anything yet.'

'Too quick, Miss Rose. Too quick. I'll see your notes then.

She sulked her chin over to one side and tipped her glass up. 'Are you going to sack me?'

'It depends.'

'We could make a deal.'

'What sort? Are you going to sell me your body?'

'I could take a smaller salary.'

'I don't care about your salary.'

'Oh! Well then, double it.'

'What I care about is having disingenuous little frauds in my office.'

'I didn't mean,' she said, 'to behave like some spy or something. You make me feel as if I've been caught out in industrial espionage.'

I privately thought to myself that she would be extremely good at it. 'It's what comes,' I said drily, 'of letting women work. They go in for such ungentlemanly behaviour.'

After that it was a sopping wet descent into London and non-speaks across the tarmac. Far from being conscience-stricken she took out from her handluggage a candy-floss coloured cape of plastic and pranced, dry as a bone, just ahead of me. Greasy rain splashing on to the cuffs of my trousers and a cleaner version of the national product going down the back of my neck, I waded disgustedly towards the entrance. Polly for all her delicate ways was a human camouflaged armoured car and I wasn't going to forget it again in a hurry. Still her explanation was a better one than might have been forthcoming. If in fact the Greek connection . . .

'Damn it, where's my passport?'

She turned and gave me a cool look. 'Did you leave it on the plane?'

I looked back through the swing doors.

'Or in that plastic bag?'

I took it out. 'Thanks.'

She smiled at me. 'Friends?'

'OK. Friends.'

I didn't really care about her American corporation or what they thought of European broking. I had plenty of other worries on my mind and after that diversion they came right back and settled where they belonged. I'd come back to London to see Roger, not to quarrel with Polly. She put her hand into mine and I found it very nice.

'I'll drop you off at your flat,' I said. 'I'll have to go then. I may catch Roger before he leaves the office.'

In the City the streets were emptying fast. The surreal atmosphere of after-office hours settled like dust over Eastcheap and the Monument. The place where thousands work and no-one lives was undergoing its familiar metamorphosis from life to death. In another few hours the buildings and narrow alleyways would have the stillness of a town whose population had died of the plague.

I parked my car near the Monument and walked up. The quick shoe repair and key cutting shop was still open. The cobbles glistened.

Roger's office is north of Eastcheap up past Lloyd's. I walked towards it rehearsing in my mind how to speak to him, how to disentangle the lines of our relationship so that he would listen to the news I brought him, and act to save the business.

When I got to the building I thought at first that I was too late and the porters had locked up. But the heavy revolving door moved round when I pushed it and at the back of the entrance lobby the porter was still there. He looked up, one hand reaching into the back of the desk, the keys already on the counter.

'Evening Roberts,' I said. 'Is Mr Collingham still in his office? I want to speak to him.'

'Good evening, sir. Mr Collingham leaves very late these days – if at all. Go straight up sir. I'll call through to tell him you're coming.'

I nodded and walked towards the stairs instead of taking the lift. Unconsciously I chose the method of approach that took

51

the most time. I doubt if any messengers with bad news like to hurry. At the third floor I walked along to where his office door stood slightly ajar. The muted sound of my own steps in the apparently empty building sounded intolerably bleak. The passage was wide and carpeted over stone. Not a sound came from Roger's office. I tapped the door and stood in the entrance. The room was empty. That is to say the great antique desk that had come from some British Embassy in the Middle East with Roger's great uncle was neatly littered with papers and files. Of the four black telephones one was off the hook. The door into the inner office was closed.

While I still stood there taking in the room and making up my mind what to do the inner office door opened slowly. Roger, his left hand on the door knob, his right in his trouser pocket, moving with the deliberation of a robot, confronted me. Behind him the room had been converted into a private study bedroom. I could see a divan bed and somewhere or other, when I looked at the picture again in my mind's eye there was a cup and saucer. I was shocked. I struggled to find the words to begin.

I heard my voice say, 'Hello Roger.' I waited. 'Look – no hard feelings. I suppose Sylvie's explained that she made it all up?' He made no reply at all.

His head was bent slightly to the right in what was an exaggeration of a familiar mannerism. He didn't look at me. His eyes remained for some seconds fixed on the carpet just in front of his right foot. Like most people I had only the vaguest idea of what a nervous breakdown was but I was suddenly aware that here was a man having one.

'I wondered if we might have a talk?'

He looked up.

'About business.'

The look in his eye as he at last brought his gaze to meet mine froze my nerve in mid-air like a waterfall turning into ice. He still said absolutely nothing.

'Roger.' I fought to speak like someone resisting paralysis. I said something like,'You've always understood me so well and been such a good friend. You have to know I would never have done anything to damage you. Sylvie made it up.'

'Have you come to tell me that?' he said at last.

'No. Not only that. I've got bad news about the business.'

He tipped his head back slightly and gave one short quiet bark of a laugh. I began to wonder if he was drunk, except that it didn't affect him that way. He let go of the doorknob now and came into the room. When he got to the desk he sat down and slowly put the dead phone back on the hook.

'I wouldn't listen to you,' he said, 'if you came to tell me that the Japs were making container ships out of fibreglass and brown paper.'

I felt sick. For God's sake how could he imagine that I would let him down. All I said was, 'Is it likely that I'd cheat you?'

He made no answer for a while. He took up a pen from the blotter and turned it end up by running his fingers slowly down the shaft.

'Right,' he said at last, 'what is it?'

'I went to Greece.'

He nodded. I found it difficult. It sounded such a hopeless story: such a farce.

'In a restaurant last night where I happened to be sitting I overheard a conversation between Stavros Spitsodopoulos and four others.'

He remained immobile while I told him the story. Not once, not even when I leant over the desk to try to make sure that I was getting across the point about Andrea Saldi did he look at me or lift his eyes from the point of the pencil on the desk.

When I'd finished he asked no questions. There was a silence.

'Well, what do you think?' I said eventually. 'Do we try to stop him with the law or arrange facultative R.I. to get Reinsurance for this particular eventuality in advance. Or both?'

He put the pen down and sat back in the chair. He didn't seem at all shocked by the story. He ran the fingers of his right hand through his hair and rubbed his ear and then the cold blue eyes travelled carefully to my face. He thought for a moment and then he said, 'Get out.'

'What!'

'Get out,' he said again.

'But Roger . . .'

I was so taken aback I could feel tears constricting the back of my throat. His icy stare cut me short. My mind floundered. I gripped the bridge of my nose with the fingers of my right hand and my eyes cleared. As I returned my gaze to him his attention wandered. He looked like an old man remembering a half empty glass in another room. His brow clouded with the weight of effort and he got up from the chair leaning heavily on the desk. He stopped, and turning back to one of the drawers opened it and took out three sheets of paper. Then before closing the drawer, with great deliberation, he changed his mind and took out a fourth. He seemed to have forgotten my existence.

I left the office. Like a man on tiptoe going out of church I left the book-lined, telephone-scattered grave of my brother and, silent as a ghost, made my way in my own mechanised coffin through the streets back to Polly's flat.

Chapter
7

I WOKE VERY early in the morning, and waited. Eventually I said, 'Polly.'

'Why hello there. Are you feeling better?'

'A lot better.' I stroked her hair on the pillow. 'It's morning. I've got to get up. Can I use your phone?'

'Sure. Help yourself. I'll make breakfast.'

I found her in the kitchen fifteen minutes later wrapped in a silk kimono frying eggs.

I sat down, my mind overcrowded with impressions of the disastrous interview with Roger, my dinner with Polly and everything that followed mixed in with plans for how to proceed on all fronts.

'Eat that,' she said, 'and haven't you got anything to be pleased about?'

She dumped the plate across the table smiling with her weight on her palms and the cloth of the kimono falling away so that her naked body gleamed inside like a lamp. It cheered me up a good deal.

'David will be in the office at 8.15,' I said. 'Do you want to come with me or skip it?'

'Sure I'll come. I'll get ready.'

I'd also made an appointment with Jasper Wentworth for 10.30, but Sylvie was abroad until the middle of the week. While Polly was dressing I ate breakfast and assembled the plan of campaign in my mind.

Our first job on arriving at the office was to look up the *Aenaftis* and the *Chios* in our own records and also in the confidential index. I also had a feeling that we had broked shipping for Stefanidis' company, Action Line, and we had no difficulty tracing two ULCCs corresponding to the date and destination. Similarly we were working on Kinneston when the lift came and Anne, our secretary arrived early. She was as shocked to see me there as if she had believed me dead rather than away on holiday.

'I thought we'd been burgled,' she said, her hand on her heart, 'the door not being locked.'

'No, no. Nothing wrong,' I lied. 'Something just came up. I'll be off again in a day or two.'

'That's alright then,' she said, smiling faithfully. She wasn't stupid. She went quietly into her own room and presumably did what she always did, which was to hang up her coat, change her shoes and settle down at her desk by the switchboard. I got up and looked at my watch.

'David will be here in a minute,' Polly said. 'I'll make coffee.'

I was pondering the details of the *Chios* when he came in: registered in Liberia, paid cargo oil belonging to British Petrol, pre-sold to a customer in Lagos, Greek Master, Greek and French conglomerate owner, and it sinks in Arab waters.

'Look at that,' I said, forestalling his reaction to finding me back in the office.

He picked it put.

'Whose baby is it? The Greek Government, the British, the French, the African, the Liberian or the Arab?'

'Tell me all,' David said, throwing himself into his chair. 'I don't get up this early for conundrums. Who gave you that black eye?'

I thought it had more or less faded. I recounted the whole story. He didn't seem to enjoy it half as much as I'd expected. He said, 'So Polly's quite involved is she? Going back with you?'

'She speaks Greek fluently,' I said. 'It could be very useful.'

'Watch out if I were you.'

I didn't know what he meant and there wasn't time to ask as at that moment she came back with coffee. She wasn't going out again either. She pulled up a chair and sat down.

'Well, to business.' I said. 'Ideas. What do we do?'

'You realise it's August the first today,' David said after a brief pause. 'Collingham Ward Kaye could give fourteen day notice.'

'I'm seeing Jasper at 10.30,' I said. 'I'll bring it up. Also Facultative RI, etc, etc.'

'You know there's been talk on the market about the normal reinsurances refusing to play ball already,' David said. 'Even with everything thrown in Collingham's couldn't hope to cover this kind of disaster. There'll be other ships beside the designated twelve.'

'Can't we get some sort of police action? Who's available?'

I looked glumly at the details of the *Chios*, and passed them over to David again. He ran his hand through his hair for the first time and immediately it reverted into the habitual mane of blond fluff.

'What about FERIT?' said Polly.

'What do you know about FERIT?'

She bridled coolly and said, 'Far East Regional Investigation Team. What else? I've heard about them is all.'

'I don't think they'd be much good for this,' I put in.

'We're so short of time, and they are east of Iran. Still . . . we could try.'

We spent five or ten minutes finding who to get in touch with when David suddenly said, 'I know who to use!'

We both looked at him expectantly.

'SIS.'

'Oh come on David. Collingham's not some government department.'

'You don't understand. Not Secret Intelligence Service. Shipping Investigation Securities.'

'Never heard of it.'

'It was set up by an ex-official from a Port Authority specifically to combat this kind of marine fraud: crime. I only heard of it the other day from Dick Hanson.'

'Doesn't seem much to go on.'

'I'll ring Dick.'

He pulled the phone forward and started dialling.

'Watch how you put it,' I said.

'Sure. Mr Hanson please. Yes. Dick? Shipping Investigation Securities. Yes.' Pause. 'No. Not at all. Just a friend of mine writing an article and I thought they'd find it useful. Quite. What's his name? Phillip Bomb. Yes. Yes. OK, I've got that number. Thanks very much. That's fine; I'm in a bit of a rush myself. Bye.' He slammed down the phone with a triumphant glitter. 'Good. Now let's try them. Shall I ring, Leo?'

'Make an appointment for today if you can,' I said, getting up. 'I'm off to see Jasper Wentworth. I should be back here by twelve.'

I left them and walked up to Collingham's. It was an eerie feeling going up the stairs of the building knowing that my brother was there in that suite of rooms, unapproachable and cut off. Jasper Wentworth's office was on the other side of the building. I negotiated the acreage of corridor with a familiar sense of awe at the vast commitment financially that the whole thing represented. It wasn't a structure that could balance very well on a wheel turned by a madman.

Jasper Wentworth greeted me with his usual urbane manner but tinged with an additional gravity. He was not a man easily moved, or when moved likely to show it. His dark suit with a thin blue stripe clothed his well proportioned figure with an air of substantial comfort and good judgement. The perfect lie of the cloth, filled with a powerful but not fat frame, tall and somewhat massive but still elegant; I noticed it all with a sharpened sense of urgency. A lot might depend on him, but I had always estimated him as a man well educated socially but intellectually only just competent and experienced.

'Coffee?'

'Thanks,' I said.

He turned and poured carefully from a high-tech percolator on a tray. He smiled a slight smile as he handed me the cup. 'Happier days,' he said. 'Sit down and tell me what I can do for you. I thought you had gone off on holiday.'

'I had,' I said.

'Did you come back on Roger's account? He's not well you know.'

'I came back because of some news I had to give him. But it was a shock to find him in such a state.'

Jasper held his cup in both hands and balanced it on his knee, gazing down with a grave and measured concern.

'I think perhaps I had better tell you,' I continued, 'what I came to tell my brother. I doubt he's even mentioned it.' And in response to his barely perceptible nod of consent I unleashed the news. At the end of my story he put his cup on the desk and said, 'Good God. That's it.'

'It's too good to be true isn't it?' I said. 'The underwriter's nightmare.'

His face was blanched. 'The point is the timing,' he said. He put his hand briefly up and drew one hard line across his brow, 'Even without this we're in a very bad way. For God's sake don't pass the word around but we've been asked to give an account to the Committee. You saw Roger.' I certainly did. 'You saw the state he's in. And the syndicate's in trouble with the reinsurers. They have refused to go along with the new terms and are charging still for blocking and trapping for twelve months, leaving us alone for six months.'

'I thought they might,' I said. 'It was obvious. I did try to talk Roger out of it in the beginning but of course it's not really my field. This means if these shipowners pull off their ghastly coup Collingham's will have to pay out the total sum on all shipping trapped.'

'It will just simply be the end,' he said. 'We could have as many as twenty-five ships. What would it be? Two hundred and fifty million? The Names of our syndicate would of course get a horrid pasting. There'd be need for Lloyd's Central Fund because of pure deficiency – nobody reserves enough for this kind of thing. And Roger? Myself? It doesn't bear thinking of. It would probably be the biggest catastrophe the market has ever known, and after recent events that's saying something.'

'How about Facultative RI?'

'Out of the question now that everyone knows the extent of our involvement. In view of our exposure reinsurers would smell a rat. I'm afraid they already have. '

He got up and poured himself a drink, sat down, but jumped up again with a self-deprecating smile of apology. 'Not an omission worthy of a direct descendent of Sir Philip Sydney,' he said. 'Join me in something stronger.' His hand was as steady as a rock and either my ears were deceiving me or that was a joke.

'Could you,' I began. He looked up and waited.

'Sack your brother? My dear fellow, I know how fond of him you are but quite honestly we'd have done it already if it were possible. We're consulting lawyers. But your brother is the main shareholder of Collingham's. We had a board meeting on Monday to discuss this terrible situation on reinsurance and at that meeting Roger's condition became obvious to everyone. But the only way he can be forcibly removed is if Lloyd's debar him. Which they may, considering the reinsurance situation. At this stage even that will hardly help. The harm's been done and the devil has chosen to collect compound interest on it.'

'We haven't started yet,' I pointed out to him. 'I've come here to tell you what I found out by chance – a lucky chance don't forget. But when I leave I intend to move heaven and earth to stop this fraud happening. Nothing's impossible. And in the meantime, Jasper, with the help of the lawyers and Lloyd's Committee, we may dream up some reinsurances against the possibility of my failing. How about fourteen days' notice by the way?'

He nodded and made a compliant gesture with his hand, but it was obviously like prescribing junior aspirin for an amputation. We went through a replica of the conversation I had had in my own office, and I made the best of Shipping Investigation Securities. I didn't want him jumping out of the window.

'Funds?'

'Yes,' I said. 'It would be helpful if I knew I could call on you.'

'You certainly can. Dear boy, anything we at Collingham's can do. And I'd be grateful if you keep in touch.'

'I will.' I got up to leave just as there was a knock on the

door and a messenger came in from the hall with two letters. Jasper held up a cautionary finger, opened them one by one, and handed them over to me. Both were from Agencies giving notice that they intended taking their Names off the syndicates. Politely phrased of course, even kindly, but definite.

'You see? And they don't even know about the news you've brought me,' he said. 'We're already on trial. Believe me, unless you can stop this, we'll be hanged, drawn and quartered.'

Chapter
8

MALDWYN HARRIS FROM SIS was waiting for me when I got back. Nobody else was. Polly and David had gone out. Anne was in her office. As far as Mr Harris was concerned I never saw a weedier looking fellow, and I felt clean out of luck. He wasn't a desk man either but what they called an Operative. Small, nervous looking, with thin dark wavy hair, the bone structure of his face was slightly cadaverous and poetic like the faces of miners in photographs from the nineteenth century. His age I guessed at around thirty-five.

'You're disappointed Mr Turner.'

'Not at all. Not at all,' I said hastily, betraying the fact that I knew at once what he was talking about.

'I beg your pardon, I don't mean to be impolite but I'm used to it and it's best to get things straight in the beginning.'

'Sit down,' I invited desperately.

'Thank you very much,' he replied. 'It's true you see' – he had a mild voice and a Welsh accent – 'I don't look like the sort of man a person would turn to when they're in trouble. Not this sort of trouble. Muscle swinging frighteners perhaps or steely numbers, seven foot tall, but not me.' He paused.

'And I am sea sick too, although I was brought up in Tiger Bay in Cardiff and went to sea when I was fourteen.'

I just looked at him. I thought perhaps he was joking, but

then he did smile and it wasn't because he had thought of anything funny.

'But don't you worry,' he said, 'I always win.' He sat back then as if he'd sorted everything out.

'And you work for Phillip Bomb at SIS?' I said. Just to make sure that there wasn't some ridiculous mistake.

'That's correct,' he said precisely. 'And do you know, Mr Turner, that in the last ten years shipping frauds have accounted for six hundred million dollars worth of equipment and cargo.' I nodded politely. As a matter of fact the figure did surprise me. He carried on in his thick Welsh accent which, while still being just comprehensible, was oddly soothing.

'I look upon it as my hobby,' he continued in the same mild conversational tone. I waited for him to carry on.

'I won't tell you the figure if you will excuse me, but in the five years I have worked for Mr Bomb I have accounted for a certain sum which criminal elements have tried to add to their tally and failed as a result of my personal intervention. How those two figures relate, you see, is a very interesting hobby.' I nodded again. It was a nice clear point.

'Now this little problem of yours . . .' He leant helpfully towards me over the desk as if waiting for me to speak; but before I actually had a chance to do so, he said unexpectedly, 'How much is it worth?'

'Fees do you mean?' I said hesitantly.

But he cut me off with a wave of the hand.

'Remember my hobby Mr Turner. Just to whet the appetite as it were. How much might I be able to put on my side of the statistic?'

'How much is at stake you mean? How much damage they're planning?'

He nodded expectantly. Remembering Wentworth's words I said, 'Two hundred, two hundred and fifty million?' His eyes positively glittered.

'Very satisfactory,' he said. 'Very satisfactory indeed.' I could have thought of a better way of putting it but I held my peace.

'I can certainly promise you my total co-operation Mr Turner. And now the details if you please. Treat me as if I know nothing about the Lloyd's market and give me all the information.'

I thought I might as well. I settled myself in to give a clear account of it.

It was becoming too familiar as far as I was concerned, the ships in the conspiracy going through into the Gulf, and the two remaining slamming the gate shut behind them, as it were: locking the Straits of Hormuz for long enough for them to collect ten million each on blocking and trapping.

'So what do you think?' I said.

'Very nice. Very nice indeed, sir.'

Again I could have quarrelled with his terminology. But I let it pass.

'All the same, a bit simple if you take my meaning.'

'How come?'

He took out of the breast pocket of his coat a minutely folded piece of paper which he tidily unwrapped until a flimsy marine chart covered half my desk.

'Depth chart, you see.'

I didn't.

'Here are the Straits. Here is the navigable channel. Here's the scale, two times 200,000 tons *could* block it, but only sunk spot on mind you. And they might drift. I wouldn't like to have my shirt on it, sir.'

'Are you saying we don't have to worry?'

'No. By no means. Not if the man I've got in mind has got the contract. He'll have something on those ships beside oil. That's what I'm thinking. And if he's promised political complications he'll have those too.'

'Who is it?'

The chaps on *t*he demolition site opposite who had been trying to smash an iron pillar in half for a week and had been throwing slabs of concrete on it from a crane all morning had gone to lunch, and in the silence I could hear the sound of Mal's thumb nail clicking slowly over the stubble on his cheek as, apparently deep in thought, he drew a line down to his chin. I gave him a sharp look to prod him on, but he only took the sheet of paper and started to fold it meticulously again.

'Well?'

'May I see those figures sir?'

I passed him over the copy of the printed details on the two main ships, from Lloyd's list.

'*Aenaftis* 290,580 tons dead weight, 15 knots on 36–37, mix. 1,000 secs. 3100t, Greek. Built 1977, delivery Kuwait, spot market. Trip via Cape. Redelivery Shaw $10,500 per day. Attic Bulk Carriers.' And the same sort of thing on the *Chios*, '*Stavrosattica*. The 200,000 tdw *Chios* has been fixed for six months trading by Shell with delivery in the Persian Gulf and redelivery East Coast Africa. $8.50 per ton d.w.'

He folded that too, put it in the same pocket and stood up.

'I'd better get to work on this one, sir. You definitely require our co-operation then?'

I nodded.

'I'll leave that to Mr Bomb, sir. He'll contact you this afternoon.'

He looked more like a sinner terminating an interview with the vicar than a tough investigator as he stood, his eyebrows lifted in mild acknowledgement by way of a goodbye. When the door closed behind him, I remarked to Polly, who had just come in, 'I don't know what to make of him. He doesn't look much good.'

I happen to remember that she said in reply, 'Appearances aren't everything'.

Chapter
9

THAT AFTERNOON I spoke to Phillip Bomb and agreed terms with him. The high opinion he seemed to have of his eccentric employee went some way towards reassuring me, but Harris was not in any case free to take over for four days. I said that in the meantime I would return to Piraeus and, in reply to his question, that I'd be taking Polly Rose with me. I also gave him, since he asked, basic personal details from her file for him to check out. But the change in my relationship with her made it impossible to voice my suspicions about her motives and connections, so in conflict with the pleasure and usefulness of having her with me.

Shipping I.S. agreed that the *Aenaftis* and the *Chios* were our targets, since the fortunes of the rest depended on that part of the conspiracy which centred on the two ships used to close the Gulf. Also that the organisation for it was bound to originate in Piraeus since as well as being the world's main centre for marine fraud it was also the home ground of Spitsodopoulos and Andrea Saldi. Phillip and Mal Harris had compiled a short list of likely contacts for Spitsodopoulos' commission. A man called Kasteros headed the list but there were four others. Beside each man's name there were several addresses. With Polly's help I might make useful headway, and I'd find it less of a strain than being idle. Or so I thought. Harris would reach Piraeus at the end of the week.

I made other essential arrangements to do with work and had another talk with Jasper Wentworth. But the main problem was seeing Sylvie. Fortunately she was up in town, in their London flat.

'I know,' I said, in reply to her astonishment at hearing my voice. 'I had to come back briefly. Can you manage lunch?'

'Oh!' She was embarrassed. I could hear it. Polly, phoning the travel agent on the other line, gave me a quick glance.

'I'd love to meet you Leo, but . . .'

'I've seen Roger,' I interrupted her.

'Yes.' She paused a long time. 'One thirty?'

We agreed a restaurant and rang off.

When the time approached, I picked up a taxi in Lime Street and arrived early to make sure of a quiet table inside. I didn't want to be out in the glitter of their little garden for once, sun or no sun. And while I waited I had time to assemble my thoughts. Time to review the charmed *ménage à trois* – Roger, Sylvie and myself – that had been the focus of my emotional life until last week. No matter that we had not actually lived together all the time, or that I had never challenged Roger's role as a husband. The description more or less covered the facts.

I drank a glass of cold white wine over my valedictory meditation and took no notice of the menu. My role of romantic admirer – the one who lifted Sylvie over the barbed wire fence while her husband, secure and friendly, walked ahead, would change now that it had been subjected to the acid lash of angry words. Without shame and with surprisingly little regret, in that half hour I let slip my grasp on the vivid memory of Sylvie as she first appeared – a miracle of sophisticated warmth and beauty – into my adolescent life. The image that had kept, as I grew older, the Charlottes and the Pollys in the suburbs of my affections.

I sighed in spite of myself. And standing right by my elbow she said 'Leo!' in a voice so contrite and soft that I nearly got off to a wrong start.

'Don't get up.' She sank into the seat opposite me and I was aware, as I always was with her, of beautiful clothes and a kind of vulnerable and radiant attention. She said, 'I am a witch.'

'Yes, you are,' I said smiling. 'But don't let's talk about that. We don't need to. Honest.' I poured her a glass of wine and turned the menu the right way up.

'You saw Roger,' she said, not raising her eyes from the card.

'I must admit it was a shock,' I said. 'I came back because some information surfaced which needed his intervention.'

'What information?'

'I'll tell you later.'

She was still looking down and said, 'I think I'll have salmon mousse and a salad.'

The waiter wrote down our orders.

'Please tell me Leo,' she said when he was gone, lifting her face at me and not smiling, 'what happened to bring you home? What was this information?'

'A fraud.'

'Oh.' It wasn't what she had expected. 'Against whom?'

'Planned against Collingham. But it hasn't happened yet.'

'Then . . .', She was losing interest until she suddenly remembered the risk angle of the new rates. 'Is it blocking and trapping? The possibility you were afraid of?'

'Well,' I said painfully, 'I hadn't exactly expected this. Just some bad luck was always a very damaging possibility. But this is a deliberate plan on the part of some shipowners to get back their capital on fourteen ships.'

It didn't mean all that much to her except in so much as she could see that I thought it was important. I could have pressed home the point by mentioning a few figures but my mission in this case was to mend some fences, not give her more to worry about.

'The point is,' I said, 'it was very important to secure Roger's cooperation and I couldn't get it.'

She blushed slightly. 'Honestly Leo, I tried . . .'

I leaned across the table and took her hand. 'I told you, you don't have to explain,' I said. 'I'm not blaming you. He's ill. He needs looking after. That row was just . . .'

'Unimportant?' she cut in hopefully. Her expression made me laugh.

'OK,' I said. 'He probably wouldn't have listened to me

anyway. He wasn't exactly straining to hear every word I said before.'

She took away her hand ostensibly to pick up her wine glass. I suppressed an observing sigh. A nuance of the gesture marked the damage done.

'The point,' I went on, 'is what do we do now to help Roger? I don't mean in business. I'm going to take care of that. But himself; he needs help, just like a man with heart failure or a broken leg.'

'*Psychiatriste*,' she said, in a very dead tone in French.

I was taken aback.

'Yes, Leo. I am not exactly enchanted with things the way they are.'

'You're not meant to be!' I said. 'Look Sylvie.' I pushed aside my plate. 'In Guienne where your family lives with your mother with her eighteenth century retired outlook and your father being treated like a national heirloom by the Academie Française I suppose no one ever takes too much mental strain. But here, in this fighting market they do from time to time, and my brother, who loves you and keeps his hair washed and speaks quite decent French has simply got the equivalent of a dose of mental flu and needs your help.'

Instead of being offended she squeaked with laughter, and the neighbouring table produced eyes instead of the backs of heads for a polite second.

'I am sorry. I am sorry.' She pressed her hand on her mouth and shook her head still suppressing a laugh. 'I know it is not funny.'

'No,' I smiled reluctantly. 'It isn't.'

'You don't realise,' she said. 'It doesn't much matter whether I laugh or cry, I feel the same. You say he is ill. All I know is how he has changed to me.'

'Whatever he's done wrong,' I said decisively, trying for all I was worth to convey conviction to her, 'he's not responsible for it.'

'I've been so miserable.'

'I bet you have, darling. I knew it.'

She rested her brow on the spread fingers of her right hand and a tear fell through them onto the table. I made a go away gesture to the waiter who had come to collect plates.

'We were always such friends and he turned against me.'

'Not really.'

'Every evening, this wrong, that wrong, no speaking.'

I shook my head.

'Now this last week I hardly see him.'

'He's in his office,' I said. 'Sleeping there. He doesn't know what's hit him.'

'Really!'

'He's got a divan bed and, I suppose, a change of clothes. I saw it all.'

'When his suitcase and the spare clothes went I thought . . .'

'Never mind,' I said. She looked amazingly confused. She murmured, as if experimentally, 'Poor Roger.'

'Yes,' I said. 'We must get him to a doctor, and you will look after him now Sylvie, won't you? Now that you really understand what's wrong?' The tears had melted her mascara and stuck her ridiculously long eyelashes together in spikes. 'Here's the chap's name,' I said, producing the paper on which I'd written in advance the telephone number and address of a psychiatrist friend in Chelsea. 'You can trust this man. I know something of his professional history and he will be able to sort things out.'

She took the paper, and with the other hand extracted a tiny little handkerchief from her pocket and blew her nose.

'When will you ring him up?'

'As soon as I get home. To the flat.'

'Good girl,' I said.

'And when will you be back Leo?'

That brought the more brutal aspect of my immediate future back into focus with a jerk. I looked around this restaurant in central London; the well organised interior, the Italian waiters smiling as if they liked their jobs, the clientele cool, rather beautifully arranged. Different from the sweating melée of Piraeus and the job I had to do there.

'If you get Roger into that doctor's care immediately,' I said, 'you should be able to have him back on the rails ready for my return. I'll be another two to three weeks.'

★ ★ ★

When we got there Piraeus was, if anything, hotter than before. Electra's hotel had no air-conditioning. We had the same rooms as before and it was true that attached to the bedroom wall just below the metal window frame an ancient air conditioning unit, looking something like a clapped out 1940s copper car radio core, was hitched on metal brackets (one broken) – but of course it didn't work.

'Christ Polly,' I said, 'can't we move to the Hilton or something.'

She stretched her eyes wide and lifted the palms of her hands in a pantomime of helpless sympathy. She looked cool and fresh. She hadn't even creased her dress sitting on it in the plane. I fished out my handkerchief and mopped my face. I had already taken off my coat, and now the only thing to do seemed to wash in cold water and put on a fresh shirt.

'I'll leave you to it,' Polly said. 'I'll be in my room across the way.'

I walked over to the basin and turned the cold tap. There was a burst of air and a handful of iron filings fell out on to the enamel. A few seconds later a trickle of cold water followed. I blotted my face with the starched hand towel that had Hotel Agamemnon and three stars, believe it or not, embroidered across one corner in shaky green chainstitch. Feeling more or less refreshed I crossed the small tiled landing and knocked on Polly's door. She called, 'Come in.' She was standing by the window dressed in a delicate ivory silk petticoat holding a tall glass with ice in it.

I walked over and took it gratefully. She was pointing at the sun with her glass through the open window. I squinted at it. Perhaps the glare was slightly less. It was poised, incandescent and fuming above the line of the horizon as the distant ocean smoked beneath it.

'In a minute it will touch,' she said, 'and there will be a hiss of water meeting fire, a puff of green steam and it will sink into the sea.'

I waited silently and it did exactly as she said.

'Polly you're a genius.'

She laughed. She looked delicious.

'I feel hungry,' I said. 'What's for dinner? I hope you've been supervising the kitchen.'

Her glasses began to steam up and I kissed her.

Sometime later I lay on her bed worrying about the hour. By the process of miraculous transference I was cool and easy, and Polly in a warm and crumpled heap said, 'Oh but I'm hot.'

'Didn't Mal Harris say that someone was to call here at 7.30?' I asked her.

'Holy snakes.'

I dressed leisurely as Polly hurtled in and out of the shower. In my opinion if an Oriental ever arrived on time and left because the person he had appointed to meet was ten minutes late it would be the eighth wonder of the world. The Americans' Foreign Office designate Greece as the Middle East and in my opinion they had got it right. Polly reappeared, combed her hair and we went downstairs where, just to prove me half wrong at least, a certain Costas Amides was waiting.

He wore a beige linen jacket, a shirt and tie, a gold ring as big as an ashtray on his left hand, oatmeal linen trousers and party-coloured shoes. At that moment Electra burst through the string curtains in mid-sentence, her words directed at Mr Amides until she saw me and Polly. Although I didn't understand Greek, to judge by her tone I suspected that Costas had come to remove the furniture. At the sight of us she threw up her hands with a slightly quieter replica of the greeting she had given us earlier on in the day, and then turned to Polly with a vigorous explanation in Greek of the arrival of Costas Amides. Polly seemed to sort everything out. Electra retreated back to the kitchen, Costas Amides came forward and shook hands and we followed Polly through the main room where a number of guests were sitting, to a small private bar beyond the dining room.

'My aunt,' Polly explained to me, 'dislikes Mr Amides visiting the hotel because he works for the port police.'

'Oh yes?'

'And her son – also Costas – was recently fined for illegal fishing.'

Mr Amides nodded dismissively. He found a chair and sat

down indicating another seat to me. He spoke for the first time in perfect English with a slight Manchester accent and I thought, 'Here we go again. My entire life has developed an irretrievable bent for the eccentric.'

He said, 'Mr Harris was here last month and he never mentioned this to me.'

'It wasn't known about then, Mr . . . Amides?'

I felt doubtful about the name because of his voice but he nodded.

'I was brought up in England. My father was waiter in a hotel.'

'Right. Well – how can you help us? Presuming that's what you're here for?'

'You tell me,' he said. 'Phones are too public here and Mr Harris just said to speak to you.'

I explained the situation and he listened. Polly sat on the arm of the chair at an angle to him and Mr Amides never glanced at her. There was something about the way his hand rested on his knee – that and the ashtray on his finger – that explained why. When I had finished my explanation he said nothing for a while but sat tapping the chair arm. He was a very unsympathetic character; he didn't smile or look concerned. An observer who couldn't hear what was being said might assume he was bored, or making a calculation to do with time or money. Eventually he brought his unsmiling eyes back to my face and said in his flat voice,

'May I see Mr Bomb's list?'

I took from my pocket the single sheet of paper on which was writen the names of the four men, one of whom SIS considered must be the main contractor. He held it in front of him for about a minute and then folded it up and put it in his own pocket. Disregarding my likely unease he said impassively, 'I'll keep this, and let you know in a few hours' time which contact you should go for. It happens that we've just completed an investigation of which certain details would rule out the involvement of some of these on your list here.'

His manner, even while saying this, was indefinably offensive.

'I need to go back to headquarters and check. I'll send my

findings with a man who you may use to help you. Pay him well.' He got up imperturbably and held out his hand. 'I can't be of more active use to you myself,' he said, 'because I'm known for what I am. But you can depend on me,' he emphasised the word 'depend', 'for official help and I'll pass on any relevant information that comes through the grapevine.'

It didn't seem much but I thanked him all the same.

'I'll see myself out,' he said, 'the back way.'

And he was gone. Polly turned to me with a face.

'Quite,' I said, 'Still, you never know. He may be more use than he looks.'

She made a saucy joke, and led the way to the kitchen where we were eating with the family.

'The trouble with you,' I said, 'is you'll come to a bad end.'

And she said, 'Promise.'

Chapter 10

IT WAS DURING that meal with the crossfire of incomprehensible Greek going on all around me that I became aware for the first time of what an impossible task I had set myself. Assuming Mr Amides seeded out one or two of those names and we were left with a specific target for our investigations, how on earth would one go about it? While in London I had vaguely imagined various possibilities: a bribed clerk, a bit more fortuitous eavesdropping, perhaps some breaking and entering. A question of fools wading in . . . I stood now, or sat as it happened, with chill reality lapping round my ankles and wondered what the hell to do next. Any man hired by Spitsodopoulos in this instance was a professional. Any professional operating in the highly technical and ruthless field of marine fraud would have bolted all his boathouse doors. He wouldn't be keeping clerks or servants or gardeners who could be exchanged for one of Mr Amides' cat's paws, or suborned. If so, it would have been done before. This after all was one operation in a chain of naughty deeds. Neither would whoever it was be writing it all down. He wouldn't be keeping books – even ones that could be removed before the auditors called by unscrewing the back of the filing cabinet. I shovelled down Electra's food in a daze of frustration, impervious to the excuses Polly was making on my behalf. Electra apparently said I had still not recovered from my 'fall downstairs'. I agreed. I damn well had not.

There was a series of interruptions at the back door during dinner and a continual scurry to and fro of waiters between the kitchen and the restaurant. At one stage a villainous looking figure in sea boots and ragged jeans and a crate of fish looked a likely candidate for Mr Amides' messenger, but he retreated after some loud bargaining with Electra leaving nothing but a scattering of fish scales and some grit on the tiles where he had stood.

We were having coffee when the local doctor made his appearance. The back door was a deep arch, like a residual passageway, with a square door set in it. He came forward into the light, quite an old man with a priestly manner, greeted by Electra with a hushed affectionate tone the clergy would have liked to have and in Greece probably didn't get. I was still deep in my frustrating self-catechism, observing only irrelevant details of the scene around me when, shaking hands with the doctor, I felt to my surprise, a fold of paper pressed into my palm. I was so surprised I dropped it. 'Look' he said in Greek (the one word I understood because of that famous 'Ecce homo') and pointed at the white scrap lying on the floor between us. The inference was that I had dropped it in the first place. He was too old and solid to bend. I darted down and picked it up as he scraped forward a chair.

'This is good,' he said, with a radiant sunny humour and in English as he seated himself. He then carried on in Greek with Polly interpreting.

'He doesn't know much English,' translated Polly, and I said in reply that if one had to limit oneself to one sentence in this life he'd picked a winner.

So had Mr Amides. I casually unfolded the paper before putting it into my pocket. The name Kasteros was on it: all the others crossed out.

After another twenty minutes of unintelligible conviviality with intermittent interpretations from Polly, the doctor turned with finality to me, said something, tapped my arm jerkily with the back of his hand and slowly stood up.

'He is going to take a look at you and see if the contusion of your head has caused the headaches you've been getting,' Polly said.

I stood up. The doctor growled another sentence as he made towards the door.

'You're to go with him,' Polly said. 'I'll come too. He says it's too noisy in here.'

Electra seeing him move away from the table came forward still talking to several people at the same time, but mainly the doctor, wiping her hands on her skirt, nodding her gold teeth, putting her arm around my shoulder, kissing Polly's cheek, shouting at the waiter banging plates, shaking the doctor's hand, pressing on him another glass of brandy, giving it to Polly to hold, filling two more glasses and putting all three on a tray, giving it to me to carry and shooing us all out with as much energy as she had used to delay our exit.

Polly led the way by a passage which avoided the public lounge back to the staircase and up to my room. The doctor immediately settled his vast frame in the only wooden armchair and reached up pleasantly for the brandy which he took off the tray I was still holding. Neither actually fat nor much over six foot he yet seemed a massive man simply because his bones were huge and age had made him stiff. He swallowed a gulp of the brandy and waved us both to sit down. He began to speak. He growled out one long sentence at a time addressing himself to Polly and then turning to watch my reaction as she translated. Apparently Mr Amides suffered from chronic asthma that made it necessary for him to see the doctor at regular intervals. Costas Demetrio, one of the names crossed off the list, needed regular attention for a stomach ulcer. Someone called Julio Drach who apparently did a lot of illegal fishing had a sickly sister living in the house with him. I began to get the picture. Of course, he said, he was only a harmless old man, a doctor who had been serving the same community now for thirty years. Some members of that simple community treated him with more respect than an extravagant old hedonist like himself – thank you, he would drink Polly's brandy – deserved. But they were used to him. Some he had known as boys had grown into rich powerful men. Stavros Spitsodopoulos, for example. He had attended him in school holidays when he had been injured in a boating accident. He didn't attend him now of course. The man was never ill and if he was would want some fancy name from the big cities. But his personal secretary in the Piraeus office – he was a sickly chap. He was off colour so often that the doctor had formed a habit of calling to attend him at the office at least once a week. And one of the filing clerks had a boy with a bone deficiency in his leg. The doctor went off into a lengthy dissertation on malfunctions of the growth process in adolescents which Polly patiently translated.

'Ask him,' I said to Polly, 'if Kasteros is ever ill.'

I repeated the name, keeping my glance casual. And however much one doubts in retrospect a fleeting impression received, for a moment I knew the name meant something to her. 'Does that name mean something?'

Thelamion watched in silence.

She said, 'No. What makes you think so?' and the sheer candour of her look would have convinced me of duplicity if it hadn't mixed, as I looked at her, with memories of another kind.

Thelamion stirred like a great whale in his chair when he heard the question and threw me a wicked glance. He smiled innocently at Polly as he answered that alas it happened to be the case that poor old Kasteros had had two fingers shot off in a sort of game that he was playing one night with friends after dinner. Hardly a serious matter, but a mild blood infection had set in, which made the wound inordinately painful. The doctor was able to be very helpful in his humble way and they had struck up something of a friendship. Since Kasteros had a big estate and large offices attached he needed quite a number of staff and servants. They couldn't all be healthy of course, and so it had become an understood thing for the old doctor to call. His presence was almost as unremarked about the place as Kasteros himself, and of course he had to deal more or less confidentially with whoever needed his services. Lask week it had been the cook. This week – who knows? He spread his hands wide and laughed a great roar. I guessed that just about every Greek alive now must have seen the film of Zorba. And when he had finished laughing, still smiling benevolently at Polly and myself, he started to get up.

'I think,' he said very deliberately, 'that you need regular attention to make sure that you recover completely from that injury of yours. Head wounds can be tricky.' Polly's translation had taken on a certain dry classroom recitation tone. 'My fees are £500 for each consultation.' Good heavens, I thought, he must be trying to buy the Bank of Athens.

'If this is acceptable I will call once a day.'

I nodded. Polly said more than just yes and the old villain laughed and made a *sotto voce* reply that was not translated. I was amazed to see Polly going pink at the edges. He took a pad out of his coat pocket. It was a prescription pad. He dashed off a line with a flourish and handed it to me.

'You're to take that to the chemist,' Polly translated. 'He says it's very important for your health and also for his own.'

'I bet it is.'

The old reprobate said something like, 'What did he say?' but Polly just laughed. She refused to translate. It wasn't much of course, but it kept him guessing. She was a girl who usually got her own back. He shook hands and left with Polly still in attendance. I walked over to the window and looked at my watch. It was nearly midnight.

Chapter 11

I WOKE UP the next morning curiously aware, as if I had suddenly developed a twin soul, of Kasteros, the one name left on the list – the man marked out by Amides, waking to the same daylight within the radius of the same sounds. This, I thought, is what it feels like to have an opponent. Roger, who fancied he had had an opponent for some time, no doubt felt the same about Richard Brock. I could feel almost a bond; a potential for transcending normal reality as if Kasteros was in some way linked to myself by more than just the inevitable repercussions of his plans. This man who was probably stirring in his sleep not far away could turn his mind if he chose to the shipping conspiracy and go over the details item by item; the method of sinking the blockade, who would do it, how the act of sabotage should be rendered especially lethal and also political and, if Harris was right, what extra cargo there might be.

'Wake up,' Polly said.

'I am awake.'

I went back to my room to wash and dress.

Then I laid a map of the town on the undisturbed cover of the bed. One long commercial road, the Acti Maouli, ran the whole length of the Piraeus bay. At the end of it the huge building of the Posidonia housed the yearly shipping fair held in June, like the Motor Show in England. The Acti Maouli was lined with hotels, restaurants, souvenir shops and commercial offices. Our own hotel was on it – I traced on the map the main road up from the Acti Maouli to the Platia and deduced from that the more or less precise location of Kasteros' offices of Webb Draft International. To find the location of his private house on the map I had to follow the road out of Piraeus towards Salamis through the district called the Perama to where the suburbs gave way to more open land and there was space for his palatial estate.

'We're going to have a look,' I said to Polly, who had come in behind me with no shoes on her feet, 'at this man's offices and generally sort out the geography. OK? So get something on your feet and let's be off.'

'No breakfast?'

'Yes, breakfast first. But step out, Miss Rose. I want to cover some ground before lunch.'

Needless to say she stepped out fine – I was the one whose skin was gradually shed on to the inner soles of a pair of thoroughly unsuitable London shoes. I eventually bought some sandals and by lunchtime we got back to that place I'd marked out on the Acti Maouli. Alongside the water's edge was a restaurant and across the road the villainous facade of Kasteros' thriving business with Webb International in gold letters above the door. We sat down, turning our backs to the sea where darts of fiery sunlight sprang from every lapping wave. The office had the advantage of being one quite small building in the line up of commercial premises occupied solely by Webb Draft International and whoever went in or out must have business with the firm; presumably cargo, charter, personnel, or of course piracy of one sort or another.

We ate our lunch of charcoal-grilled fish and green salad, drank some white wine and watched the glass office door. In the space of about half an hour three people came and went. A Greek or Turkish businessman of middle age, a badly dressed young man and a very gross woman in a frightful cheap frock who came across to the booth by the tables and bought cigarettes. Her fingers were stained with nicotine and carbon. The waiter made some remark to her as he sorted the change and she responded, addressing Polly. Her hands looked small and delicate and dirty as she answered with animation, the deep green of her dress walloping in folds across her vast behind. The conversation went on for some minutes until she spotted someone in the crowd whose approach precipitated her in a rush of consternation back to the glass door and out of sight. I followed the line of Polly's gaze. A man was walking along the pavement whose appearance even from a distance drew the eye. Although he had curly ginger hair one could not have mistaken him for a European tourist. His heavy features, in bizarre contrast, were lit with an expression of unequivocal good humour that was endorsed by all his movements. His legs, his arms, his hat, his suit, were all as good humoured as his face. He waved across to the cafe and the waiter bowed happily. I thought I saw his eye take in Polly with a sharp interest which she was certainly returning, before he turned aside and flung open the glass door.

'Mr Kasteros,' she said to me. She had pushed her chair back when we first sat down, exhausted and sweaty-footed so that her conversation with the waiter and woman had been carried on at some distance. The waiter now acknowledged me with a smile and had time to say, 'Very rich man,' and with an expansive circular gesture, 'Palikari,' before being forced to respond to the demands of another customer.

'What's palikari?' I asked Polly.

'A kind of virile, wild fellow: a typical Greek romantic man's man who is a dare-devil outlaw, good at heart. The gypsies sing songs about them the whole time. It's a kind of national ideal.'

'And Kasteros is one of them!'

She stretched her eyes and nodded. 'He says so.'

I laughed. I liked the look of Kasteros: a generous villain; a worthy opponent. 'What was the fat lady talking about?'

'She was complaining about the work,' Polly said.

'How come?'

I was keeping my eyes fixed on the building, half distracted, half attentive, the image of Kasteros burnt on the retina of my inner eye. The picture revealed so far – the people, the buildings, the surrounding scene – seemed solid, matt and impregnable. But somewhere there must be a crack.

'What do you mean how come?'

She was turned half away trying to catch the waiter's eye to ask for another drink, but he was talking with great animation at the water's edge to someone below the wall, presumably in a boat.

'Her friend's ill. You know – the girl who normally works with her in the office.'

'Why don't you offer to help out for a day or two?'

'I did.'

'And what did she say?'

'Impossible. Apparently they never use temps of any kind. Office policy.'

I glanced at my watch. It was four forty-five. 'Let's go,' I said. I got up and walked across to where the waiter was still standing and paid our bill. As I turned back to the table the office door opened and the fat girl came out again and started to hurry across the road. I paused taking longer than I needed to put the notes back in my wallet and sort out my change. She went straight over to Polly. A bunch of sea-gulls dive-bombed a scattering of scraps thrown into the water. From the distance on the other side of the bay a ship blew its horn as it moved out to sea. The warning note sounded deeply across the background of the churning mass of tourist activity. After a brief conversation with Polly, the over-worked typist hurried back across the road and Polly stood up.

'What was all that about?' I said as I joined her.

'Apparently I can work in the office after all,' she said brilliantly, 'or at least probably. They'll see me in the morning. I told them I can type, you see, and speak Greek and English. Isn't that great?'

'Terrific,' I said, 'but why the change of mind?'

I wasn't looking at her carefully; we were walking side by side back in the direction of the hotel.

'I really don't know', she said. 'Come quickly. You don't want them looking at us.'

I was all too aware of it. I could feel a tingling sensation down the back of my neck.

'My God, I'm scared,' she said unconvincingly. I had an unpleasant feeling like a swimmer who was being caught in an undertow and noticed for the first time that all his efforts were taking him in the wrong direction.

'You don't already know that man do you?'

'What do you mean?' she said.

I pictured Kasteros again sharply in my mind; a large, easy man with his curly ginger hair and expansive expression looking alertly about him as he walked, turning his head to the cafe, greeting the waiter, his glance briefly on Polly, myself?

'What do you mean, Leo?'

'Kasteros.'

'What about him?' She wasn't usually so slow on the uptake.

'Do you know him?'

I half expected her to be annoyed but that wasn't her reaction either. She just turned her face incredulously towards me, her large innocent eyes blatantly magnified behind the spectacles, and then laughed.

'Honestly!' she exclaimed. 'Do you think I wouldn't have told you if I did.'

Her saying that put an idea into my mind but I kept it to myself. Life has taught me that when people intend to do the dirty on you they often volunteer unsolicited reassurance along the opposite lines.

We got back to the hotel and went straight up to our rooms. I temporarily put business out of my mind and concentrated on the physical pleasure of getting clean and cool again, and in her room across the landing Polly was doing the same. The dim green light that filtered through the shutters which I had left drawn, and the cool of the green terrazza tiles of the floor against my scorched and naked feet was balm of a memorable kind. I was wrapped in a towel combing my wet hair when there was a knock at the door. I leaned over and opened it with one hand while still running the cold tap, but it wasn't Polly. A man I didn't recognise looked at me silently for a moment, made what I assumed to be an apology – he had mistaken the room number, the name, the floor, I couldn't tell – and receded noisily down the stairs. I dressed, picked up the map and crossed the narrow landing to Polly's door. She was still in the shower but she called to me to come in and I sat down at the table, identical to the one in my own room, and laid out the map. In each of our rooms the shower consisted of a glass cube set into the wall which leaked copiously on to the tiles. The wash basin was in the main part of the room with the mirror above it.

'I'd do anything for a glass of gin and tonic,' she said.

'I'll get one.'

I got up.

'Make sure they don't put soda.'

I had to queue at the bar. In the semi-darkness of this shabby inner room a crowd of exhausted holiday-makers made the air throb with the aftermath of heat and exertion. I bought a bottle of gin and two of tonic to save on future expeditions. Just as I took up two glasses and turned to go Electra emerged from the door to the family's part of the hotel, deferentially leading Dr Thelamion. Her face lit up at the sight of me and she seized my face in both her hands and patted me on the cheek as she handed over the great man. He looked just like he had done yesterday; dignified, slightly dirty, admirable, his expression edged with the minute glimmer of complicity at his own deceit. The way he shook my hand demonstrated no knowledge of anatomy. I massaged the cracked bones as I reloaded, plus glasses, and walked upstairs ahead of him, thinking to myself that Polly would know that we were coming because of the noise. She opened the door ahead of us and greeted him exuberantly. As soon as the door of the room was closed behind the three of us, however, he put his bag down on the table and turned to Polly with a change of expression, speaking rapidly to her in Greek. She said eventually to me, 'He saw one of K's men leave the hotel as he arrived.'

I said nothing. For some reason I felt sure that it was the man who had knocked on my door while I was washing but I saved the idea for later. Thelamion stood by the window holding his bottom lip with the fingers of his right hand and staring fixedly through the slats of the blind. But then he roused himself, clapped his hands together and started to talk again. His theatrical commentary on his own words might have made it possible to understand him if one even had a rudimentary knowledge of Greek. As it was Polly explained that he had gone out to K's house in the morning. The cook needed to be persuaded to have an operation for a hernia and two men had called whose visit would have gone unremarked by Thelamion if it were not for the fact that he had been offered a very special drink as a result. These two men had apparently been to the estate on business some five times in the past month, driving from Athens in a car with an Athens registration, and bringing with them on the second visit the crate of bottles unobtainable outside Russia. What vodka! What a drink! What a spirit of man's own fire from the gut of nature. Knowing bloody well that the drink itself was immaterial to me compared to the donors of this life blood, Thelamion ranted with histrionic splendour, sinking his voice to a whisper, like a preacher talking of heaven to the condemned, and rose to a crescendo putting the points of his fingers to his mouth and rolling his eyes.

'Does he have the car number?' I asked Polly.

She relayed the question.

He took a piece of paper out of his waistcoat pocket and handed it over. I couldn't think what to do with it or what it might prove either way. Kasteros would likely have, at any moment, a number of pots on the boil. There was no reason why this should be ours. However, as a straight charter firm, Webb would not have anything to do with the Russian fleet. Although the list of the Russian maritime fleet is so huge it takes up nine to ten pages of the Lloyd's List, their voyages, fixings and insurance are all kept to the national state companies, so even a London broker would only know about them through reinsurance, which they still farm out to Lloyd's and which Lloyd's still take in spite of the fact that the whole eastern block constantly attacks the fixing rates. One might wonder why on earth Lloyd's continue to have anything at all to do with Russian marine insurance. They had even found a way round the mandatory quarterly payment of premiums by introducing a premium reserve for six months; and still Lloyd's continue to take an interest because presumably the whole fleet, reinsured through them on a treaty basis, would eventually according to their contract have to pay and make money for underwriters. However, all that was beside the point. It merely flashed through my mind as if a trip switch had activated a section of my office file. What was relevant was that Webb International couldn't be fixing legitimate charter for Russian shipping.

'It is known,' I asked Polly, 'who these two Russians are?'

'Yes. They were two commercial attachés on the staff of the Russian Embassy in Athens.'

I handed over to Thelamion the equivalent in Greek drachmas of 500 English pounds and he took it.

'Is there anything else?'

Polly translated. He shook his head without smiling. He seemed suddenly to have remembered something again that disquieted him. He was packing the money down into the depths of the doctor's bag with an expression of distracted concentration. He shut the clasp and ponderously straightened his back. He could make no promises but he'd had an idea. Tomorrow or the next day he would call at the same time. Would I please not forget to appear ill and complain occasionally of headache.

Polly asked him what it was that he had on his mind but he wouldn't say. I opened the door for him. My mind was very much occupied with the news he had brought us, not the man himself. He stood a moment at the entrance to the room, his eyelids dropping slowly in a sort of double wink of farewell. Then he stepped out on to the head of the stairs and pointed in Polly's direction. 'Not good,' he mouthed and barred his lips with his fingers. Before I could close the door he whispered, 'Four o'clock,' and pointed downwards emphatically towards the entrance of the hotel. Out of sight behind me in the room Polly couldn't see him. Before I could react to ask a question he was gone. I went back into the room but I said nothing about my private arrangement with Thelamion.

Chapter
12

POLLY WANTED TO go dancing at Perama. I'd hired a car so that we could drive along the Salamina road and after dinner when the whole population of Greece was out and catching up on life we joined the melée. The plan was a good one for me. I needed some assistance to fend off Polly's psychic probings from the assignation Thelamion had made with me. The night was brilliant with stars above the electric light below breaking off with a sudden change of tone towards the incalculable darkness of the sea. Before the colonels' régime the cafés of the Perama had a special line in sleazy zip. We found one that bore unmistakable signs of its previous incarnation as a brothel with its ancient decor of scarlet wallpaper starred with tiny brilliant green flowers. It reeked of scent bedded in stale cloth and wild Greek music made the candles flicker.

'He must have international contacts,' Polly said for the second time. We were discussing Thelamion's story of the visitors with the vodka. 'Russians have cargo after all. Why should it be so unlikely for them to be involved with a shipping firm?'

'I don't know.' I said. Her body softened in a quiet phase of the music and I gathered her against me with a sudden feeling of sharp sadness. Duplicity isn't really amusing, and the childlike candour of her manner touched my heart even while I distrusted her. And Thelamion's uneasiness and the expectation of what he had to tell me in private hung over me.

'I can find out tomorrow,' she said, 'when I get my hands on his paperwork.'

'Yes, you can can't you,' I murmured. I wanted to get her home and fast asleep by three a.m. The crowd around us was in keeping with the atmosphere. Impervious to tourist instrusion the ancient habitués of the place and their generation of successors rampaged through their night life as they always had done. Two huge and tough-looking Greek sailors in a close embrace danced a tango. Prostitutes and gypsies made careful forays among the crowds. An old woman pushed her way across the crowded dance floor and thrust a bunch of flowers in Polly's hand. Polly spoke to her in Grek and I felt around in my pocket for some change. When we eventually got rid of her I said, 'What was all that about?'

'Oh, you know – the usual.' She seemed suddenly to have had enough of the place.

'I'm tired,' she said, 'let's go home.' I wasn't waiting for a second offer. It was already half past one.

Later on I found it was I who was tired. More so than I thought. Simulating sleep beside Polly dreams came up and nudged the inside of my eyelids.

'I'm going into my own bed, Pol,' I said in a whisper. 'It's too hot here.'

I did as I said I would. I shut the door, threw back the sheet and lay down with my eyes closed and waited. After about ten minutes I heard a slight sound and the handle of my door started to turn. I watched it inch round the minus side of the clock. She had plenty of patience. When it stopped I closed my eyes and breathed deeply. I couldn't even hear her enter the room but I knew she was there. When she had checked up on me she went. I opened my eyes to see, in the dim shadow, the final minute settling of the lock. When I had found out what Thelamion had to say to me it would be time to ask Polly Rose a few straight questions.

My watch showed 3.40. I waited another five minutes and then got up and put on my clothes.

Even then I was conscious of every sound I made. Polly's room and mine were the only two opening off the short flight of steps from this side of the foyer. I used her technique for opening the door. The perpetual racket of the daytime was stilled. I tiptoed down the stone steps and looked into reception. No one. The door was bolted but not locked. The bolt sprung with what would have been a crash if I hadn't used all my strength to control it. I stepped out and waited.

The street was deserted. Glimmers from the water made no sound. I jumped when something jabbed me on the thigh. A child much too small for anything around at this hour ran a few yards and then stopped and looked back. I followed. He kept up that routine until we were on the open road and the houses had given way to scrub land on one side and the sea on the other. It took hours. I looked at my watch; 4.45. Tired out.

Now we were leaving the road and going down to the sea. My guide ran from cover to cover. I tried it and felt a fool. I'd walk. If he made himself invisible I'd lose him with any luck and I could go home to bed. The stones slid under my feet as I climbed down to a group of huge rocks where I'd last seen him. There was no-one there. Just the water whose unseemly struggle took no account of the hours of rest. I sat down and waited. I'd give it ten more minutes and then I'd have to go back to be there when Polly woke.

A fall of stone behind brought me to my feet. Thelamion's hand on my shoulder made me collapse again as if a tree trunk had tipped on me. He crouched beside me, still with his arm on my shoulder. His strength in his youth must have been phenomenal. Just before my spine became permanently crushed he relaxed and sat down with his back against a rock.

'Friend.'

It was only the second time I'd heard him speak any English.

'This is too dangerous for an old man.'

'Young ones too,' I said.

He took a small fold of paper out of his pocket, opened it briefly, folded it again and handed it to me with a sigh. He said, 'This come with vodka.'

I was about to speak (I wanted to ask him about Polly) when there was a sudden noise of a car engine. He listened. I thought it was just a car going somewhere at 5 o'clock in the morning.

He put his hand on my shoulder again to keep me where I was and stood up.

'What is it, Thelamion?'

He stood for a moment quite still not answering. I could see his expression dimly in the moonlight.

'That was just a car on the coast road wasn't it?'

His whispered reply sounded distant, as if it already came from the land of the dead. 'The car stopped, turned off it's lights. Listen.'

I could hear nothing except perhaps from the land direction just the faint rattle of stones.

'They are gone,' he said, but paused, lacking conviction.

'Who?'

'I must go. You wait.' He never looked back down at me where I still crouched by the rock, but kept his face toward the dark recesses of the beach. 'Goodbye my friend.'

I did as he said.

He began to walk back across the rock-strewn margin of the bay. I watched him, losing sight every now and then of the black shadow of his body against the black shadow of the rocks. There was no sound but the uneasy shifting of the water and the occasional rattle of stones as he climbed the bank with the ponderous dignified motion of a strong old man. My body, crouched against the rock, ached with more than the tension of physical discomfort. Suddenly the inherent menace of the scene was let loose as if the gates of hell had burst and the car, which much have been drawn up facing the beach, switched its headlights full on. Thelamion was caught right in the beam, his body stooped slightly forward with the climb. I crouched, my heart and circulation eliminated by the light as if it had gutted me. For an instant Thelamion merely stood there. He didn't even shade his eyes. The more-than-silence of the shore at night, with a deadly last whisper of water and stones, clung about him and then shattered in a scream of gunfire. Not one explosion but a pack of them, like a sudden hysteria of mechanical wolves that ripped into his body, lifting it into the air with the impact and tossing him back down the bank. And then immediately the headlamps swivelled round, dismissing Thelamion to darkness before I could even be sure he was dead, and now I knew that they were after me. The whole shore sprang with lurid cuts of light sweeping from side to side as the lamp, presumably on a swivel, raked across the rocks and the crash and shouts of men hunting took over from the nightmare intrusion of the guns. They were all around me. The impulse to run was so strong that the effort alone of supressing it almost made me sick. But I knew my only chance was not to move. I crammed my body into the crack of the group of rocks where Thelamion had pushed me down. Suddenly a figure ran past with that tell-tale different motion of the pursued as opposed to the pursuer. With a yell they had the light on him, missed him, caught him again and fired. It was the boy. Even they in the excitement of their ghastly chase could surely see the size he was. I thought he'd gone but he must have hidden nearby and now through a crack in the rock I saw intermittently the brutal recovery of his remains from the edge of the water and witnessed although I couldn't understand the words, the poor thing's practical obsequies. At least they had no further use for me. Assuming they'd found Thelamion's contact they prepared to give up the search but the delay seemed endless. In the glare of the lamp I could clearly see the man who turned full into its beam. There was the tramp of another footfall on the far side of the rock. Fear scorched through me as I realised my leg would be seen unless I drew it away from the gap. To do so I'd shift into this man's line of vision. At the very moment that my heart seemed to have climbed into my throat and my brain locked with tension he raised his arm and signalled to the land with a shout, and the light was extinguished.

In its wake the blackness of night was absolute. The men stumbled cursing away from the water.

I waited long after they had gone. The sea endlessly moving and utterly unmoved took on a corpse-pale tinge of light. I stood up. My own sweat acted like a refrigerator and I was freezing cold. I walked for a long time along the edge of the water not risking the land until I reached the town. Feeling like a rat in the empty streets I slunk back to the hotel. The door was still unbolted. I let myself in and tiptoed up to my room.

I opened the door as Polly had and as silently closed it again. I took off my clothes and threw them on the floor the other side of the bed. I read the words on Thelamion's piece of paper. I was glad Thelamion had at least enjoyed the vodka since it had had such a cruel aftermath. A lethal delayed hangover. I put it in my wallet and the wallet under some clothes in the drawer.

Eventually I lay down on the bed and pulled the sheet over me. In spite of everything – in spite of Thelamion lying on that cold shore and in spite of the words on that piece of paper – I slept. I slept like a tired man and he slept the sleep of the dead.

Chapter
13

'LEO.'

'Sssh.'

I opened my eyes a fraction. Polly was standing over me. Daylight filtered through the slanted slats of the shutters. The green tinged light gave her silken hair and beautiful innocent skin a nymph-like radiance. I remembered Othello's words – 'Are you honest?'

'I've got to go. What's wrong?' she said.

I should tell her that I'd been up half the night and that Thelamion had been murdered: she should know what her hand was in. I said nothing except that I had a headache, but in my heart I knew something else was the real source of the pain, if I had any.

'You poor thing!' the nice girl said, and laid her cool lips against my forehead. Perhaps she knew nothing. Perhaps Thelamion was only cautious about women. Perhaps she had only had a brief conversation, last night in the Perama, with a gipsy and bought some flowers. Here after all was the world itself bathed in sunshine again where four hours ago it had been wrapped in darkness, evil, vicious and uneasy. At whose door should I lay that?

'Do wake up,' she said. 'I've got to go to work.'

'You're going then?'

'You know I am.' She laughed. 'Leo, what's wrong with you?'

I sat up and took hold of her hand. She put her head on one side and crouched by the bed.

'I'll be back for lunch.'

'What time?'

'One o'clock?' She was smiling. 'If that's the lunch hour in the lion's den. You're worried aren't you.'

'Take off your glasses.'

'Oh Leo, I must go. What will they say if I'm late?'

'I don't know what they'll say,' I said, 'do you?'

She pressed her lips together and frowned. I took a handful of her hair and pulled it gently until her face was close enough to kiss, then she stood up. I still held her hand. The fingers trembled slightly. I could see nothing in her face. It was like looking into the clearest water. Not a shadow moved.

'I told you. Don't worry. I'll be back for lunch.'

There was that too I supposed. If she thought I was worried for her safety little did she know with what mixed feelings I contemplated the possibility of her being perfectly secure in the company of my enemy. I shifted my gaze before she could catch me. Are you honest?

'Well I'm going,' she said with a little debonaire wiggle of her hips, 'so let go my hand.'

I kissed it before releasing it, with an irrational tender compassion.

'And if you've got such a bad headache as all that, at least Dr Thelamion will be pleased!'

Would he though? So she had no idea. I watched her walk over to the door. She seemed to hesitate a moment but then turned and left.

I lay quite still. I couldn't sleep again. The sounds from outside began to gather pace: the as yet muted clamour from the sea and the road along its edge. Suddenly in the street a woman started to wail. The sound, so unfamiliar and so close at hand, broke the incipient pattern of the day like someone throwing a brick through a plate glass window. I jumped off the bed. The slatted shutters were still drawn. I foraged for the catch. Whatever was going on down below was reaching a crescendo with now more than one voice raised in a frighteningly abandoned lament. The cortège, since that was what it turned out to be when at last I got the shutter catch open, had stopped just below my window. A bier made of a broken door of which an old bolt was being used for a handle at one corner, bore the body of a large person covered from head to foot, but I knew at once who it was. I didn't need to identify the tearful voice of Electra in the crowd or look more than once at that friendly massive outline under the pall, to know that it was Thelamion. I pulled the shutter close again and turned back into the room. I did the things that people always do. I dressed and washed and shaved – the noise from the street returned to a more familiar pattern. I took my wallet out of the drawer and put it in my breast pocket. The words on the paper were Tri Nitron Coagulant 60. Didn't mean a thing to me, but it had meant a lot to Thelamion. I hurried down the stairs. Some tourists stood about in the foyer.

'What's happened,' I said. 'Do you know?' I thought they might be English, but they stared at me in French.

'*Qu'est ce qui'il y a?*' I said. '*Savez-vous qui est mort?*'

'*Un Grecque, je crois,*' the man said indifferently. The woman looked at me. I stepped behind the unmanned desk in the foyer and through the string curtain. There was no sound until I turned the corner in the passage. One of the men who worked as a waiter was assembling equipment on a trolley. On the other side the kitchen was empty. He looked up, was about to order me away, recognised me and said, 'Electra no here.' He was one of the very few who could speak some English. I said, 'What has happened?' He frowned in concentration. I said more slowly, 'Happened? Has there been an accident?'

'Yes. Very bad. Doctor found on rocks early this morning. He is dead.' He spread his hands, one with a drying–up cloth in it and shrugged in a concerned and care worn way.

'A good man,' I said. 'Can I go out this way?' He took a few quick steps across the room and opened the outside door for me. The bell from the reception desk rang from the passage.

'Thanks,' I said, leaving him to it, and stepped out into the side street.

I decided to go straight to the Hilton, it being the biggest and most impersonal hotel in Piraeus with an efficient phone system. There was no sign of the cortège. It had disappeared. The road was thronging with people just as on the day before. I turned left past Webb Draft International and up towards the Platia. Inside the Hilton it was cool, indirectly lit and efficient, as in any Hilton in any part of the world. I bought a newspaper and ordered some coffee just to establish my presence before using the phones. I considered taking a room in order to make the calls in comfort and possibly to have an alternative hideout from the Agamemnon. I had an obscure feeling of being not so much watched as known, like an intruder who has triggered off the burglar alarm but not yet been seen. The nice public call boxes with their glass enclosures and the crowded foyer made me feel more safe.

I read my paper from cover to cover or at least the business section, since it contained news of several hiccoughs in the smooth running of some Lloyd's syndicates which were destined to assume significant proportions. A few years ago the fashion in scandal had all been for falsified loading bills, stolen cargoes at sea, dual claims on damaged goods and so on. Now, ironically, since the Kasteros/Spitsodopoulos conspiracy promised to re-establish the old fashion with a vengeance, there were currently two or three cases of the mismanagement of the roll-over funds on reinsurances or unorthodox deployment of members' money which had hit the world headlines. Roger before the outset of recent disasters, had talked a good deal of one underwriter who had issued a Binding Authority to a colleague in Brazil, with disasterous results. I read about it now spread over half a page. At the bottom of a small column was a news item about the reinsurance arrangements of Syndicate 3X15. I remembered that that was the number of Richard Brock's box and then passed on to the racing news and from that to my calls. I had given the number of Mal Harris's office and my own to the desk. The man signalled to me now to go into the booth across the foyer and I stepped into it and let the smoked glass door close gently at my back. I picked up the phone and listened to it ringing in my own office in London. A strange girl's voice answered. I'd forgotten that David would have to get someone in to temp for Polly. I asked for David without introducing myself and she put me through.

'What's it like there?' I said. 'Any news?'

'I should say. You'll have your work cut out to draw any attention in the Press just now. It's all going on here.'

'I read xxx.'

'Shorty Culver and his magic pen,' he said, referring in market slang to the Broker with his binding authority in Peru.

'Is our business with them alright? I remember I put some through about a week before leaving.'

'Of course. When did Lloyd's ever not pay up? It's just the poor old Names with burnt pockets who are crying out to the big Committee in the sky for refunds and reparation.'

'How's Roger?'

'Ah ha!'

'What do you mean?' I said with sudden alarm.

'Just that he's reported to have perked up remarkably,' David said. 'Owing to a certain event.'

'What event?'

'Brock's name was posted at Lloyd's yesterday.'

'Posted on the board,' I said incredulously. 'What for?'

'I gather it's net accounting.'

'It can't be!' I said that, not particularly as an intelligent comment but as an exclamation. The fact was that at one time net accounting, although against the rules, was carried on by a number of underwriters as an ingenious way of exceeding their premium limits without letting it appear as such in the books. Lloyd's sets a limit on the amount of business every syndicate can do, measured in terms of total premiums which they may accept. Net accounting is a device whereby the underwriter can exceed that limit by deducting concealed reinsurances from the totals in the accounts; showing in fact the net figure. Brock must have been desperate to replace the business he had lost to Collingham, and I felt a twinge of sympathy for him.

'I think it's just the beginning of something else, and net accounting's not the half of it,' said David.

'But he'll be suspended for a whole year.'

'And won't that just delight Collingham. There was a photograph of him in one paper going into Lloyd's with a smile on his face.' I talked the details over for a few minutes and then asked news of a few purely office affairs; some accounts late in being paid, a broker who had suggested some mutual business.

'Any idea when you'll be back?' David asked.

'Just cross your fingers that I get back,' I said dryly.

Sitting in the same old office in London I shouldn't think he took me seriously for a moment. I said goodbye and rang off. I went back to the desk with my thoughts concentrated on Brock and the tragedy of such an afficionado being debarred the practice of his skill. On the other hand perhaps it was a pity that it hadn't happened sooner and my brother would not have found it necessary to launch his suicidal challenge for supremacy in the War Marine field. It took another five minutes for the desk to put me through to SIS and I went back into the same glass booth.

This time the note of lighthearted irony inseparable from any conversations with David Wigan was replaced with deadly seriousness. My name was taken in clipped tones and I was passed to Phillip Bomb who took the phone with an anxiety that was anything but reassuring. I gave him the details off Thelamion's piece of paper and my story did a great deal to make him feel worse. He said Mal Harris would be on a flight from Heathrow at 1300 hours and would contact me at the Agamemnon.

'Good,' I said, with feeling. 'And have you by any chance checked out Polly Rose?'

'Yes. 'Fraid so.'

'Oh!' I said. I didn't really need him to say much more.

'Mr Harris will give you details. But be careful.'

'Goodbye then.' I put down the phone and preoccupied as I was, pushed the swing door and nearly walked straight into Kasteros. If it hadn't been for the fact that the door was made of smoked glass I've no doubt that Kasteros would have seen me. He was just walking past the phones, his manner of alert expansive well-being expressed in a smiling face and the maximum attention to his surroundings. I let the half-opened door swing back against my shoulder and pretended to retrieve something forgotten on the shelf. He was holding a largish green plastic disc in his hand which I later discovered he must have collected at the desk. It had the number thirty-three stamped on it. He shouldered his way benignly through the backwash of his own powerful aura and disappeared through a door at the back of the large entrance hall. I went over to the desk to pay for my calls.

The typical melée of the well-fed bourgeoisie who patronise the tasteless, mass-produced, international de luxe hotels crowded the various offices. I had to wait while the deskman who had dealt with my calls disposed of other business with a group of Americans. Beside him several receptionists plied a constant trade with arriving and departing guests, and queries of residents. It was not by any means an unlikely place to see the famous come and go and I thought I recognised several faces. The desk clerk being momentarily rushed off his feet, made a move half to apologise for keeping me waiting and half to produce my sheet, when a bell called him away and with another holding gesture he threw a switch and became involved with a series of calculations down a speaking tube let into the desk. I waited patiently and it was then that I saw two Arabs come into the hotel, one of whom I recognised. His dishevelled head-dress, loose jacket and familiar robes were common but particularly recognisable as his especial uniform, and the raffish handsome aging face was unmistakable. He moved very quietly and unobtrusively with his one companion over to the desk. The second man spoke to one of the receptionists who nodded, looked through some cubby-holes under the desk, and produced a green plastic disc which he handed over. The Arab took it, and the two of them walked past me towards the back of the hall, but the younger man held the disc with his fingers spaced round the rim as if it was a framed negative, and it was easy for me to see the number, which was thirty-three.

'Mr Turner. Thank you, sir.' I took the phone call account sheet from the clerk and opened my wallet.

'What is the system you have here with the numbered plastic discs?' I said, as I extracted my credit card and handed it over to him. 'Daytime gambling?' He smiled politely at my friendly curiosity.

'Just a system of private room hire, sir,' he said, 'for business meetings.'

100

'Oh really. That could be useful to me,' I said.

'Speak to the receptionist if you'd like further details, sir,' he said, holding the carbon for me to sign.

I hesitated. 'Just a moment. I need to make another call to London. This number again please.'

He supressed any irritation he might have felt and I went back to my seat. In due course he signed me into one of the booths and I gave my name and asked again for Phillip Bomb. After a wait of several minutes he came back on the line.

'PLO?' His voice was incredulous but cautious. 'Are you sure, Mr Turner? PLO and Kasteros meeting in a private room?'

'Certain,' I said. 'Who could mistake that face? I'm sure I'm not wrong.'

'Did anyone else follow?'

'I can't be certain but probably not. In the space of about a quarter of an hour or twenty minutes several others have collected discs.'

'Right. We'll make what enquiries we can this end and I'm also going to contact certain members of the Embassy staff in Athens; but if you'll just wait now for Mal Harris to contact you this afternoon we'll take it from there. Has anyone noticed you, do you think?'

'Not here,' I said. 'I'm pretty sure not while I've been making these calls.'

'This afternoon then.' The line went dead. He was one of those who don't say goodbye.

This time I looked carefully through the glass before venturing out. There was a temporary lull in business in the foyer. Lunch time was approaching. I collected my sheet again, paid in full and left. It was time to go back to the Agamemnon to meet Polly for lunch.

At the entrace to the Agamemnon I looked up the crowded street to see if I could catch sight of her on her way, and turned into the hotel. She wasn't in the restaurant and not wanting to be the solitary focus of Electra's or Iphigenia's or the whole family's attentions if they discovered me there alone, I collected a cool beer at the bar and went up to my room. By half past one she still hadn't turned up. I assumed the lunch hour was one thirty to two thirty but I was beginning to get hungry. Fortunately the hotel cooking was not at all bad for Greece. The idea of a really well made *tamouli* for example and perhaps some grilled fish or a kebab began to seem very tempting. I went downstairs with my empty glass to check that Polly hadn't arrived and gone straight into the restaurant. Lunch was in full swing. The waiters Costas and Steven, and Iphigenia's little niece were busy among the cloth covered metal framed tables and multiple string chairs, but there was no sign of Polly. I went back into the entrance and out along the street half expecting to see her appear just at that very minute. The office lunch hour might be two to three after all. I preferred that to the alternative explanation.

For one last check in the bedroom I went back up the stairs and opened her door without knocking. Her small hand-case was open on the bed and bending over it just carefully arranging some clothes was a stranger. I could best describe the immediate impression he created by saying that a dog on encountering him would go rigid and snarl in its throat and raise its hackles; not the exuberant aggression so often shown by silly dogs to perfectly charming people but of serious alarm. The fellow raised his eyes to me and carried on with what he was doing. I hung on to the door handle and said firmly, 'What exactly do you think you're doing?' He straightened up resting the middle finger of his right hand on the opened lid of the case. His composure was oddly repellent. In soft sharp tones he gave me an unhurried explanation in Greek of which I couldn't of course understand a word. He then looked carefully about him: took the hairbrush off the dressing table, put it in the bag, closed the lid and picked it up. I thought, 'Could he possibly be acting under Polly's instructions?' There was something so unconcerned about his manner, so confident. I said, 'Don't you speak English?'

He shook his head but I had a strong suspicion he did. He walked towards me speaking briefly in tones that sounded apologetic but dismissive. I felt at a loss for what to do. I said, 'Wait. You can't take those things without an explanation.'

The man didn't react but reached the door with every apparent intention of going through it. I remembered the waiter who spoke some English. I put out one hand to stall the man's approach, and with my body still blocking the door, I leaned out onto the landing to shout down to the restaurant, 'Steven!' at the top of my voice. Whether I actually shouted or not I still don't know, since painlessly and without any apparent sensation I lost consciousness. The man took hold of my lower arm in a pressure that did not seem particularly urgent or even aggressive, but I felt a numbness up the left side of my neck and then passed out. When I woke up the only damage was a bruised shoulder from falling against the step. I looked at my watch. It was two-thirty. The man, of course, had gone.

Chapter
14

MR AMIDES LOOKED at me with a curt authoritarian impoliteness that implied a quite unnecessary defiance of what he took to be my social status. He had insisted on my queuing up in his outer office and he now listened to the details of Thelamion's murder and Polly's disappearance with controlled rage. He wanted me to know that he regarded me as a criminally stupid gentleman amateur and a liability. I restrained myself from flicking a speck of dust from the impeccable Mechlin lace at my sleeve but only barely.

'Can I explain something to you, Mr Turner?' he said. He leaned forwards and with one hand caught his office door a swing and it skimmed shut.

'This man Kasteros is a professional. You know what a professional means in terms of your own business no doubt. What do you suppose it means in another line of business? It means the same thing.' He prodded at the khaki painted metal top of his desk with his index finger. 'The same thing. There are highly professional surgeons, and brokers, and portrait painters, and electricians. In that meaning of the word Kasteros is a professional. How do you think he's evaded justice all this time? Luck?' He spat the word out.

He waited in silence for effect and I was glad of it. Just when he was ready to begin again I said unhurriedly, 'Mr Amides.'

He had to store the breath he'd taken in to continue the harangue.

'Polly Rose has taken on temporary employment at Webb Draft International and failed to turn up for an appointment. A strange man collected her clothes and incapacitated me rather than give an explanation. I suggest that you send someone round to the office immediately to make enquiries.'

He tapped the bell on his desk without replying. A curly haired youth in a short sleeved shirt pushed open the door with a decisive quasi-military air and stood to tangled attention.

'Dobbs,' Amides demanded. The youth shot out. Evidently Amides had picked up more than a Midlands accent in Manchester. Within seconds another officer appeared. Amides spoke to him in Greek while he stood before the desk at attention and then left smartly.

'That will be done, Mr Turner,' Amides said dryly. 'I expect the personnel at Webb Draft International will deny all knowledge of her.'

'What will you do then?'

He braced his back against his chair. 'Do you think Webb Draft International will have any record of her being hired?'

I supposed it was unlikely.

'You probably imagined that, this not being England, we can just break in there without any sort of warrant and throw our weight about.'

He had hit the nail on the head but I declined to admit it. I got up to go since the little creep was obviously obsessed with the idea of being as unhelpful as possible. I gave him just a curt nod and said briefly, 'Thank you, Mr Amides,' as I walked towards the door. I had a feeling that whatever activity he was capable of would be strictly delayed until I had left with the impression that none would be forthcoming. In which case he might as well be allowed to get on with it.

I walked in the direction of the Platia in search of something to eat and killed an anxious hour with a plate of kebab and a copy of the *Financial Times*. By the time I was back in the Agamemnon it was late afternoon. Polly would have been about to come back from the office. I sat on the bed. It was four o'clock. The London plane must have landed and I'd have more news for Mal Harris. I went downstairs rather belatedly and booked him a room, and then wandered out into the street and started to walk in the direction of Webb Draft International but turned back. Across the road something, the movement of a newspaper, the turning of a shoulder, caught my eye. I was level again with the Agamemnon. On the other side of the road the man who had knocked on my bedroom door the previous evening and who Thelamion had probably seen leaving, pretended a relaxed but obsessive interest in the sea. Anger took the place of my apprehension about Polly, grief and horror for Thelamion, frustration at all intruders. I walked over to him, and without a pause, put my hand in the small of his back and pushed hard. It must have surprised him as much as it did me. He staggered forward and a metal ring sticking out of a stone about six inches from the water's edge completed the job so that he fell clumsily into the sea. 'Ha ha ha!' I laughed a great jolly good natured laugh. 'Got you Bill. I told you I would!' I leaned over to give him a hand out of the water and the tourists, provided with an implicit explanation, gawped at the joke. The man hesitated to take my hand but he hadn't much choice since the onlookers, thinking we were friends, were leaving him to me. When he finally made his mind up and reached up to take it I ducked him. I held out my hand again. His eyes, like the teeth of a man-eating fish glittered up at me in silence. He decided to swim for it. He was wearing lace-up shoes. The nearest steps on to the road were at least a hundred yards away. One or two of the more interested onlookers came over in time to see him swim away, his gold watch strap gleaming under the water, his newspaper camouflage settling nearer at hand like a huge untidy dirty bird. Chuckling amicably and calling after him, 'See you for a drink at the hotel in half an hour Bill,' I walked off, and back into the Agamemnon. I was perhaps, as Mr Amides would have been only too keen to point out, totally unaware of what the professional criminal charges for loss of face.

Chapter
15

FIVE MINUTES AFTER this episode Mal Harris arrived at the Agamemnon, paid off his taxi and walked into the foyer carrying a polished brown cardboard suitcase and wearing, in spite of the climate, his best suit. I was relieved to see him but still not as relieved as I might have been if he looked anything like the part he was expected to play.

'Any fresh news, sir?' he asked as soon as we had got to his room. We had brought up some beer from the bar and he immediately threw off his jacket to reveal sturdy braces, took a long draft of the beer, and ran water into the basin with the other hand.

'Yes,' I said. 'Polly Rose managed to get a temporary job helping out in the offices of Webb Draft International, and now she's disappeared.' I filled in the details.

'I'm afraid that's very worrying,' he said, 'in the circumstances.'

'I agree with you,' I said dryly. 'But you don't seem too surprised. What did you find out when you checked up on her in London?'

He folded the towel neatly over the rail, picked up what was left of his beer and drained it. 'There's an extensive Greek side to her family.'

'Of course. For heaven's sake, that's partly why she accompanied me here in the first place.'

'Because of her aunt, sir. Presumably she didn't mention her cousin.'

I just nodded wearily. I didn't even hear him say the name. Kasteros, of course. I doubt if it was planned. She just played along with events as they happened.

'Who told you about Kasteros?' I asked.

'Amides.' He was knotting his tie, and glanced back at me in the mirror.

'That's impossible, isn't it,' I frowned. 'You must have been on the plane by the time I got to his office this afternoon.'

'Yesterday, sir.'

'You mean he knew that when I called to see him today! He just played me for a fool then.'

'He's got an odd sense of humour, sir.'

'You can call it that,' I said bitterly. 'And how about Electra?'

'You don't have to worry there, sir.'

'Don't tempt me!'

He changed tack. 'Would you think that one of my brothers was a Methodist minister, sir?'

As a matter of fact I wouldn't put it past him, but I could see he was trying to be helpful.

'It's the same thing with Mrs Christopoulos. She feels about Kasteros like Gwynn feels about me. They aren't in each other's confidence.'

'That's alright then.'

'I wouldn't like to minimise our difficulties, sir.'

'Don't worry, you're not,' I said. 'And how about Thelamion?'

'Definitely not. That I'm sure of. And of course she doesn't know what you found out about the meeting between Kasteros and the PLO at the Hilton.'

'I never had a chance to tell her. I probably would have done.'

'But she does know we've pin-pointed Kasteros as the Contractor, so now he knows that. And she passed on a message about the meeting with Thelamion here. Well, there we are sir.'

And I supposed that was all there was to be said really.

Presumably she'd decided to skip when she got to the office and heard about the murder of Thelamion. And one of Kasteros' men had collected her things for her. And even yet, her cheating child-like gaze, her skin, shone in the back of my mind. I regretted her.

'Do you want to know about TriNitron Coagulant 60, sir?'

'Yes, I certainly do,' I said. 'What is it?'

'A nerve gas.'

'Nothing to do with us then.' I meant it. I didn't immediately see the connection. It was his lack of response that brought me up short.

Eventually he said, 'It's almost certain that that has been pumped into number five tank of the *Aenaftis* at Gdansk.'

'But that ship didn't go to Gdansk. I remember the details from the Index.'

'Officially it didn't, but unofficially's another matter.'

'What on earth do you mean?'

'That ship went up to Gdansk from Rotterdam, two deck hands died during loading, no record in the ship's log.'

'That's impossible! I checked the *Aenaftis* out in the Confidential Index and an additional journey like that would be bound to go in.'

'People don't always keep to the rules, sir,' he said rather acidly.

'There's a Lloyd's reporting station at Elsinore. They couldn't miss it.'

'The watcher made no report I'm afraid,' he said in a tone of tactful regret. 'But the ship had a pilot, of course, between Elsinore and Halsingborg – it has all been checked.'

'Well, I suppose it was managed then. Somehow.' There was no point arguing. 'My God! And Thelamion?'

'Thelamion came across the information by chance probably but he knew what it was because of his medical training.'

'And what is it?'

'A formula that probably paralyses the nervous system instantaneously at the same time as thickening the blood. It probably has the capacity to remain in suspension over water for an unspecified period; it is not combustible.'

At the end of this semi-official recitation he looked at me

and said in a different tone, 'We can find out this sort of thing quite easily with our network, you know. Various organisations are very helpful to Shipping I.S., and that is the extra cargo they are carrying.'

I said, 'You thought there'd be one.' I was too stunned to say more. I've always had a horror of poisons, especially the hell-inspired notion of poison warfare, which presumably this was.

'What has this got to do with insurance fraud?' I said quietly. I got up and walked over to the window. Compared to my state of mind the waterfront seemed quiet and orderly. Harris took a small newspaper cutting out of his inner pocket and handed it to me. It was an account of a speech made by Sheik Yamani in 1981. It said:

> Sheik Yamani, the Saudi Arabian Oil Minister, claims the Soviet Union intends to gain control of the Persian Gulf oil fields. He told the German Society for Foreign Policy that the West was under-estimating the Soviet threat to its oil supplies and must take preventive measure. 'Hitler in principle granted the Russians domination over the Persian Gulf,' he said. 'Since then Russian ambitions have not changed. They want to rule the Gulf. But when the Soviets control the oil fields it will be all over with the Western economy and you will have to give up.' He said that by 1986 East European energy needs would exceed Soviet oil production and the Soviets could have to spend 50% of their hard currency for oil purchases. This would force them to find suppliers who would sell oil for roubles instead of dollars. 'The simplest way to do this is by conquering the oil fields,' he said. In line with this strategy, the Soviet Union was increasing its influence in Iran and aiding revolutionary movements in the Near East and Africa. Asked by a member of the audience what could be done about this Sheik Yamani answered: 'We cannot fight against the Soviet Union. That is your job.' He said the Soviet danger made urgently necessary a settlement of the

Israeli–Arab dispute. If Israel accepted a Palestinian state in West Jordan and in the Gaza Strip, the Arabs would recognise Israel and negotiate with it.

Harris saw I'd come to the end. 'You see, sir,' he said, 'that report appeared in 1984. Now, a fraud is basically a conspiracy between a number of people, who don't respect the law, to make money illegally Right?'

'Sure.' I was still staring at the paper. It seemed extraordinarily apt.

'But once such a situation has been set up it's a convenient launching pad for other schemes besides the original fraud.'

I could see that.

'Kasteros, having been commissioned to organise the initial set-up, can see his way to selling the facilities three times over and who's to stop him? He's keeping the shipowners happy because he's getting them their pay off. He's selling the political aggravation involved to the PLO who are also happy. And he's selling to the Russians who can give a real live test to a new chemical weapon at the same time as contributing to the fouling-up of an area essential to Western trade, and the aggravation of Israeli–Arab relations.'

I just wondered what Polly, dabbling speculatively in the dirty waters of international crime with her dainty little fingers, would think of this one. I said aloud, 'Presumably your London office has contacted . . .' I paused wondering who on earth one would contact. ' . . . the Ministry of Defence? The Foreign Office?'

'Yes sir,' he said.

'And then?'

'They asked to be kept informed.'

'Eh?'

'They will verify of course.'

'But it's . . .' I looked at my watch, controlled an impulse to hit my wrist against the window frame, and then said with deliberate calm, 'It's August the 3rd. On the 15th they plan to let it off.'

'I know sir. But officials very rarely believe the information from their own security services, let alone outsiders. They realise eventually of course.'

'But not in time to act.' I felt more tired than if I'd had five nights without sleep instead of just one. Roger's bank balance had turned into a right Pandora's box.

'The Foreign Office has requested that we meet a member of the Diplomatic Corps here in Athens at six o'clock.'

'Well in that case . . .'

He checked me with a polite and melancholy smile. 'It will be one of their SIS men – Secret Intelligence Service, not shipping – unfortunately.'

'How do you know?' I said.

'It's happened before, sir. Every legation has its quota of SIS. We'll probably get a first secretary this time but a fat lot of good it will do us.'

'Well let's persuade him,' I said with some exasperation. I thought he was being too pessimistic. I thought a lot of things, including that a British spy would be a highly trained expert and not some drunken charmer with a licence to get other people into trouble.

My first five minutes in the company of James Milton helped me to sort this out. Our appointment was in the Hilton where Mal walked straight over to the desk and collected one of those green discs which he glanced at and put in his pocket. We went to the back of the entrance, up one flight in a lift and along to a small open office where the disc was exchanged for a room key. With it, when we got to Room 50, Mal unlocked the door and politely motioned for me to go in. The light was already on and seated at a high chair by a private bar was a handsome, well-dressed man of about my own age and about a quarter drunk.

'You're from Lloyd's aren't you?' James Milton said to me when the introductions were over.

'Well. Not exactly.'

'Not my bag anyway. Never could stand the bloody City.'

He held up his glass and said, with a friendly and charming smile, 'Mud in your eye,' laughed and drank deeply before putting his glass back on the table. I laughed as well. It was impossible not to like him.

'Sit down. I'll pour it for you myself. Everything's here. Gin, tonic, beer, whisky, cointreau, bourbon. Mr Harris?'

'Beer please sir.'

'Don't call me sir. Can't bear being called sir. Blast, this stuff froths all over the place.'

Mal took it off him while he mopped his hands with a clean handkerchief, grimaced, and turned his attention back to the mixing for my benefit.

'Our firm,' he suddenly disconcertingly veered into business and sobriety in one move, 'our firm, not the Foreign Office but my firm, says that Kasteros' contact with the Russians and Palestinians is linked. We don't know what he's doing. Nobody apparently ever does know what Kasteros is doing while he's doing it. What is your involvement at the moment?'

'He's contracted to sink two ships and incapacitate twelve others for a consortium of Greek shipowners conspiring to defraud the insurers. I'm a broker. '

'And the brother of the underwriter with some very bad business on his plate.'

I shrugged.

'Quite right. None of my business. And what's your involvement at this time, Mr Harris? My office tells me you have some special news.'

Mal told him about the Tri Nitron Coagulant 60. He tossed back another mouthful of whisky as if it was all in the day's work.

'What are you going to do about it?' I said.

'Do about it? What do you mean do about it?' His tone held an immediate flash of aggression.

'I'm an amateur,' I said. 'You tell me.'

'Christ!' He dumped his empty glass on the table and looked at me nodding his head very slightly as if confirming some unheard inner conversation according to which I had absolutely no doubt I was the terminal exhibit in the line of fools.

'Would you say this gas is harmless then?' I said.

'No.'

'Or that it's not on the ship?'

Patience made him thirsty so that he needed to pour himself another drink as he said no a second time and a third time.

When I challenged him with the consequences of its dispersal in the Straits he just said, 'Now let me ask you some questions.'

He took the whisky bottle and walked over to an armchair, sank into it and, with a self-mocking smile, poured himself another treble.

'What makes you think we don't get some nut charging into our office every day of the week with tales of fiendish foreign plots. Mind you . . .' He flattened his hand in the air as if smoothing down an angry man – and who's to say he wasn't. 'I'm not doubting your word. But people can be mistaken. It's a bit late to start apologising when Her Majesty's Government has moved in like some bloody combine harvester and executed, thrashed and tied up the opposition. It's embarrassing then to have to admit that someone got it wrong.'

'I'd have thought your firm, as you call it, would be impervious to embarrassment by now.'

He smiled, unperturbed. 'Well you're wrong. But I'm glad to see you've got some guts because you may be going to need them.'

He stopped, drank another inch or so and sat back to look at me and at Mal. A combative, slightly spiteful assessing look came over his face. I braced myself for his reaction. An ordinary-looking man with no apparent experience of anything except English public school and City life, and an emaciated, air-sick, Welsh eccentric from the slums of Cardiff docks couldn't be too impressive.

'So what are you going to do about it?' he said.

'What do you mean?'

'It's obvious isn't it?' I was right. He wasn't impressed. He looked at me with a mocking, spiteful stare and then slammed down his glass saying, 'Jesus Christ!'

I got up and poured myself another drink. 'Don't take it too hard,' I said. 'We may not be as useless as we look.'

He laughed and took another hefty draught from the glass. 'I can't stand businessmen,' he said as an explanation. He smiled at me as he said it, looking up like a handsome talented schoolboy goading an inept teacher.

'Funnily enough I don't particularly mind drunken diplomats,' I replied.

'Spies,' he corrected me between mouthfuls, 'spies. Between these four walls let's call a spade a spade. You're a bloody stuffed shirt of a fucking upper class English businessman and I'm . . .' he stumbled over the words, laughed at the implied joke at his own expense, ' . . . a drunken spy.'

He got up surprisingly steadily and fetched a small bottle of soda off the bar. Getting the top off gave him some trouble but he managed it and muttering, 'Time to take it easy,' poured about an inch of the soda into another two inches of scotch.

'Come on Mal Harris,' he said, 'you're not drunk, you'd better have a scotch. It goes with beer.' Mal said he was quite willing but, expecting opposition, James carried on as he poured out and handed the glass to him, 'Come on, come, I insist. Drink up and I'll tell Mr Turner about his girlfriend. One spy should always help another and so I've helped her,' he carried on unstoppably. 'I've taken Miss Rose home.'

'What! That fellow who called at the Agamemnon to collect her things was one of your men?'

'Why do you think, when she offered to help out in the Webb Draft office she was first turned down and then taken on after Kasteros had walked past the cafe. She's his cousin.'

'We know that,' I said.

'Now you do!' He was caught on the hop but not showing it.

'As soon as we had the message from London about your having spotted the PLO meeting with Kasteros at the Hilton I realised you would tell her all about it when she came back from the office, so we had her picked up.'

'Where is she now?'

'Why ask a stupid question like that? What does it matter to you where she is?'

I looked at him. He knew perfectly well. I was silent for a minute and James was busy with the bottle.

'This has to be the last one,' he said. 'I've got another appointment. The Head of Chancery is giving a dinner party at eight.' I pitied the hostess who was going to have to greet him in an hour's time. Mal gave an apologetic cough and recrossed his legs. He spoke like someone in chapel – a strained expression of mild attention on his face, his deep set eyes in shadow. James nodded in the act of lowering his glass after yet another mouth to mouth resuscitation.

'Go on.'

'I just wanted to make it plain, sir, so that you personally know, that my office confirms . . .' he paused on that word until it had plenty of time to sink in,' . . . that the Tri Nitron Coagulant 60 has been loaded into number five tank of the *Aenaftis*. That we know, sir.'

'Right.' Suddenly James Milton seemed quite reasonable. He listened like a normal businessman at a board meeting. Perish the thought that the unpredictable bastard should read my mind at that moment.

'If we don't get official help we will be trying by other means to divert this ship and keep the cargo intact for international inspection.'

'Fair enough.'

'And we'll also be trying to survive a PLO terrorist attack on the ship.'

'You'll have your hands full,' he said and laughed as he drained his glass. 'Anything else?'

'If we're not going to have any help, sir, can we at least have cooperation and non-interference.'

'Funny you mention that,' he said. I looked at him sharply. James flexed the skin around his eyes in a peculiar characteristic gesture between goodwill and contempt. 'Those PLO . . .' He put down his glass. 'My firm has been informed that the PLO's whole objective in this enterprise is to discredit the Israelis. When you think of it why should they want to blow up a tanker?' He paused to register the reaction of his audience. 'Why should they?'

Mal said nothing. Neither did I.

'I'll tell you why. The Israelis have all the advantages. For heaven's sake they practise almost genocide and still western governments feel they're "one of us". Just because they're not Arabs nothing they do seems to smell quite so bad. Well if they get the credit for sabotaging a couple of ULCCs in the Straits of Hormuz (and I can promise you that's exactly what the PLO are planning) and damaging western trade where it hurts, that's going to change.'

Mal said, 'Is this supposition or fact, sir?'

'Call it information,' James snapped. 'And if so it could be that the Foreign Office will want such a useful bit of public relations to go ahead without interference.'

'Public relations! It's mass murder they're planning.'

'Yes, yes. Explain it to him for Chrissake,' he said to Mal Harris. 'Tell him what Macchiavelli said about the ends justifying the means.'

'But the gas!'

'And then they'll have your phantom bloody gas all over the Gulf. *Touché*. I'll be late.'

He shook hands with Mal and then with me, laughed at some private joke, and passed out in one sense, the other to be deferred with any luck for an hour or so.

Mal and I, alone in the room, were aware of the furniture for the first time, the joyless green walls and hideous light fittings. I said, 'Shall we go?'

Chapter 16

I SAID, 'THAT'S it then. Finish. We can't go on.'

Back in the Agamemnon after a silent walk over from the Hilton I pondered the appalling escalation of Roger's personal problems and came to the obvious conclusion. Although Mal said nothing immediately, I wasn't banking on his agreement. I turned round on him.

'Right – I want you to understand this Mr Harris – I'm . . . oh, thanks.'

I took the glass he was holding out to me. I suppose he noticed that my hand was trembling and it may have contributed to the melancholy of his expression.

'I'm pulling out. I'm sorry,' I stated. 'Sorry to get you into something and then pull out. But it's beyond us as individuals to deal with the situation that's developed. In London we saw things differently. That was bad enough. But this is different. This is international terrorism and top level politics on a different scale. Roger will just have to start his business over again like anyone else.' I paused for breath. 'And I'm not going to be argued into doing anything more energetic in the morning than going back to London and getting a good rest in my office.'

He didn't argue. Neither was I going to stop talking. I should have been drunk by that time but I wasn't. My emotions burned up the whisky as fast as I swallowed it. I forgot that I had ever disliked the taste.

In retrospect I still can't work out what his response consisted of. I must have ranted on for half an hour and that small, tough, consumptive looking fellow couldn't be moved. He looked sympathetic, he didn't argue; he gave me his respectful attention. But behind the mild facade of his inoffensive expression was a visionary determination against which I knew my arguments were making no headway.

At about 9.30 there was a knock at the bedroom door. Evidently Mal expected someone as he got up at once with a gesture as if he would have given me the details in advance if there'd been a chance. My first thought was that it might be Polly. But it was not. However, the smiling fellow in the doorway was a welcome reminder of the real world. Curly black hair, puppy fat physique, about thirty. I shook hands with him automatically, not knowing what aspect of Mal's plans he fitted in to and wishing not to be involved anyway. He spoke English with a thick gutteral fluency and with a sinking heart I heard he was a ship's mechanic.

But he was also hungry. If he hadn't been I don't think I would ever have become re-involved. My determination might have held out on an empty stomach in that wretched room fresh with the defection and disappearance of Polly, and the equally demoralising appearance of James Milton. I went along with them to the restaurant because it seemed the obvious thing to do. At the bottom of the stairs Electra suddenly appeared from the kitchen passage, saw me, flung out her arms with a loud cry and, uninhibited by her own perfect awareness that I couldn't understand a word of Greek, broke into a lengthy and passionate monologue. After the first outburst Mal interjected a word or two in Greek, at which she turned eagerly to him and carried on as before, still speaking at me for all the world as if I understood but now including Mal. Eventually she stopped and asked some questions which he answered, appeared satisfied, reiterated passionately part of her former speech, brushing the corner of her eye hastily with the back of her hand, reached up and gave my head a motherly pat, called down to someone in the direction of the kitchen and hurried off.

'Tell me,' I said to Mal, 'where did you learn Greek and what was she saying.' He smiled.

'I had to learn the language for this job, sir.' I dodged the bumper of a yet larger car that crammed past as we went out into the street.

'And apparently she is under the impression that Polly had to go back to London because of some business to do with your office.'

'Will the FO send her back to England?'

'I daresay they'll be able to persuade her, sir,' he said drily.

Out here on the road none of the day's heat seemed to have found anywhere else to go and it lay on the stones in the dusk like another sort of stone, a different dimension of weight, heavy and immovable. The uncrushable vitality of the local population and the dogged determination of the holidaymakers pushed it aside with every possible device of noise and movement. We stopped at some tables beside the water. Over the water to be more exact. The wooden floor built out on piles into the edge of the sea was seamed with the glinting reflections of water between the cracks.

Until the food came I found it difficult to concentrate. Mal was giving the mechanic – he was called David Kazantsis – an edited account of our problem. He didn't mention the gas and he didn't mention the PLO. I was wishing we were alone so that I could ask Mal Harris, now that I thought of it, how a reputable security organisation like SIS could have failed to check up on the credentials of Polly Rose quickly enough to avoid letting me go off to Piraeus with the cousin of their chief suspect. Now, of course, I remembered Mal's reticence in my office in London. I ordered without thinking and ate at first without thinking. But human beings are animals not machines, and before I knew it the food I ate consumed my bleak dispirited resolve to go home and leave them to get on with it.

'What was that you said?'

Mal looked up at me. There was no heightened attention on his face to alert me to get back behind the cover of my indifference.

'Polly,' he said.

'Yes exactly. What about her?'

He registered a sort of impassive solemnity and volunteered the opinion that things had turned out surprisingly well.

'How do you make that out?'

David Kazantsis looked from one to the other and switched his concentration to his food.

'We are in a position to know exactly where we stand now.'

'And how does that help us? Everything is for the best in the best of all possible worlds.' I was thinking not only of the shambles we were in but also of Polly: the transparent, lily-like texture of her skin and certain aspects of the private time we spent together.

'She wasn't candid enough, sir,' he said, the facade of mild sobriety cracking momentarily under the impact of his own wit.

I laughed unwillingly. 'So we know where we are now do we, Pangloss?'

'I think so sir.'

'And where, besides in the S H one T are we?'

'On our way to immobilise the *Aenaftis* in the Gulf of Oman.'

'Before the Straits then?' I said humouring him.

'Easy,' David Kazantsis broke in. 'Simple my friend. I show you. Here is the *Aenaftis*.'

'Don't mention that name again loud, boyo. We must learn by other people's mistake.'

'Sorry. Sorry. I am sorry.' He hunched his shoulders and peered round. In the road a car jammed just alongside our restaurant blew a horn like an amplified mouth organ and another replied. An angry woman shouted at the driver, and our waiter yelled an order across the tarmac. The restaurant on the left was playing Beatles music and ours was playing Greek. Then far out on the sea a tanker blew its horn.

'Alright, alright,' Mal said, 'carry on boyo.'

David held a chart up between his plate and mine. It had been xeroxed in reduced size and the diagram that covered most of the sheet could have been a printed circuit board for an icecream making machine as far as I was concerned. ULCCs don't look like ships at all. They can easily be a quarter of a mile long from stem to stern, and the contents of that elongated box shape were drawn on David's chart in section, with other items in detail. I already knew the practical problems of getting these ships around the oceans of the world through my broking activities. To manoeuvre at all they have to have a 60 ft keel and although this colossal draught means trouble, it's not deep enough to give real leverage. It takes several miles of water for the vessel to respond to direction, three miles to stop and anchors are virtually useless.

'She is diesel,' said David. His voice held deep satisfaction.

'Not steam you mean.'

He thumped me in the back. 'We're lucky!'

I shelved that point for the moment. 'There aren't many diesels,' I said. 'Are you sure?'

He just pointed to the evidence and I supposed he must be right. Of the many details that appeared on the hundreds of ships I dealt with every week I wouldn't now, remember if the *Aenaftis* had had this peculiarity. All the same . . .

'Mal,' I said, 'for heaven's sake. What's the point of this. You know how we're fixed.'

'But it is easy,' David protested. 'One switch. That is all you need. One switch in UMMS.'

'Unmanned machine space,' Mal muttered. 'I've got a plan, sir.'

'Tell me about it on the plane in the morning.'

He paused. There was something like a silence. Between us at least.

'You'd better know, sir, that I am not leaving that ship to sail unhampered up to the Gulf.'

I could have laughed. I felt very angry. 'And what exactly do you think you can do about it?'

'I don't care about being paid, sir. I'll telegraph my resignation to SIS in the morning. I've done it twice before.'

'And then what?'

'If this ship is stranded, with its cargo intact if possible, before the Straits, there will be no ULCCs trapped in the Gulf and a very interesting cargo for international judicial inspection.'

'And how does Mr Jennings become shot?'

'I've got my crewman's papers, my discharge book and all

that, sir,' he said, ignoring my literary jibe. 'The ship stops at Durban on the 10th. I intend to join her.'

'Just like that.'

'There's not much in it. There's no one harbour for a ULCC where crew are taken on and discharged as you know. It costs too much for them to stay anywhere an hour longer than they can help. They load or discharge and go. And some crew leave and some join: always. I'll join at Durban.'

'And then you'll walk down to the engine room and throw a switch.'

I never heard anything more far fetched in my life. If you could switch these ships off like light bulbs their already legendary vulnerability would go out of sight.

'You realise how far fetched it sounds.'

'I don't think it sounds far fetched,' he said.

'Well, then, your experience is a darn sight broader than mine.'

He nodded. *Touché*, to quote James Milton. 'Let David explain, sir. It's not that simple.'

I listened, unwillingly at first. I've always rather liked the subject of mechanics without having spared the time to actually become knowledgeable. In spite of myself, I was fascinated. Apparently a diesel-driven tanker, once on the high seas and free of obstacles, switches over to bunker fuel, which is a cruder cheaper oil, to save money. But bunker fuel only remains liquid at high temperature. Consequently, when a ship approaches an area where she must slow down for manoeuvrability and the rev count will drop, the engine must be switched back on to the lighter oil. If it isn't, and the engine runs too low or is stopped for so much as three or four seconds, bunker fuel freezes in the pipes and the whole engine has to be stripped down before it can be restarted. During that time the ship is helpless with no control. You can't anchor a ULCC. And the obstacles, whatever they were, that caused the ship to slow down to manoeuvre in the first place, more than likely become the grave on which she founders.

'And where exactly would we be with the *Aenaftis* broken on rocks and spilling the contents of her tanks out on to the sea?'

'Pollution. Very bad. Very bad,' David said, but you could see he didn't really care. Mal, however, knew what I was referring to.

'In the Gulf of Oman,' he said, 'there are sandbanks. Failing that, delay would make the ship late at its rendezvous and the terrorists who are meant to attack the ship and release the gas have a very exact contract regarding time.'

The waiter came over and poured out some more wine. Mal asked for the bill and he went away with the empty plates.

'Really,' I said. 'I wonder. There's a possibility I suppose.'

That was the moment when I could have gone back to a relatively peaceful life and didn't.

Chapter
17

BACK IN THE Agamemnon Mal unfolded more detailed charts of the *Aenaftis* and also laid out on the table a well-thumbed seaman's book and discharge papers. They both had my name on, or more accurately of someone called Len Tanner, which was near enough for me to answer to, but not actually inviting identification on a crew list, and with an identity snap that must have been a careful bit of photomontage since I recognised myself but to my knowledge never looked that scruffy.

'Where did you get this?' I asked incredulously.

Judging by his expression Mal Harris read my reaction as wholly admiring. According to him his office turned out excellent forgeries as a matter of routine. The snap was an old one borrowed from the office.

'And the four days growth of beard?'

'We thought it best, sir.'

'Like hell you did. I can't stand being unshaven.'

But it was, nevertheless, a mesmeric bit of work, not only the photograph and the authentic-looking documentation, but the timing. It was as if my identity had been really trapped in the mirror of another dimension so that any remaining doubts I had about the enterprise seemed like quibbling over a certainty.

'Won't they know these papers are false as soon as they find out how new I am to the business?'

Mal stood at my elbow and thumbed back the pages of the discharge book. Although it looked reassuringly less than new it was, as he pointed out, mostly blank. I had only done one voyage and that on an African grain-carrier.

'They won't be surprised, sir.'

I knew about the heterogenous mixed Asiatic crews. They could consist of any variety of youth, age, skill and ignorance. Still, I had never imagined myself living in some hell hole below decks with a bunch of navvies trying to spin out an unrealistic impersonation of the kind of job I know absolutely nothing about.

David Kazantsis on the other hand was a happy man. While my last feeble gestures of doubt were being demolished, he had deliciously unfolded three charts. With one he had now covered the table, another was draped over the chair, and the last was on the bed. Between these, with the delicacy typical of fat men, he stepped, absorbed and picking his teeth.

'You ready David?' Mal said.

David was concentrating. He kept his gaze on the chart in question, marked a point with his left hand, gestured to Mal with his right. He held the toothpick between the thumb and index finger, and the other three fingers extended in a gesture of attention. The fat curves of the palm of his hand looked surprisingly delicate for a mechanic.

'Yes. Is OK.'

He looked up with a beam of satisfaction, having come to a conclusion.

'I show you.'

We grouped around the charts. The first schematised the layout of the *Aenaftis* in general, but was mainly taken up with the engine. It was only a part of this we had to understand. The second was an electrical chart and fortunately not required reading as I had never seen anything more complicated. The third was the nautical navigational chart of the Gulf of Oman. Normally the course lay from Durban north and then diagonally across to the Straits of Hormuz. The ship would be on bunker fuel until within two miles of the Straits. It would normally avoid veering actually into the Gulf of Oman. The point at which we should incapacitate the engine was precisely marked out for us where the drift would carry the *Aenaftis* among those three long slicks of shallow water.

'What's the draft there?' I pointed at the longest sandbank shaped like a fish and sloping at an angle to the shore line.

'Can't say for sure,' Mal said. 'Every attempt to chart the sea bed ends up inaccurate in so far as the contours are always shifting. But here at least,' he pointed at a place on the chart which was marked with a clutch of numbers, 'the sandbank is above water. And it's definitely too shallow for our draft up to here.'

I followed the area he marked out. 'We could miss it.'

David shook his head but I suspected that if our hopes were on the opposite side his goodwill and optimism would be equally available.

By the time we finally parted company for the night I felt I had lived at least three years in one day. I suppose I was more used to a regular life than either Mal or David but I stumbled wearily down the stairs from Mal's room on my way to the separate flight that led from the entrance lobby to my own.

There was one man in the entrance as I came in from the other side and started towards the stairs. David had made a move to leave at the same time as I did but stayed to have another drink and some more seaman talk with his old friend. It was too bad he hadn't come with me. As I said there was one man in the entrance lobby, and it didn't occur to me that I was what he was waiting for. I didn't even look carefully at him or have the least qualm of insecurity when, as I made to pass him, he reached out towards me. At first I remember thinking, for some reason, that he wanted to know the time. Then I recognised him.

Demetrios Chia did not intend to leave me alive. It was his one slip-up in what was otherwise a very thorough job. From the hotel foyer into a car drawn up right across the entrance took only seconds. If I'd known what I was in for I would have struggled harder in the beginning, but I minimised the embarrassment of being coerced by another man in public by putting up less resistance, thinking I could talk my way out of it later. I had a lot to learn. I skinned my hand trying not to fall as he crammed me into the car and a man at the wheel, without turning his head, gave a preliminary blast of his horn just to warn everyone to get out the way, and drove off. I had a split second in which to take in the real threat of the inside of the closed car and flung myself as heavily as I could at the door, grabbing for the lock and hoping to throw myself into the street.

Just the way Chia reached out and stopped me was a frightening indication of what was to come. Real violence is not familiar outside of war. You keep your arms and legs intact in a normal fight. There is an underlying long-term view about the human body that stops short of mutilation. But not now. This man had no such inhibitions. I hadn't seen that he had a knife but with a muscular rapid thrust across the car he literally cut my hand off the door. The knife was thick and strong. The blade sliced as deep as he could drive it across the back of my hand biting into the bone and releasing only with a jerk. I was astounded. Before the pain hit me and took up every cell of my brain's capacity for awareness, the realisation that he was actually trying to cut my hand clean off unhinged my assumptions: that he would have if he could. I was not about to be punched up and get a few black eyes or even break a leg. A whole new range of experience was opening up before me and I felt sick, and not only from pain and loss of blood which was pumping all over the car. I struggled to think. Like someone fighting to close the shutters in a storm, I grappled for the latches of my mind while the pain howled in my head and drove my thoughts before it like torn up scraps of paper in a cyclone. When I looked at my hand it seemed that only the palm was still holding it together. I looked at my companions. The driver's face I hadn't seen but beside me in the back seat sat the well clothed figure of my swimming friend. He turned to me, the mechanical shark's eyes observing with bitter remorseless contempt the state I was in. I said something like, 'For Christ's sake, don't be mad. Nothing's worth this. Let me out. Let's talk.'

He was quite unmoved. The only tension in him was a sort of elastic satisfaction: a snake satisfyingly aware of its poison. In his own time he replied with one sneering sentence in Greek. The driver half turned his head and hunched his shoulders in a soundless laugh.

'You don't speak English at all?' I shouted at him. It seemed all of a sudden a matter of utter desperation to be killed by a man who wouldn't even understand what you said as you died. He turned on me savagely and hit the side of my face with the back of his hand. He brought his hand back and held it up for me to see his ring. He pointed at it. It was covered with blood but not his own. It was a heavy ring with three metal blades shaped sharply in leaves pointing upwards; decoration was only their secondary purpose. Blood poured down the sides of my neck and into my jacket.

He had missed my left eye, but not on purpose. I had a choking feeling that the blood had somehow got loose inside. A suffocating constriction closed my throat. We had reached a lonely stretch of flat ground quite high above the sea, and far enough inland not to hear the waves. The driver braked with a jerk and I grabbed the loose flap of my hand spitting out some of the blood which ran down my face into my mouth. The car door was opened. A sense of space and night wind. No trees. Bushes. No people. Only starlight. Chia hit the side of my face and shouted. I was afraid he'd notice how easy it would be to cut off the rest of my left hand so I tried to hit him as hard as I could with my right. The other man reached into the car and grabbed my shirt collar from behind. The front of the shirt tore open under the impact but the sleeves and neck held well enough for him to drag me out and throw me on the ground. There was a moment's hideous silence. I felt the small stones and sharp grass under my head and the hazy lop-sided impact of the ground under the sky. The driver stood over me. Chia got out of the car on the other side and I saw his white trousered legs step round the back. The night sound of his shoes on the gravel and the intermittent flicker of the wind was unforgettable. I had to run. I rolled suddenly sideways, lashed out with my right hand and sprung to my feet. I might just have given the driver a bruise big enough to need explaining to his wife but all in all there wasn't much I could do. He lashed me across the head with contemptuous ease. I tried to shout but the sound came out in a whisper. The field tipped sideways and I leaped into unconsciousness like a burning man leaping into a lake.

Chapter 18

WHEN DAYLIGHT CAME someone apparently found me. Like my Greek friends, they thought I was dead. I wasn't but I wished I was. When I unwillingly came to focus on this world again it was night. I was in a hospital bed. The very sight of the dark made my gorge rise. I was sick. A nurse half-hidden in the dim light tended me as best she could. I was calm again. I waited for the cacophony of pain to become less shrill, and remembered. My left hand was in plaster up to the elbow. I could move both my legs although not without considerable pain. I had a bandage over half my face including one eye. It seemed that the gods, disgusted with my timidity, were determined to show me just how low down on the losing side they'd marked my starting place. It was then, rather than in the restaurant or doing homework over the charts, that I made my mind up. The version of myself who had half-heartedly complied with the seduction of the forged papers and the technical lessons had been partly play-acting. But the brutality of my attackers had taught me a lesson in seriousness of purpose.

In the morning a doctor appeared, accompanied, much to my disgust, by Amides. The doctor explained my state to me. My left hand had been operated on and tendons stitched together. It would be in plaster for two weeks and should not cause me much trouble in the interval. Then physiotherapy and it might be almost as good as new. In addition to multiple contusions, I had been shot straight in the chest. The bullet ricoched off the sternum and by good luck came to rest against the third rib. It had caused shock, i.e., collapse of the cardio-vascular system, which fortunately they were optimistic enough to mistake for death, and left me. Luckily I had been found at daybreak by a woman walking into Piraeus to sell eggs and prompt hospital action had saved my life. I had been unconscious for ten hours. But all other damage was compara-tively superficial.

I felt sick. I felt a loathing for my own body that had provoked such a bestial attack: a loathing for myself. I caught Amides' eye looking at me and managed to twist my lips into what I hoped was a smile.

'And now doctor, you're going to tell me that I have been very lucky.'

He laughed companionably, holding my board in one hand and clipping his pen back into his pocket with the other. 'In one way yes, Mr Turner, in another no. That's life.'

I was desperately tired, but Amides didn't leave with the doctor. My nurse had also gone.

'I'm too tired to talk to you now Amides,' I said, in a bid to get rid of him by appealing to his highly-developed neurosis of British upper class authority. When I opened my eyes a minute later he was still there.

I gave him all the details. He said he wouldn't bother me about anything else at the moment, thereby managing to leave me with the unpleasant certainty that he would another time.

When I next woke the square of light which was my window no longer framed the glare of the midday sun. Someone was sitting on a chair on my blind side. I moved my head round as far as I could and he got up.

'Hello Mal,' I said.

He ducked his head in sympathetic acknowledgement and remained silent for a moment.

'Anything the matter?'

His melancholy face became humourous with a remote inner smile.

131

'Our ship's in Durban in five days, sir. I'm just worried about your health.'

I laughed, and we all know that joke. A stabbing pain in my chest was followed by a warm feeling of blood. He gave me some water.

'I'm alright,' I said when I could speak again. 'The doctor's language makes it sound terminal but all I've got is some cuts and a broken hand.'

He didn't argue. But his silence was not the forbearance of a protective nurse. More speculative.

'Give me another twelve hours,' I said.

He nodded.

'Or twenty-four. What's happened about Demetrios Chia? I've had Amides inflicted on me once already.'

'They've got him safely under lock and key. Costa Amides is very pleased about that, sir.'

'What did he say about it?'

'You wouldn't want to know what he said, sir.'

I could guess.

I noticed I was feeling dizzy. Also very tired. I moved one leg under the sheet and tried lifting the plastercast on my left hand. It was a bloody disappointing experiment. I caught Mal's eye watching me. I suppose I'd been a liability to him in the first place before the Greeks tried to kill me.

He said, 'The wonders of modern science, sir, combined with man's natural need to win will get you on board that ship, or I'll eat my grandmother.'

'Anybody who's prepared to dispose of their grandmother on my account I reckon a damn good friend,' I said.

The next morning, when Mal came in I eyed him askance. His grandmother's days were numbered. But he was not alone. James Milton, his laconic provocative eye taking in the hospital furniture with distaste, strolled beside him with one hand in his pocket and I thought at once that he was up to no good.

'How's the hunchback of Notre Dame?'

'Fine thanks. Hello Mal.' Mal raised his eyebrows at me in his characteristic gesture and nodded from behind Milton's shoulder but said nothing. A wise precaution in the presence

of someone who treated all words uttered by other people as so
many gazelles on whom to set the tiger of his bloodthirsty wit.

'You don't look fine to me,' James said now in characteristic
form, 'but the police are very pleased with you if that's any
consolation.

He looked around for somewhere to sit down and chose the
side of the bed. I tried to move my leg in time but failed. He
didn't notice but took some cigarettes out of his pocket and lit
one, dropping the match on the floor. I felt the same irrational
attraction to his bloody-minded rather elegant ruthless style as
I had the first time.

'We're going to take you home.'

'Who's we?'

'Foreign Office, old sport. First class plane service by order
of Her Majesty. Bunch of flowers, nurse in attendance, Mal
for company, the lot.'

Mal had remained standing. I could feel the magnetism of
his modest silence willing me to hold my tongue so I held it.

'So that's alright then.'

'When is this?'

'Thursday, OK? One of the girls has packed up all your
things.'

I just nodded.

'Lucky bastard if you ask me,' he carried on. 'If I could
escape another year of blasted *kleftikas* and *dolmas* for the price
of a beating you'd find me in the queue.'

'The locals are very obliging around here,' I said. 'I'm sure
you could be fixed up.'

He laughed good naturedly. Somewhere inside that complicated jungle of his personality there lurked what Hollywood
calls a real human being.

'Your next of kin have been informed, by the way.'

'What do you mean?'

'Name of Collingham.'

'Oh. I wish you hadn't bothered them.'

'Routine,' he said, looking sharply at me with undisguised
curiosity. And whatever effect that information was going to
have on Roger and Sylvie I didn't want it printed on my face
for him to read. I closed my eyes and rested back on the

pillow. The FO had no doubt said I'd had a road accident or fallen off a ladder. They wouldn't give the other end the chance to put two and two together.

He stubbed out his cigarette on the floor. 'Time to go.' He stood up. 'I'll be off then. Enjoy the journey. Goodbye Mal.' He shook hands with him, waved to me and was gone. I waited for the door to close and then looked round at Mal. 'The trouble with him,' I said, 'is that he doesn't know about your grandmother. In view of the terrible fate that threatens her I feel I shall have to disappoint James Milton.'

'Just what I was thinking, sir.'

'And you too? How did he work that out?'

'It seems that the Foreign Office have decided not to allow interference in the activities of foreign nationals on foreign soil. They say that it would be more in keeping with the interest of Her Majesty's Government to let them work things out for themselves.'

'Like blow up a few ships and close trade in the Gulf by chemical warfare.'

'Under the circumstances, yes. So it seems.'

'The circumstances being Israel getting landed in a position of irredeemable international approbation.'

'I think they'd have a knees-up in the Travellers Club, sir, and brush their teeth with champagne for a month.'

'Are we legally obliged to do what they say? I don't want to land up in a British prison.'

He looked doubtful. 'At the moment,' he said, 'I've only received advice from the British Intelligence Service, and you, as an injured tourist, are being given an assisted passage home. If they thought we weren't planning to follow their advice it would be a different matter. Neither of us has given them any reason to think we won't.'

'You just agreed with him then?'

'I gave him that impression.'

I thought for a moment. 'I can leave tomorrow night.'

'Through the front door?'

'Through the window.'

He got up and looked at it. It had a large metal frame which slid open diagonally – not ideal. He tried the pulley. The opening would make it necessary for me to bend almost double, but if I couldn't manage that I couldn't get to Durban.

'Is there a drop?'

'Four feet. Four and a half.'

'What sort of time?'

'I'll let you know tomorrow, sir. I'll give it a bit of thought. We'll have to go straight from here to the airport and catch our plane without delay or else we'll be stopped.'

'Are they keeping an eye on you?'

'Oh yes,' he said at once. His air of solemnity was a private joke.

'There's a problem though, isn't there? If you shake your tail off, he'll immediately notify his office and they'll watch the airport.'

The glitter of enjoyment in his deep-set melancholy eyes intensified. 'Don't worry, sir,' he said. 'I'll get it all worked out.'

'Yes?'

'And we've had a bit of luck.'

'You don't say!'

'Shipping IS has dug up a contact in the Oman.'

'Let's get down to business then. I've been doing some thinking and it's been on the same lines. Pull up a chair. By the way, any news of Polly?'

'I did ask,' he said, 'but you can see what they're like.'

I nodded.

He put a brown paper bag full of grapes which he'd been holding on the table. 'We should have thought of the Oman before,' he said. 'The Sultan's pro-British and his army has an English colonel.'

'Who knows him?'

'Phillip Bomb. He says he's a cautious man: not free to do what he likes either. But both he and the Sultan are willing to talk to us, confidentially. If they decide to help, the army has shore marine equipment as well as land forces. They can be at the ready in the Gulf of Oman or off the Mussandmun Peninsular.'

'Has anyone told the FO?'

'Not a word, sir.'

'So what do we do? Fly there before going to Durban? Is there time?'

'Yes. Just about. None to spare.'

'How about tonight?'

'Tomorrow will do. It had better be tomorrow. Eat your grapes, sir,' he said. 'We've got to get your strength up.'

Chapter
19

I HAD ANOTHER dose of Amides late the next afternoon. He came when I was trying to rest and he brought one of his acolytes with him. Their obvious mutual attraction sublimated in the master/underling relationship, Amides and his prodigy carefully orchestrated a boring hour of questioning and cross-questioning on every detail of the recent event least likely to be my favourite subject for discussion.

As Mal had not had the opportunity to finalise his arrangements for our flit I was still awaiting his visit and impatient to get rid of the policeman and his friend. On the other hand I was careful not to give Amides the idea that I had anything else to look forward to other than a sponsored trip home and a lengthy convalescence. I lounged on the only armchair as languidly as I could answering the interminable catalogue of questions until according to my watch the time of Mal's appearance was imminent and he had unaccountably still not arrived.

The interrogation had stuck on the driver of the car. Amides needed a clearer account of the man's appearance to enable a positive identification whereas I could only produce an untalented category of commonplace details: dark hair, straight, no beard or moustache, middle height, etc. Preoccupied as I was, I only wanted Amides to go so that I could get on with the essential arrangements.

I looked again at my watch. It was nearly six. Mal could surely not delay longer. Amides referred to his notes with a dissatisfied but somehow conspiratorial air which I certainly hadn't noticed before or had put down to the dialogue with the young neophyte. He was up to something. I became alert at the moment when it was too late. He nodded at the sergeant or whatever he called him, and stood up at last.

'If you'd be so good as to come with us then Mr Turner, we can settle this by an identity parade. I asked the men to be prepared in case we should need them at the station.'

'I can't go with you now,' I said.

Amides was enjoying himself. He unsuccessfully tried to supress his satisfaction at overriding me. He regretted the necessity, but they had the right to expect my co-operation and the hospital had agreed that I was fit to make the journey to the station if it was needed. I looked again at my watch. If Mal came and found me missing, how would it affect his plans? On the other hand we had a whole night before us. But then again, he would have fixed on a particular plane.

'How long will it take?'

Amides was determined not to give me a clue but the boyfriend happened not to be looking at him for once nor could he resist the temptation to practice his English.

'Half hour,' he said, with a descriptive gesture wiping the air between us with the flat of his hand. He had the sort of lips that turn out at the corners and a passably classical Greek face.

I picked up my coat. I hadn't tried much walking. My left hand made it impossible to actually put a jacket on but I could carry the thing. The wounds on my body looked negligible now and didn't show under the shirt. My left leg was the most painful item since a bruised muscle behaved like a strain and stabbed at each step. What with all this it wasn't difficult to give a convincing performance as an invalid who had better not be kept on his feet too long. The sergeant held open the door.

Two police cars were waiting for us in the road. I was going automatically to get in, as one of the men held the door, when a sudden sensation like vertigo made me stagger. It passed as evidence of physical weakness but in fact the sight of the interior of a car and the sensation of being handed in through the door nearly turned my stomach.

The hospital seemed to be situated just outside the main town of Piraeus. Within minutes we were back in the turmoil and commotion of the busy streets, the evening trade just getting under way and the sea a mixture of black and dazzling facets of water like a smashed mirror hung between day and night.

The police station was right in the middle of the town and up behind the Platia. I followed Amides with the boyfriend just behind, through the outer layers of the establishment where Amides obviously ruled with a rod of iron and into an inner yard. Amides gave the word and one man walked smartly over to a door, gave an order, and stood to attention. About ten men, under the control of another police officer came unwillingly through and lined up.

I spotted my friend of the torture session before they had even stopped walking. He looked at me as if I was a man in a crowd. In fact his dispassion was almost noble. This was the body and face that I had last seen outlined black against the phosphorescent night sky, looming between me and the stars as I lay on the ground. I could feel again the sharp bristle of dry thorn under my head and scattered stones and the coolness of the late night air. And this man, unmoved, indifferent, his face a paler shadow, standing there at a slight angle, the short light sleeve of his shirt palpitating slightly in the fitful breeze like a butterfly's wings. Now, like then, he waited heartlessly for the next move. Perhaps he had been one of those who had done the same, but more, for Thelamion.

I said to Amides, 'That's him. Third from the right.'

'Sure Mr Turner?'

'I've every reason to know.'

He made a gesture and a police officer walked over to the file. Amides himself turned and let us out of the yard, and back to the waiting police car. It was 7 o'clock. I was tired like a man who'd done a day's work. There was a change of transport and this time a police van drove us off, and Amides, to my slight surprise, was still included. It was easier to rest my leg on the upholstered bench in the back of the van than it had been in the car. The teeming streets made less impact through the high set minimal window space of the van's side. Amides sat next to the driver, and I, separated by the hostility and awkwardness of our surroundings, travelled in silence. The boyfriend and the fellow policeman also with me appeared to be on bad terms and ignored each other. Prompted by an uneasy thought I stood up and looked out of the window. 'Aren't we going the wrong way?' The policeman ignored me as much as the boyfriend.

I forgot my leg and it pulled me back down towards the seat when the van lurched on a corner.

'Sit down please,' the boyfriend commanded officiously. I ignored him. I banged my plastercast against the partition trying to cross the van and Amides turned round with a sharp command in Greek. Both policemen were on their feet.

'What's going on?' I shouted to Amides. 'This is the wrong road.'

The boyfriend with an insolence which bit as hard as the pain in my hand, gestured to the seat with his gun.

'Amides,' I shouted, 'give some explanation or I'll do my best to smash this van to pieces if it's the last thing I do.'

For a moment the two police officers backed off and Amides swivelled round in his seat, his twisted little eyes whirling in his blasted head, his ugly flat voice sharp with authority.

The second officer stepped towards me. I swung my plastercast at his throat. He caught my arm with surprising neatness and forced me down into the seat. At that moment the van stopped. Both men took hold of me and frogmarched me out onto the tarmac. Amides took his time to stroll round. We were at the airport.

'What are we doing here?' I said.

Amides snapped, 'What do you think, you fool.'

Before I could reply I caught sight of Mal. He was just getting out of a car that had drawn up twenty feet away. The driver unloaded suitcases one of which was mine. The departure annexe of the airport was fifty yards away to the left. I choked down the overwhelming animosity I felt towards the insufferable Amides. I saw that I'd been made a fool of. He cooperated with Mal Harris as a fellow officer of sorts in pursuit of a criminal they both wanted. This ruse had got us to the airport without FO interference. But for myself personally Amides wouldn't have helped me out of the path of a runaway truck.

Mal took in the situation at a glance but there was unfinished business with Amides and his manner was non-committal.

'I hope everything's alright sir,' he said, coming towards me as I approached him.

'Bloody well just about.'

'The police are going to escort us through the first barrier. Mr Amides.' He spoke the name with a little formal duck of the head as Amides joined us, and then added, 'Are we ready? The plane leaves in seven minutes.'

We started to walk towards the terminus. I felt deathly tired. Standing upright and moving was a gruelling chore. We were almost at the barrier. We were past the barrier and walking to the gate. The startled glances of one or two other travellers penetrated the membrane of my disorientated consciousness. I could have done without the fight in the van.

Mal said, 'For God's sake don't faint sir. We're almost there.' I did no such thing.

Chapter
20

THE NATIONAL AIRPORT of Muscat and Oman is Seeb – small, modestly equipped, looking from the air like an allotment with a garden shed. After a one hour stop-off at Dubai with it's flashy modern equipment and ostentatious grandeur, we made the descent towards the tiny conning tower of Seeb with first the sea appearing on the left with the beach running parallel with our course and then, as the wing tipped, across the gangway through the windows on the right just visible across the thin chest of a sleeping itinerant Indian worker, the moon-lit, spiney foothills of the Jebel Akbhar.

The contents of the plane on this last leg of its flight matched the modesty of its destination; five Indian men, two heavily wrapped Arab women and an elderly Omani gentleman, an airsick Welshman and one half dead Englishman. Activity at the airport was also in proportion; a couple of police in military uniforms, a scattering of Omani men in white dishdashes, turbans and Kunjahs, and, to our relief, no reception committee for us. The Indian baggage handlers who eventually extracted our suitcases from the plane smiled, making flicking gestures with their fingers. Big hotel? Intercontinental Hotel, Ruwi, very grand OK? And to the taxi driver, Arabic, slamming doors that sound like tin sandwiches packed with plasticine and we drive straight out of the airport and turn left onto the main highway leading to Muscat.

Ruwi, a purpose-built maze of twentieth century concrete, lit with bare bulbs, might have lacked charm in the eyes of some foreigners, but to us the Intercontinental rose like an oasis out of the sharp light and shadow. Plumbing, air-conditioning, soft beds, woven rugs, a bar; the silk of my shirt flapped loose again between my shoulder blades. The hotel was almost empty. We took the two best rooms and ordered drinks and food. After the Agamemnon, a bathroom with real hot and cold water, a bath that I could partially fill and climb carefully into, a clean floor and fresh thick towels brought the first glimmer of well-being, even to me. Mal knocked on the interconnecting door óf our rooms to say that dinner was ready. He had had it brought up, two waiters wheeling a loaded white-swathed trolley to a table near the window, and we sat down to eat.

I thought it was too late to call London because of the time difference. I was half glad; too tired to do it anyway. I had already fallen asleep twice where I sat when the phone rang. Mal went to pick it up and I drew aside the heavy curtain and looked down into the street.

Rather like a hotel that carpets the stairs only up to the first floor, the streets of Ruwi reverted to dried earth behind the facade of the main road. Bare electric bulbs hung from some street corners. A man with a brown paper bag stepped out from the open front of the sort of shop that stocks anything from car parts to dried beans and toothpaste. He was dressed in clothes his ancestors would have worn five hundred years ago and what's more they looked as if they probably had. I took a sip of champagne and let the curtain fall back with a thud, as Mal came back into the room.

'We're wanted down the road,' he said.

'What, now? Where?' I doubted if I could stay awake, even standing up.

'Who was it?'

'Phillip Bomb.'

'London? We're wanted in London?'

'No. Mr Bomb calling from London to say that the car is on its way from Muscat to pick up us.'

I groaned, whether at the convoluted effort of messages

from Muscat to Ruwi being phoned via London or the prospect of imminent physical effort I wouldn't know. I'd have to dress. It would take time. While Mal got the trolley removed and smartened himself up I struggled into my clothes and stood in front of the mirror only to discover a small red stain of blood had seeped through onto my shirt. The phone rang again, this time from reception to announce the arrival of the car. My hair, snipped by the nurses in the hospital when bandaging my face, made me look as if I'd been in a dogfight.

'Sit down sir,' Mal said, 'Leave it to me.'

He put on my shoes and socks, combed my hair. 'The jacket will do.'

'I can't get it on over the plaster.'

'Let's see sir.' He eased it deftly so far, but the cuff stuck. He had a pair of scissors in his kit, and prepared to cut an inch or so near the seam where it would show least.

'You go.'

'There're expecting two of us sir. Everything depends on our credibility. If they think you're too badly injured they'll look for other means: maybe pull out altogether. We need them.' Bang went a jacket that cost me three hundred pounds. The last thing I did was swallow a pill he gave me. The coat hid the blood stain as long as I didn't move my good arm too much or put my hand in my pocket. I was suffering what hospitals call discomfort.

Downstairs we got into the car whose driver, dressed in immaculate white turban, trousers and embroidered sash held open the door. We both got in and the driver started down the almost empty road, the lemonade coloured street lighting adding to the timeless squalor of the streets.

'What do we want from them? Let's get that clear,' I said.

'We want their army with shore marine equipment to be available off the Gulf of Oman and the Mussandam Peninsular.'

'In case we miss.'

'In case. And a salvage vessel in case we don't. And we want them to monitor events and be ready to intervene.'

'No more?'

'See what they offer, sir.'

'How much do we tell them?'

'We don't specify Tri Nitron Coagulant 60. They're very wary of any contraband cargo. Leave it at that with the Minister of Defence. He's the man we're going to see. The Sultan's in Dhofar.'

'And the British military commander?'

'A Colonel Brandon. He's not here. If we get the all-clear from the Minister of Defence, they'll fly us out to Mussandam in the morning.'

The drive into Muscat was only about fifteen minutes along the highway, originally built to link the Sultan's summer palace with the Queen Mother's palace beyond Seeb.

When we arrived at our destination it was a building disconcertingly reminiscent of a tent, a public library and a grand hotel. I walked with careful deliberation, unable to bend at all or make any casual gestures.

The Minister was a very short man. He waited for us in the middle of a vast room of which every surface reflected light except the chairs. When the introductions were over and we were all seated he lit a cigarette – a Gauloise – and screwed it into an onyx holder. There was something handsome and simultaneously ill fated about him that reminded me of Toulouse Lautrec. He had decided to fix the main focus of his attention on the Palestinian involvement in the case. Collingham's bankruptcy was too small an issue, however manipulated. Russian involvement perhaps too large.

'The Palestinians . . .'

We waited. He flattened the palm of his left hand towards the ceiling as if indicating a group of them flying silently across the gold moulding.

'So much to be pitied.'

I nodded.

'So much to be feared. So much to be admired.'

Which did he do most I wondered.

'You know we call them the new Jews of the Middle East.' He laughed. 'You call it ironic?' He spoke perfect English so he knew well enough. 'As Allah said, *"Fi effic cursum adillah"*: The mirror creates its image. Just as governments needed the Jews to finance them in the past, we need the Palestinians to survive our bureaucracies today. Look all through the Middle East. Who are the administrators of business, of offices? Palestinians. The managerial posts? Palestinians. The only personnel who understand AWAC? Palestinian. How then,' he said, and paused, an inch of ash suspended momentarily over the polished marble floor which reflected images in a faint replica of the way in which Sylvie's table had once mirrored the lace-capped hydrangeas, 'How then can you suggest that we refuse entry to Palestinians coming into this country or try to restrict the movements of those already here?'

'On an individual level surely you can act to repress criminals regardless of their nationality.'

'Ah, but I am not an individual.' He made this extraordinary remark with such smiling urbanity that I didn't get his drift. 'I am a Minister of Government. You are an individual, and you think and want to act as an individual. I am the State, and must act on the level of government.'

He sat looking entirely satisfied with himself as well he might. He had without any difficulty at all brought us both to the point. On an issue of this importance, if indeed it was as we described it, why did our application for help not have British official backing? A government doesn't reach an official agreement with two private gentlemen. A government only makes an agreement with representatives of another government. The only way to convince him was to take him entirely into our confidence.

I looked across at Mal. His pale features and fragile angular bone structure made him look, in this setting, like a man from another world. We were both men from another world. But perhaps with luck a world that His Excellency had a sentimental regard for. He also had been educated in England.

We took the only path open to us. I left most of the recital to Mal. His Excellency chain-smoked Gauloises and listened. He looked serious over Lloyd's and commented that it was high time the Middle East had its own insurance market. He had met James Milton at a party in Kuwait. The other details he heard in silence.

Finally he made a gesture, scarcely noticeable, with the

146

hand that held the cigarette and a servant at the door some twenty feet away turned and disappeared at the signal.

He looked from one of us to the other. His lips had a groove around them – a familiar feature, as if drawn with a mahogany crayon. If the shape of the mouth was brutal it could be very unattractive but in this case his lips were soft and curvaceous, as if perhaps he had somewhere in his past Persian ancestry. It didn't help to remove the air of slight decadence from his person. There was nothing one could do but wait.

Eventually he said, 'Mr Turner. Thank you. Mr Harris.'

I wondered if it was dismissal, but apparently not, the servant was making his way back across the floor accompanied by two others.

I looked at the tray being held out to me.

'Please take one, Mr Turner. You will find it very refreshing. A concoction of herbs . . .' His voice tailed off. I would have willingly taken one of the little glasses but the movement needed was too delicate for my broken hand and reaching upwards with my other would make the coat swing open. Eventually I managed. Concoction of herbs my foot – it was neat whisky.

'Please come.'

He was standing up and we followed him across the floor to an alcove where on a high table against a wall a map was laid out, and a neat pile of papers. When we were grouped around it he said, pointing at a place on the map,

'Here is Dibba Hisn. It is from here your attackers will come.'

He paused for effect. Mal said, 'Not in the Oman then, sir.'

'Unfortunately not.'

'Are you informed of that, sir?'

'We are. Now here, as you see, the curve of coastline forms a large bay which is divided between three countries, Dibbah Muhallab in Fujairah, Dibbah Hisn in Sharjah, and Dibbah Bayah in Mussandam. You will see from this that any attempt on our part to interfere from the land would be futile.'

'But the sea?'

'Precisely. Both here,' his small tapered finger rested on the eliptical stretch of coast along the Gulf of Oman, 'and here just off the Mussandam Peninsula it happens that Colonel Brandon wishes to organise practice military manoeuvres in approximately ten days' time. I see no reason to discourage him. Naturally they will need MTBs and other shore marine equipment.'

'And salvage vessels, sir?'

'We have them,' he exclaimed, as if the implication was of their not having any. 'We have them. And where shall they be but in the sea!'

'Will you be contacting the Foreign Office, sir?'

'Why should we? They have not contacted me.' He raised a hand and snapped his fingers. The tray of herbs reappeared and we each took a fresh glass. The servant retreated with the patient tread of a man in bare feet used to distances. When we were alone again the Minister said, 'Excuse me,' and delicately drew aside the edge of my jacket and let it fall back in place.

He sighed. I drank my herbs.

'You are brave men, if what you say is true. And I,' another pause 'can only offer you an arrangement between friends. I, not His Highness Minister of Defence. You understand.'

'We understand.'

'And my friend Colonel Brandon will meet you in the morning. I have a plane. It is at your service. My car will collect you at seven. Will this suffice? Make your arrangements with him.'

I smiled at him and he looked solemnly back and then the voluptuous lips curved regretfully.

'I too would be quite content for the Palestinian –' he paused, 'Public relations exercise did Mr Milton call it? – to succeed. But not the other thing. No, not the other.'

Chapter 21

THE NEXT MORNING, from the point of view of a sick man dragged out of bed at dawn, the trip to the Mussandam Peninsula seemed a waste of time. All we needed was to talk to Colonel Brandon, and what were bloody phones for.

'Shipping I S advise it sir. The Colonel wants a meeting.'

'Alright Mal, but for Chrissake lift this arm for me will you.'

I was trying to ease on my shirt. Bed at two and up at six racketing around all over the place was something I'd had enough of for the time being.

'Shipping I S just rang sir . . .'

'Don't they sleep either,' I said. 'Do you mean to say they've been through already this morning?'

'An hour ago. And not too pleased either.'

'Oh?'

'The Foreign Office.'

'What about them?'

'They were requesting our return to Britain.'

'I hope your office said they'd no idea where we'd gone.'

'Not exactly.'

'Where did they say we were then?'

'In jail. In Piraeus.'

I laughed recklessly. 'Good old Amides,' I gasped. 'I never thought I'd like that guy.'

'He's co-operating with the FO sir.'

It took me a minute to see the point.

'You mean refusing his phantom jail-birds a Consular visit?'

'Exactly.'

'Very neat!'

More than could be said for our flight to Mussandam. The small army plane shot up in every thermal lift and dropped like a stone into every air pocket; both of which are features of desert flying. By the time we were at journey's end Mal looked as ill as I felt. Through the plane window one could see an eagle drop of empty stone and just further on, unnecessarily marked out in the endless runway expanse of desert, a runway. As far as the eye could see dry sandy earth pricked with stones shimmered into distance and at first nothing moved. St Exupery landing for the second time in search of the little prince might have chosen it. Then I noticed the khaki Mercedes standing at some distance with a soldier holding open the door while another man in army uniform stepped smartly out. He stood and waited for us a moment and then walked the last couple of paces forward and held out his hand.

'Colonel Brandon.'

I tried to assume an equally business-like air. 'How do you do. Leo Turner. Maldwyn Harris.'

Disconcertingly he gave a short sigh before nodding unsmilingly and shaking hands. It seemed to be just a habit. His eyes flicked around the perimeter of where we stood as if his attention was repeatedly called for. His watchful glance only flushed the occasional dry brown bird from cover.

'Right. Let's be off. I'll sit in front with you, Cooper.'

The driver opened the doors and we got in.

'Have a decent flight, did you?'

'Perfectly alright sir. Bumpy.'

'That's the desert for you! Watch it Cooper, that dog's going to run.' The driver braked. A tan coloured dog leaned forward with its nose towards the road, sprang back and cantered off.

I looked at the back of the Colonel's neck as we drove along; short coarse hair like the dog, weathered skin, about fifty-eight and the abrupt manners of authority superimposed on shyness. After ten minutes we stopped in front of a hideous house in a little compound. Quarter of a mile away across the flat desert was a clutch of barracks.

'Don't forget the cigarettes Cooper.'

'No sir.'

'And get the Monday edition if you can.'

The driver's smart energetic responses collided with the stifling wave of heat which surged into the car as soon as he opened the door. Around the house a rectangle of grass the colour of a hyped seed packet was bordered with a hedge of oleander in full flower. Beyond it where the gardener's watering can didn't reach not a blade of vegetation disturbed the absolute symmetry of the desert until a far distant clump of palm trees marked the edge of the mountains.

Inside the house the Colonel's wife was waiting to meet us. This was no surprise as Shipping I S in the morning's briefing from London had drawn a graphic picture of her, coupled with the warning that to succeed with the Colonel we'd have to win over his wife. Their assessment of the situation was confirmed at once by the Colonel's manner as he made the introductions; his touchingly obvious admiration, pride and devotion combining incongruously with authoritarian shyness. 'Rosemary, my dear,' he said, 'here are Mr Turner and Mr Harris. My wife, Lady Rosemary.'

He supervised the introduction with watchful satisfaction as we shook hands. Lady Rosemary was cast in the time-honoured mould of the English eccentric, with an aristocractic bony face, rather like Wellington to whom she was distantly related, iron grey hair and height of over six foot. She also had the pleasant gravelly voice of a middle-aged women who drinks and smokes.

'What a treat to see you all,' she beamed, and in the same breath, 'Ahmed, what have I told you? Start with the guests.' An Arab servant with a loaded tray stepped guiltily back from the Colonel to whom he was about to offer a drink.

'Come and sit down. Poor Mr Harris looks a trifle pale. Ahmed, fetch my flying mixture.'

Mal shifted nervously under her scrutiny. Bent half double to look into Mal's face, Lady Rosemary gave him a really charming smile and said, enunciating rather clearly. 'I'm always upset when I fly you know. Aeroplanes leap about so over the desert.'

'Please don't worry about me Lady Rosemary,' Mal said desperately, but she cut him short.

'Don't be nervous. It will make you feel a lot better.'

'Thank you,' the poor chap said, giving in and taking the glass from her. We all watched with varying degrees of apprehension or interest as he raised the dark brown fluid to his lips and took a sip of it. He gasped.

'Drink it down man! Swallow the lot!' the Colonel ejaculated, his face a study in paternalistic zeal as he stood in the middle of the floor, his coffee cup to his lips. Mal drank it.

'Tastes a bit awful I know,' said Lady Rosemary. 'I won't tell you what's in it. But admit, now don't you feel better?'

Mal opened his mouth to speak but at first no sound came out.

'He feels much better, don't you Mal?' The poor man looked at me with his mildest expression but suddenly his face cleared and he put his head on one side like somebody contemplating the inner workings of a clock. A look of astonishment took the place of the former mild and uncomplaining expression. He still didn't seem able to speak but Lady Rosemary was satisfied.

'You see. It always works. Now sit down all of you. Before my husband takes you off I want to hear about everything. Go away Ahmed.'

The room we sat in had dove grey painted plaster walls and shiny green terrazza tile floor overlaid with rugs, good English furniture and curiously enough an English Victorian fireplace with carved marble surround, and on top of it all chintz loose covers on the armchairs and lined and inter-lined chintz curtains.

'Surprising isn't it?'

'Yes, it is rather.'

The Colonel had been watching me but the expression on his face showed not the uncertain suspicions of a man with doubts. Rather the unquestioning pride of ownership so that I could voice my astonishment without any fear of causing offence, since he would assume one's predominant feeling was admiration. And really it was. If one were going to sidestep local artifacts completely then it couldn't have been better done.

'Never mind the furniture Guy,' Lady Rosemary broke in. 'I want to know, Mr Turner, if it's true that someone tried to kill you in Greece? You needn't look so surprised. That naughty fellow James Milton told me.'

'Does he know we're here?' I said at once.

'No. Better not mention it. He gets drunk you know.' She gave me a very wicked smile.

I had an aunt like her once – dimly remembered. She died in the Suez fiasco because she enjoyed the excitement so much she refused to be rescued. It was a useful cross reference. If the Colonel was inordinately fond and proud of his wife, I, in the little time I'd known her, had been very keen on my aunt.

Fortunately Lady Rosemary had a strong practical streak. She raised the question immediately of contact between the *Aenaftis* and the Colonel's forces and got us a loan of radio equipment with a twenty-five mile range. We would need the salvage vessel to be out to sea between the Gulf of Oman and the Straits of Hormuz from the 14th to the 18th. Mal itemised the stages of our plan to join the ship at Durban and run her aground on the sandbanks of the Gulf of Oman. If, however, we failed and the ship reached the Straits, if Omani MTBs with their crews were on hand, they could intervene when the *Aenaftis* was attacked.

In mid-sentence she suddenly picked up a little bell and said, 'Ahmed, champagne,' to the servant who appeared so quickly I hoped his understanding was limited to kitchen English. He approached her with an open bottle on a tray which she felt briefly to test its temperatue and nodded. Colonel looked at his watch.

'My dear, we shall have to be going.'

'Not yet darling. Ahmed is just pouring the champagne. I must be allowed to wish you luck.'

Colonel Brandon sat back with a degree of complacency which was almost touching. Obviously if his wife said there was time then as far as he was concerned there was time and he knew she would never let him down. I could imagine the charm of living within Lady Rosemary's orbit. No uncertainties, no meannesses, no nagging doubts and always a timetable. We drank and when I remember Lady Rosemary I see her invariably in my mind's eye smiling in acknowledgement or benediction, over the rim of her champagne glass, her sinuous good-looking face bright with encouragement.

Since it would take an hour driving on bad roads to reach the peninsula, a picnic had been prepared for us. The sergeant loaded this into the accompanying jeep and Mal climbed in beside the driver leaving the Colonel and myself to share the other car. This seating arrangement was ideal for a private brainwashing session which was exactly what Brandon had in mind.

'The Sultan and I were at Sandhurst together,' he began. 'Long time ago now.' He stared out of the window. Not at me.

'You haven't made a whole career out here though, have you Colonel?' I thought I might as well let him know he wasn't the only one who'd done his homework.

'No.'

Short. Staccato. Uninformative. Having weakened his opponent with the abruptness of his reply, he let the effect sink in with a second's silence and then turned his face inwards from the window and gave me a charming smile.

'Now you . . . Tell me the exact situation with your brother. We were at school together you know. Lot older than you. You haven't got the same name as him have you? Mother married again, what?'

I explained carefully about the blocking and trapping cover. I began at the beginning with Roger's exaggerated sense of grievance towards Richard Brock and his measures to recover business.

'What does your brother make?' The question took me aback. But it was not surprising that he should want to know. I remembered leaning out of the window of Court House when I had consciously added up for the first time the likely burden of commitment in those perfect parterres and herbaceous borders, the immaculate box hedges and the shaped yews and the water. I went over it in my mind, but couldn't manage the

154

mental arithmetic, fished around in my pocket for a scrap of paper and my pen, then accepted the small neat notepad from Brandon and started to work it out. Roughly speaking, Roger got a percentage of the management agency income, say five per cent since he owns fifty-five per cent of the shares. The management agency is paid one per cent of the premium income of syndicate 3X15. The premium income of Collingham's was about eighty million pounds. One per cent of eighty million pounds is eight hundred thousand pounds. His fifty-five per cent share would, therefore, bring him in around four hundred thousand pounds from that alone, minus point two five per cent paid back by the managing agency to the members' agency. Subtract then about two hundred thousand pounds from eight hundred thousand pounds and you get six hundred thousand pounds, fifty-five per cent of which (three hundred and thirty thousand pounds) would be Roger's stake. From that subtract approximately two hundred and fifty thousand pounds (his share of that) in outgoing salaries and rent. Then add profit commission (Collingham's year), ie six million, of which he got about eight hundred thousand pounds plus his own Lloyd's membership returns, plus investments.

I eventually tore the sheet off and handed the pad back to Colonel Brandon. 'Income in a good year about a million.'

'I suppose you're going to say that's not much after tax.'

'You're not in the Civil Service yourself, you know,' I rejoined.

'The Oman's not the UAE. Look at these roads. Dirt tracks. No oil. Roger's done very well. Nice chap though. Always liked him. Shouldn't wish to see him go down.' He paused. 'Do you mind if I have a look at that paper?'

I handed it to him. I didn't know if it was natural curiosity on his part or an element in his thinking with regard to the whole episode but either way I was there to answer his questions.

'What you've told me is that your brother stands to lose far more than he can cover.'

'Other people will lose too,' I said. 'Every Name on the syndicate will take a punch in the pocket hard enough to knock some out for good. And this part of the world could be written off for a long time. Who knows?'

'Doesn't Lloyd's have a fund?'

'It certainly does. The policyholders have got cast iron security. But they're very strict about passing any of that on to the Names of working underwriters. My brother will be ruined but so also will the trade in the Gulf and so will the market as a whole.'

He nodded crisply. 'I can see that.'

The palm trees were getting nearer. Colonel Brandon was typically the type of man who prides himself on being factual; capable of reaching dispassionate conclusions, incorruptibly reflective of evidence. All the more so, in my experience, such men, when they found their minds made up, couldn't always trace the workings. A stone dropped into the well, a remark which dropped without a trace into the background of evidence radiated waves of adverse influence. He turned to me now with a frown.

'I'm a simple man, Turner,' he said. I smiled at him. Decent was what he meant but he didn't like to say so. He stuck his neck out crisply. 'Is your brother implicated in the fraud?' I was not to expect him to detail how exactly. He was no expert. But it was obvious that men who compete for financial gains could be too inventive for their own good.

'Ring London and check,' I said. 'Even if I were completely wrong about the character of my own brother, from the business angle he has nothing to gain and everything to lose. He went in on a gamble he should never have entertained.'

'One fit of temper's just like another fit of temper. See that band of trees before the mountain there, Cooper?' He had altered the pitch of his voice to reach the driver, 'How long will it take us to reach Coca Cola?'

'Half an hour, sir.'

'Stop for lunch at Suq.'

'Yes sir.'

'That band of trees,' he said to me, 'marks the beginning of the peninsula.'

At the top of one of the enfolding hills we got out of the car and saw the blue waters of the narrow straits stretch out with Iran dimly on the other side. Familiar thorny scrub underfoot, dusty sandsoil, sky of turquoise, sun of beaten gold.

We ate our picnic where the sergeant, Cooper, laid it out on folding tables overlooking the bay and immediately afterwards drove down to Dibbah.

This was where the curve of coastline passed successively through the three Arab countries, Dibbah Muhallab in Fujirah, Dibbah Hisn in Sharjah, both of the UAE, and Dibbah Bayah in the Oman. By the sea there was an horrendous smell from a carpet of tiny fish stretched out like tinfoil on the sand. It stank as it dried and decomposed in the hot sun, being only harvested for fertilizer. I looked around at the huge and lovely bay. The Dibbah village was reminiscent of fishing villages in Italy or Greece – the brilliant whitewashed walls shining so brightly they might almost make a sound. My shoe had sunk slightly into the sand. A little boat was nearing the shore further down the curve towards Dibbah Hisn. I could faintly hear the crowd of children on the water's edge shouting. The Colonel was looking in the same direction as I was. The moment seemed caught in a crystal of timelessness. I said to him eventually 'What are they shouting?'

'Oh the usual. *Hullah, hullah, hullah* – it's a whale. *Hatha 'l haut.* The man in the boat shouts with them and then they pull out these tiny things. Stink don't they! We'll have to be off.'

Mal and Cooper appeared over a rise in the sandy edge of the bay and at the same time a car, winding towards us from inland along the rough road we had followed. It was another Mercedes. It halted near the jeep.

Colonel Brandon said, 'Here's the Governor of Dibbah. Nuisance.'

I looked at my watch because although we didn't have a plane to catch in the sense that our transort would fly without us if we weren't there in time, it would still be inconvenient to be delayed. We'd need to get some sleep before the next day's departure for Durban. The sun no longer lay flat but sliced sideways with a cooler edge. We began to walk towards the cars. As we climbed up, the further curve of the bay came back into view with the palm-fringed edge of the Fujirah border lining out to sea.

'*Salaam alecum.*'

'*We alecum es Salaam,*' clipped back the Colonel, making it really sound like an obligatory, meaningless phrase by lifting his voice crisply on the last syllable. I remembered his father had been a vicar. The Governor acknowledged the introduction of the rest of us. He was extremely well dressed. His turban was immaculate and the long curved knife of the Omani uniform was fixed in the sash of his *thobe*. Fortunately he didn't seem anxious to prolong the encounter and after a civil five minutes his driver opened the door for him and the formalities were smoothly reversed into farewell like film running backwards.

'Well Cooper, let's be off.' We climbed in as before. The driver of the jeep couldn't be found at first but a couple of blasts from the horn brought him at the run from a nearby house.

We drove back to the airfield where the plane was waiting and paused while Cooper handed some boxes over to the pilot and saw them stowed.

'What is it, Cooper? Oh yes. I almost forgot.'

Colonel Brandon took a small package that Cooper held out to him.

'This is for you.' The terse and manly expression which had more and more settled on his features while awaiting the final moments of our farewell softened into remembered affection.

'For me?'

'My wife asked me to give it to you. Don't know what's in it but she would have been very disappointed if I'd forgotten it. Well done Cooper.'

I stored the small package in my pocket. With his characteristic shift of attention the Colonel was suddenly watching a group of birds on the tarmac over on his left.

'Thank you very much Colonel. Good luck.'

He gave me a caustic look and held out his hand.

'I think we understand each other. I'll do what I can. Good man. Good man.'

The two of us boarded the plane. Before it had started to taxi the Colonel walked defiantly away. Not the type to wave farewells. Not the type to let his friends down. Not the type to miss a party for the men. Mal said, echoing my thoughts, 'We didn't waste our time, sir. What's in that package?'

I took it out of my pocket and tore it open. 'Wire clippers. Is this some sort of a joke?'

He looked aghast. 'Lady Rosemary may be eccentric, sir, but there'd be method in her madness.'

'What is it?'

He shook his head. 'I can't quite make it out, sir.' But from the way he took them in his hand I could tell he had, for some reason, a nasty suspicion. They were quite small and delicate. 'Intricate electrical work I'd say.'

'When are we going to have to do intricate electrical work?' I asked.

'I sincerely hope not at all sir, not on a diesel ship. Only steam would involve disconnecting the alarms.' He didn't explain any further but put them in his pocket like a man who expected to have to use them in the near future in spite of what he said.

Chapter
22

THE FINAL ARRANGEMENTS for our departure the next morning for Durban dominated the unforgettable atmospheric cocktail of our last evening in Ruwi. We needed more suitable clothes for our role aboard the *Aenaftis* and found them in the ramshackle shops near the hotel, where crudely assimilated versions of modern European equipment shared the shelving space with local artifacts of Old Testament origin and bizarre items washed up from the backwaters of the nineteen-thirties. Inside the hotel itself an ambience owing more to the amorphous influence of twentieth century advertising than any culture gave the backup we needed for last minute contacts with London and the finalisation of our plans.

Shipping I S must have kept Mal Harris on the line for more than an hour in all, between three calls, and if I or Collingham survived to pick up the bills they'd be lucky. But their torrent of briefings and last minute checks and admonitions had no other effect on Mal beyond increasing the glitter in his eye.

'I feel sorry for them, sir,' he said, referring to his colleagues in London. He did too. He thought they were clean out of luck to be behind their desks a couple of thousand miles away like frantic nannies whose charges were getting dangerously near the water. As for myself, I had to forego any attempt to get hold of Roger or Sylvie in case the SIS got wind of it. I sat in the curtained alcove bleakly wondering what they were up to and praying that no added pressures of impending doom were queering the pitch beyond repair.

There was no more I could do. Until tomorrow.

In the morning there was one more item of news which Mal kept until we were safely on the plane.

'What was that?' I said. 'I didn't know there'd been an urgent phone call. Who from?'

'Lady Rosemary sir.'

I looked at him sharply. 'What for? Has Colonel Brandon decided not to back us?'

'Not that problem, no. We've got his support. But I found out about the wire clippers.'

'You've lost me.'

'I'm afraid you're not going to like it sir. James Milton pulled off a little coup.'

'He's not going to be waiting for us in Durban is he?'

He shook his head regretfully. 'I wish he was. I'd throttle him, boyo.'

He turned his face full towards me and said solemnly, 'He interfered with David Kazantsis.'

I stifled a laugh.

'He substituted the charts. Very nifty I must say. Quite professional for once. About twice every ten years that lot show a bit of skill.' His tone was bitter without the usual subdued humour.

'You mean it wasn't the correct chart of the *Aenaftis* we studied?'

'No.'

'What was it then?'

'The *Chios*.'

'Lady Rosemary knew all this?'

'They happen to be friends, sir. As you know, when she heard we were on the way she rang him deliberately, he being posted in Athens you see. Not giving a hint of our impending arrival. None of that. Just fishing for news. She's a very lively lady.'

'Like hell she is. Why didn't she tell us all this yesterday.'

'Embarrassing for her sir. The Colonel is sensitive. She

161

found an unexpected opportunity to telephone me this morning. Otherwise we'd have had to rely on the wire-clippers.'

'And what was the misinformation that James Milton managed to foist on us?'

'For our purposes only one important item.'

I just looked at him.

'The engine – the *Aenaftis* engine is steam, not diesel.'

I stared at him incredulously. 'What are we on this plane for then if we can't incapacitate the ship's engine?'

'That's another question.'

'You mean to say that James Milton, suspecting that we might have other plans and having made his own contact with David Kazantsis had us fed the wrong information. So now we're going to join a ship that we have no means at all of stopping.'

'Not quite sir.'

'You mean Lady Rosemary's blasted wire-clippers?'

'They do come into it. But the point I'm making is that the steam engine has its Achilles heel too sir.'

'What's that?'

'Salt.'

I braced myself. Or rather I did the opposite. I pressed the button on the armrest and tilted my seat back as far as it would go.

'Tell me all,' I said with resignation. 'We've got another three hours. Don't spare me. How are we going to do this one?'

'I don't know sir. I'm not a mechanic. I know the basic principles of the steam engine but . . .' He paused. 'Here's this steam engine. Now, the water that circulates through the pumps has to be pure. For a steam engine used on land of course that's no problem but in a ship at sea, Mun!' Mal's change of vocabulary reflected his anxiety. 'Here's a huge tanker ploughing through hundreds of miles of salt water, and it's driven by an engine that can be sabotaged by one grain of salt getting in the pumps.'

'Well . . .'

'Not an exaggeration I assure you. Diawl!'

'Speak English Mal.'

'Bloody hell, sir'

'Right. So our job's easy then.'

'What you mean, Mun?'

'Put salt in.'

'You think they put a ten million pound tanker driven by a steam engine in the middle of five hundred square miles of salt water and not work it all out?' He spread his left hand. 'One, the system is sealed. Two, a specimen of the feed water is tested every half hour. Three, the instant there is any salt in the feed tank an alarm rings.' He had two fingers left but he seemed to feel he'd made his case and I wasn't arguing.

'So there's no way of getting at it at all.'

'Oh yes there is. But I don't know it. And if I did, I don't know how to disconnect the alarm. That's what the wire clippers are for, see. Have you ever seen the electrical board of a tanker sir?'

'No I can't say I have. Wait a minute. Kazantsis had one. Good God!'

'Well it's something to look forward to, I can tell you. They done their best to wire up a replica of the human brain, Mun! Fine wires of every colour in patterns so convoluted and extensive it's beautiful if you like that sort of thing. Literally hundreds and hundreds of miniaturised connections and,' he paused dramatically and then went on, 'one of them is the alarm. Not one wire mind. A little system. And it will be all mixed and muddled in with the other systems.'

The air steward was just making a well timed round collecting orders for drinks. When we had settled back with a bit of liquid encouragement I said to Mal, 'How does it work? Give me a clear description again from the beginning.'

'Right sir.' He took a gulp from his glass. 'The water for the engine circulates through pumps. In the old days the engineer of the watch came to do a saline test every half hour. Every single half hour mind you. Round the clock. He took a specimen of feed water out of the system. He put it in a test tube to which he added silver nitrite. If there was any salt in the water a double decomposition takes place and silver chloride is formed and shows as a white precipitate.'

'And nowadays?'

'Sometimes – often – ships still have a manual check. But the more modern ones have an automatic monitoring mechanism. With that system, the first presence of salt activates an alarm which goes off in the duty engineer's room and the engine is switched off.'

'And if it isn't switched off?'

'The boiler would be put out of action.'

'One boiler or two?'

'Doesn't really matter because if there were two you'd put salt in the reserve feed tanks.'

'Well you seem to know a lot about it.'

'Not enough sir, I assure you. I could try, but I wouldn't know if I was disconnecting the alarm or the captain's bedside reading light.'

'That's an idea. Why not just sabotage essential electrics regardless of what they are.'

'They'd just mend it, wouldn't they. Rejoin the wires in seconds. No harm done. It's not every wire that monitors a chain reaction which can blow up the boiler.'

I mulled it over thoughtfully. It sounded difficult but somehow not impossible. 'I've got it!' I said.

The expression he turned towards me was unflatteringly pessimistic.

'There'll be someone on board who does know,' I said. 'We ourselves may not know enough and it's now too late for us to get the correct information from Shipping I S or another David Kazantsis. But you've got information on the ship itself.'

'Yes,' he conceded. 'I have. I got the complete crew list from London.'

'That's it then. Let's have a look at it.'

'Yes, sir. As from Rotterdam, that is.'

He unzipped his holdall and drew out the folder, leafed through that and extracted a sheet. I peered over his left arm. It didn't mean a thing to me, but he went through it with no response either until he came to the last name but one. Das Lal.

'Das Lal,' he muttered. 'Duw! We might be lucky again.'

'What you mean "again". Who is it?'

'I'm not sure mind. Das Lal.' He raised his head like a chap I knew who did crosswords used to mull over the visionary impulse of conflicting graphs of thought. 'Daisy. It could be him. Das Lal. Daisy.'

'I'm waiting.'

'A man I knew once, sir. Met him eight years ago on a tanker. The men called him Daisy but he was an Indian. I think, I'm not sure but I think, his real name was Das Lal, I don't know why he's down here as a messman mind you.'

'And if you're right?'

'That man sir – he could wire up Mars to Uranus.'

'If it's the same man.'

'Or a rabbit to an elephant.'

'Better still.'

'Or a London bus to a tonga.'

'Or a Porsche to a mine sweeper.'

We carried on like that until we landed. Maybe it was the alcohol – or the altitude – or the fact that when you're about to join a ship run by gangsters ferrying lethal gases to a rendez-vous with terrorists you might as well have a good laugh.

Chapter 23

AT DURBAN THE plane landed in a suave and steady curve and with no luggage beside our holdalls we were out on the streets in no time and in a taxi headed for the terminal.

It seemed cold after Piraeus. I had forgotten that summer in Europe was winter in South Africa. By the time we reached the port area and the pub that we were aiming for it was nearly dark. The surroundings we found ourselves in, beyond the obvious fact that they were rough and dirty, were depressing. Mal seemed to know it well and pointed out the offices of 'Stella Maris' mission to seamen where we planned to go later, a customs shed, a row of service buildings, a sort of seamen's doss house up a side street and a more brightly lit frontage which he called a pub. It was a bloody awful, ninety proof cafe, thick with the mixed fumes of smoke, men, food and alcohol. I followed Mal up to the counter. No-one took any notice of us either in the main room or the kitchen side. From one point of view it was reassuring. From another, we might starve to death.

Mal eventually managed to exchange a few words with a gorilla-like chap swathed in towels from the waist down and shouted over at me.

'Len, what do you want, boyo? Steak and kidney, some stew I can't pronounce or sausages?'

'Stew,' I said.

There must have been thirty or forty seamen in the room. Some of them looked clean and tidy. Others looked like tramps. A group of about eight of them were gathered around a table at one end of the room. Something about their attitude made me wonder what the object of their discussion was. An elderly seaman sitting down with his back to the wall and facing my way was being questioned by three men standing grouped around him. Another man, sitting on his left with an empty chair between them, had swivelled sideways in his seat to face the grey-haired seaman. Two men who looked like Indians were also sitting at the end of the table. I couldn't hear their voices which merged with the general noise. But when Mal turned round from the counter, one of the Indians who was just about to put some food in his mouth dropped the fork with a clatter and shouted his name. Men glanced briefly round.

'Good,' Mal said under his breath. 'Take these boyo.' I took the plates. He looked up at the advancing Indian with the full beam of his tubercular quiet smile. The Indian was small like himself but tougher looking. I fetched a couple of forks. Mal looked over his shoulder to see if I was following. He introduced me by the false name put on my papers; Len Tanner. Amrit seemed more than pleased at the encounter with Mal. He was leading the way over to the very table I'd noticed, while reiterating how delighted he was to see him and extending his welcome to me. He introduced us to the Indian who was sitting at the end of the table; not Das Lal. For the moment we sat down without any involvement with the other men. The table was green tin, wiped fairly clean but burned and scratched and the wall behind it was also green marked with the tawny stains of fat and smoke and scratched by the iron chairs.

Since we had come here in order to pick up all the gossip and make contact with the seafaring community, Mal's encounter with someone who was obviously a former shipmate was just what we wanted. Our story was that we had come off a ship which had been severely damaged in dock four weeks ago. We'd been up country enjoying ourselves and having a break and now were looking for a new berth. The cacophony of noise around us made it difficult for me to hear what was being said. I tried listening to different languages and identified ten before Mal's voice cut in saying, 'Wake up Len. You're not listenin' boyo. We may 'ave a job.' Amrit was calling over to the older man I had originally noticed and he nodded to us: a lugubrious northern face; name Sven.

It was odd that he should have drawn my attention the moment I came into the room. His appearance wasn't striking except that he looked old and out of condition. What was striking about him was that he was a seaman on the *Aenaftis*. The ship had been off-loading at Durban and was going in ballast to the Gulf to reload at Dubai. That much we already knew. When the tanks had been emptied some had been filled with water and others with inert gas, as is the routine, as a precaution against explosion. He threw more weight onto his elbows as he said that and looked at the other men. One of the standing men pulled out a chair and sat, calling over his shoulder at the same time to a mate at the bar. Sven's voice droned on. It was a grievance they had. Two of the crew had been badly scalded by a steam pipe bursting in the galley and had had to go to hospital. The ship's officers were in a tearing hurry to replace them and go. Mal pulled his fingers across his jawbone until he held his lower lip pinched forwards. I never said a word. Amrit said, pointing at us 'They're looking for a berth.' The Swede shook his head, although what he meant was yes but what a lousy ship. Mal arranged for us to get passes and go back with him. The master was desperate to be off without further delay. He'd take anyone. All the rest of the talk, the to-ing and fro-ing, the condensation inside the foetid building, the polite chat of the Indians, a weird chanting game that a group of Chinese were playing, a small fat fellow with a bandaged arm who looked Mexican, the melée of languages and men, all merged in my memory five minutes after I'd left the place never to return. Presumably it's still there – still full of seamen and cooking as it was the night Mal and I in company with Sven and still followed by Amrit and friend, stepped out and started on the long walk to the ship.

The air was cool and full of stars. We were in a crowded built up area but it was all pipes and machinery and the towering drums of storage and refinery in the near distance on the land side of the loading buoys. We showed our passes at each gate. We were now walking along an endless road that drove straight out to sea. I thought it had a wall on one side but suddenly the wall gave way and I realised it had been a ship all along. Another had already started on the left. Huge pipes tied in bundles edged the waterway with what looked to me like giant stopcocks and other more complicated mechanisms. Mal said, 'We should have got a taxi.' The others stopped and looked around as if one might come up at any moment. As soon as we stopped walking the unearthly atmosphere enveloped us. I wished we had arrived during the daytime when even this, to me, futuristic shipping scene must bear some resemblance to normality. Then men presumably hurried about in the sun and the sound of voices would humanise the brutish outline of the machinery. Now a light dark wind ruffled my hair and my heart lurched sickly. As if he read my mind, Amrit said in his comfortable Indian voice, 'No taxi my God. We'll keep walking.' I didn't think of asking how many miles it was. Each shape that loomed alongside I assumed to be ours until we passed it. It took about fifteen minutes to walk the length of one ship. One could see on to the deck of the loaded ships whereas those that were in ballast rode high on the water and made a barrier between us and the open sea. I'd never seen so much metal in my life. The giant lights of the jetty shone like cold moons on the unsympathetic outlines of these ocean-going shoeboxes with their unwieldy superstructures piled up on one end like a block of flats. From time to time we passed a ship that was alive with activity. But as if to deliberately counteract any inroads of normality the men at work were all masked. I guessed they were probably pumping oil off the ship we were passing, masked against the poisonous fumes. If they shouted to give or acknowledge an order their voices were muffled. On deck the men were busy mainly with the vast red painted stopcocks and coupling mechanisms to link one pipe with another.

After a brief glance my companions paid little attention but just kept walking. Their conversation was all on the cricket league tables. I'm interested in cricket but I couldn't compete with the expertise of the Indians and Sven, whose endless voyages around the world seemed to be made in the phantom company of every sportsman ever televised or otherwise reported. Just when the ache in my legs was beginning to change frequency, Sven said, 'Here we are,' and a vast ship in ballast towered between us and the now luminous sea. As we walked nearer it projected higher until it cut off our view of the water. I wondered how on earth we were expected to get on. The high rise block of flats at one end which was the bridge was peppered with lights but between them and us this unpromising cliff of iron seemed to me to pose quite a problem. As we had walked along, our journey had been enlivened by frequent mouthfuls of schnapps from a bottle which Sven kept in his jacket pocket during the brief moments he wasn't drinking it. Mal had drunk little and the Indians none at all. But I had compensated for my lack of conversation with a companionable readiness to share and share alike with Sven. Mal took my arm and started to walk along purposefully. To my surprise, camouflaged by all the shadows and painted exactly the same colour as the ship, a ridiculously narrow ladder stretched down from the deck of the *Aenaftis* to the terminal floor. Sven took hold of it and started to climb. With his huge puffy white hands his white hair and pale skin, and dappled grey jacket swinging loose at one side with the weight of the now almost empty bottle of schnapps, he looked like a fly newspaper's cartoon of an elephant walking up a wall.

'I'm glad you think it's funny, boyo,' Mal said to me in an undertone as he prodded me up before him. 'Hang on tight. There may be oil on the rungs.'

There was.

At the top a seaman waved us past and Sven, weaving slightly, beckoned us towards the lights. I looked at my watch but I'd forgotten to alter it and it read three, either am or pm but not right in either case. That light night wind that I would probably never feel again without an inward shiver flitted freely from the open sea across the deck. It sobered me up a little but not too much. I was sick of the endless walking by the time we reached the superstructure and was glad to find that our way up the bridge consisted of standing in a lift and pressing a button. We got out on the fifth floor.

The bridge was a vast space with banks of machinery in a console arrangement along one side and a row of windows along the other that overlooked the sixty foot drop or more on to the deck. One man was sitting alone in a chair listening to the radio.

'Chief officer,' Mal said in an undertone glancing at his watch. The chief officer on board ship takes the four to eight watch. I looked at Mal's wristwatch and tried to alter my own. The adjustment knob slipped. Sven shepherded us up to the man who didn't move or turn the radio down. The Indians had gone down to the crew's quarters below the main deck to visit some friends.

'What is it?' the man rapped out suddenly when we were within a few feet of him. I heard his voice with a shock of surprise. He had the black brows and curly hair of a Mexican, Spaniard, Greek, Italian – anything rather than Scots. Sven explained and the hybrid strange eyes swivelled on to Mal and me. I felt myself tighten inwardly. His look was both unfriendly and careless. He picked up a telephone and pressed a button.

'Tell the captain there are two seamen here on business to see him.' He waited, looked away towards us again and said, 'Can ye cook?' I was meant to be an ex-mess man so I nodded. He seemed to consider that. After a few more grunted remarks down the intercom he put down the receiver and said to Sven, 'Take them down to the main bridge deck Seaman.' As far as he was concerned that was the end of the conversation. It didn't take any effort to remind oneself that the officers on board this ship were probably aware of the criminal intentions of the owners.

We went back through the chartroom to the left, down a floor with also the offer of another down of schnapps. I shook my head. Perhaps I was drunk enough. The captain's suite of rooms was on the main deck and we stepped out of the left into a weirdly unseagoing world of wall to wall carperting, large bulky furniture, and all the trappings of someone's notion of a comfortable hotel. The door to the captain's rooms was open.

A wide hallway with doors on either side led in the direction of the noise. Several angry voices talking all together came from a group of men standing in the middle of a huge sitting room. Armchairs, TV, bookcases, desks, lamps: the designer had at least had the decency not to put in a fireplace – and five men, their main language being English although the accents were thick and various, so engrossed in argument that our arrival went unremarked. Mal and I stood waiting. Sven approached the group, his brow knotted, his ability to mentally grasp anything in a parlous state. The captain saw him and threw back his head with a silencing gesture to the others. There was a grumbling pause. A Mexican-looking man, very handsome and vexed, shook his curls and finished an impassioned but almost incomprehensible sentence. They were refusing to do something or other.

'Sven, my old friend,' the captain said. Sven knotted his brow to listen. The men mostly looked at us.

'I am about to read the articles to these men who say they will not go down to examine the suction valve in No 3 Tank. '

The captain – according to Shipping I S briefings; Dmitri Kolnyses, 45, born in Athens, educated in Crete where his father ran a building firm for fifteen years, married to a German woman, five children, Masters Certificate 1978, no known criminal background, which was to say precisely nothing – exuded an air of unflappable good humour.

'Are you willing to go down Sven? After it has been gas freed by Butterworthing?' He spoke to him in the rough nannyish tones of a superior whose subordinate is obviously drunk. Sven deliberated very seriously and well he might. Crude oil residue emits a lethal gas when mixed with oxygen – poisonous and highly inflammable. Going down into a tank that has been emptied is a dangerous pastime. The captain turned his broad face on Mal and myself. Most people's eyes went straight to my left arm and so did his briefly.

'Yes?' he said.

'We heard you're short of crew, sir. My friend here and I are looking for a berth, sir,' Mal said.

'Papers alright?'

'Yes sir.'

'What was your last job?'

'Ordinary seaman me, sir.'

'Second mess man, sir,' I said, opening my mouth for the first time.

The other men fidgeted.

'Very good. Very good. 'You worried?'

'Yes sir. But we need berths, sir.' The captain turned round to the other men.

'If these two men are prepared to go down for the inspection, you,' pointing, it seemed, at random to two of them, 'won't be needed. Any more argument from the rest of you – I'll read you the articles. Port police. Goodbye. Farewell.' He swept his palms together in the middle of the air as if swatting a mosquito, 'Finish!' His tone was perfunctory, informal, but bullying – used to rubbish crews and discontented men.

The men shifted their feet discontentedly. The handsome young Mexican jerked his head sharply looking from one side to the other. He would not wash the tanks. Don't bother about the articles. He was going. He looked close to tears for some reason, but I thought to myself, you don't know what you're missing mate. I had a sudden idle vision of him praying to a statue of the Virgin Mary in some little place where the noise of traffic couldn't be shut out. And the statue, painted blue with feet sticking out at the bottom, slowly lifted one arm and crossed out a name in a book that stood on a stand in front of her, under the title of the *Aenaftis*.

'Come on. Don't stand there dreaming boyo . . .' Mal prodded me. 'We got a job, mun.'

We followed the other men out of the room. The interview was over.

Once along the corridor to the left, into the lift, and down to the crew deck, abruptly the resemblance to a large hotel ended and that of a spacious, scarcely occupied, luxury modern prison began. Everything was metal – the floor, the handrails, the ceilings. The cabins went round in a long square with these daft square windows called portholes down here gazing out onto the derelict landscape like picture windows in a council block. The officer signing Mal and me on indicated two doors, ticked his chart, and left.

I opened the first door. A small passageway had a shower room on one side and cupboards on the other. Straight ahead was a room with a hand woven carpet of orange, curtains at the window, upholstered sofa, desk and table and a small bunk. It looked quite comfortable. Mal flung open the cupboard. A white boiler suit was inside it along with a couple of towels and a spare blanket.

'Put that on,' he said. 'Mine's next door.' I put my holdall on the floor. From the porthole I could see onto a sort of promenade which went round the area of the superstructure running inside the ship's hull. It was illuminated with actual round portholes called scuttles on the port and presumably the starboard side, and between these now, in the hours of darkness, lights shone. I started to take off my clothes and pull on the boiler suit. It was cool without the jersey. The sleeves were wide and loose and I could slip the plastercast through easily. I did up the belt, picked up my jersey, slung it round my neck and made for the other door.

Mal was already coming out and we started back towards the lift. The place seemed extraordinarily empty but on the main deck three seamen were assembled. The officer in charge was handing out equipment. I took my bundle without comment. We began to walk along a raised catwalk down the middle of the deck. The atmosphere was like an execution party. I thought it couldn't be that bad.

'Watch out on the ladder,' Mal hissed at me. 'Hold on with your good arm for Chrissake. I hope you like heights.'

Our ship was now brightly lit up with floodlights. When we came to the first pair of tanks five men were detailed off to the left and our group to the right. Imitating the others I slipped the mask I'd been given over my nose and mouth, and followed Mal towards the ladder. It looked alright at first. After the climb up the ship's side I'd given up expecting the sort of ladder that a safety inspector would consider adequate. I put my foot on the top rung, took one look at the mechanical sky that overhung the deck and started to climb down. After about ten rungs my eyes started to adjust to the dimly lit gloom. Through the stuffy mask an unmistakable smell of ordinary gasoline thickened each breath. The muted thud of the other seamen's boots shook the rungs, and as I gripped the handrail my fingers slid unnervingly every now and then on oil. Ignoring Mal's advice I paused a second to look down and around me. I went down another thirty rungs or so before looking again. The size of the dark cavern over which I was suspended took my breath away. I might have been a spider dangling over the well of a cathedral.

Another ladder sprung off at an angle and disappeared into the immensity of darkness, the once-white-painted structure spinning fragilely off into space until it was lost to sight. I could slide my left hand only loosely over the rail because I still had very little grip in the fingers but I was glad that it was that way round. It made me feel more secure to get a firm grab on each rung with my right as I descended.

The men below climbed on without haste. No-one seemed in any great hurry. As we neared the bottom half, vast metal supports going across the empty space at intervals began to loom up shaped like colossal buttresses splaying out towards the base until they formed a wall across the floor and up the other side. Without these web frames the tanks, when empty, would collapse under their own stress. The tank had already been washed. The so-called 'Butterworthing' process, named after the man who invented it, is a system by which boiling hot water spray washes down the tank from level to level until the final oily slop is pumped from its floor into the waiting barge alongside. But pockets of residual sludge would remain, and if disturbed by the simple process of being trodden in, emit undetectable fumes lethal enough to kill a man in four minutes. Anyone would assume that the answer would be for the men to go down into the tanks wearing masks and carrying oxygen cylinders. But the bulk of that equipment on a man's back would make his body too wide to go through the holes in the supports. If the holes were bigger it would weaken the structure too much to withstand the seas; check mate.

Once we got to the bottom and started work I could see in practice what before I had known in theory. We had been told to keep together and the first men were waiting at the foot of the ladder. I stepped aside and waited for Mal. He looked around him as he got off with big eyes like a novice.

'Duw,' he said with a soft curling of his lips, 'I must be the only seaman who likes it down here, Mun. Reminds me of the pit.'

'What pit?' I said as we walked behind the others towards the first great transept of metal. 'You weren't a miner.'

'No, but when I was a nipper I got taken down by one of my uncles. It's in the blood. See that?'

I looked where he was pointing.

'That's what you've got to watch for.'

I couldn't see a thing. There was very little reflection off the floor of the tank which was the dull uniform colour of river mud until the build-up of distance swallowed it in darkness.

'There. Look.'

Peering I could see a very slight shimmer. Just as the inside of this colossus of modern technology was structured like a cathedral half turned inside out, here was a sinister shadow in glutinous quiet half shades of the rainbow, like the lights of stained glass. And it meant death. The reverse image of the life giving force of spiritual regeneration was complete. It was a patch of oil residue.

'Stir that with your boots and breathe three times boyo, and tell St Peter that he had no business letting Scotland beat Wales in Cardiff. Look ahead of you. You can't spot the sludge close-to; get it from a distance and make sure you remember where each one is. Keep looking.'

We started forward again towards the first opening in the metal wall that formed the base of the first cross beam. In it an opening just big enough for a man to crawl through provided the only access into the next section. And the next. We tramped the whole length of the tank until we got to the suction valve which was at the end of the tank on the inboard side.

The men went mostly in silence, hating it. Regularly every three minutes the leading seaman contacted the man on deck by radio.

The smell of gas made you feel sick, but that was not the gas that killed. If you've got a headache Mal said you knew you were alive. The fumes from the sludge were different. Once stirred and mixed with oxygen, they could only be smelt with the first breath. Like most really cruel poisons, after that it could not be detected.

The tank was divided into six huge sections. Six climbs through the access hole in the transept, six glimmering moons from the Butterworth plates open on the deck above our heads. No seven. One space divided internally six times . . .

I was only tired and feeling sick. There was silence except for the muted rubberised tread of our feet. The lights had non-static switches to guard against explosions in the volatile atmosphere. The boiler suits were cotton. Boots rubber. When we were half way through a man slipped. I couldn't really see him, quite some distance away in the gloom, and at first took no notice. There was a shout and a cackle of command from the intercom. A man ran past dragging something. There was a trample of feet miles ahead that echoed down the hollow ribcage of the tank. Everyone was standing still except the seaman who was struggling to cram his bundle through the transept hole. I realised with horror that the bundle was another man. I threw down my equipment and ran towards the hole. 'In front of you,' I heard Mal's voice thunder behind me. I ran sharply round a pool of slime, grabbed the feet of the unconscious man and fed them through the hole. And then another. And another. And then the ladder. Christ, like trying to get into the hold of a Boeing 747 by climbing up a string in mid-flight. Two minutes must have already gone. They lowered an oxygen mask down through the plate. Half way up a wire pulley lowered and was hooked onto the back of his boiler suit. I let go of his heels and he swung like a pendulum banging against the rungs. I heard a tearing sound. But the cloth held.

After that, the valve was inspected and repaired. In the gloomy light the combined brutality and caution needed grotesquely misrepresented our movements as we completed the task and turned back in the direction of the access ladder.

When it was finished the climb back up to the deck was endless. The night air on deck that had tasted foul before was like champagne now, pure and spotless from the wide acres of filtering ocean. I pulled my mask off and half sat on the handrail. Two other seamen in white boiler suits like ours were tightening down the Butterworth plates and sealing off the entrance to the tank. They were always in a hurry, on these tankers. To refill an empty tank with inert gas re-cycled from the engine to obviate the chance of explosion. I looked up at the sky with all that metallic light and stars in it. Mal was talking to the man on the other side of him. Eventually he turned to me.

'Come on Len. Let's get something to eat.' We started on the long tramp up the deck. 'And I've got good news for you. Daisy's on board. Das Lal. That's him.'

'Well, thank God for that,' I said. 'When did you find out?'

'Chap told me just now. In the galley like you.'

'I still can't understand why he's down as a messman if he's an electrician.'

'That's his hobby, Mun. Not on 'is cards.'

We washed down our boots, went back to the cabins to clean up, and then back to the main deck to get something to eat.

A distant sound of sitar music played by one of the Indian seamen merged with the unlikely scene of metal and wakefulness in the unfamiliar dark of foreign seas. Mal slid back the lid of the food container and helped himself to fish soup and bread and cheese. I helped myself.

Perhaps an almost empty motorway cafe was the nearest parallel to the room we were in. Three men at one table half the room away, and another just arriving made up the entire clientele. But then it was an unsocial hour in any place. The smell and taste of oil kills hunger and I had no particular desire to eat. It was Mal's idea and a good one as it turned out. The fish soup was fantastic. I couldn't believe it.

'Everyone gets some luck,' Mal said. 'The crew list had that Frenchman on it, remember.'

'Good god,' I said, 'The chef from Maxim's taking a cheap holiday.'

'Enjoy yourself while you can, Mun,' he said. 'They've got tempers, that lot, and you'll be working with him later.'

I didn't take him seriously. I got up to see if there was some

178

rouille. Sure enough there was a whole bowl full under the hatch and a basket of rounds of bread. I took it incredulously back to the table. I forgot about not being hungry.

'I been on a ship once,' Mal said, 'with a terrible cook. I haven't forgotten him yet.'

'How many ships were you on?'

'He wasn't a cook at all. He was a Mexican pipe-welder it turned out. Any more bread?'

I passed him some.

'The ship did the run from Canada to Rotterdam and it was so damn cold, ice everywhere, Mexican oil being taken on as poisonous as ruddy cyanide, and the messmen had to be replaced, the second mate had to go to hospital, the first mate went off on a joy ride in a shore boat and crashed it into a pier. Misery. And it was all the cooking.'

I gave a shout of laughter.

'Listen to this,' he said. 'The Captain's wife, she was on board. We were going to sail the next day and when she thought of the terrible food she was going to have for the next six weeks she insisted on going ashore for one last decent meal before leaving. We were secured to another ship because the port was full; Yokohama fenders, with great huge truck tyres lashed on the outside to stop the ships from crashing in the swell; the winches frozen, the gang-plank covered with a mixture of ice and oil. It sloped sharply because of the ship being in ballast and the other one loaded. She was a pretty woman too . . .'

'Was? You don't mean she was killed?'

'Nearly boyo, nearly. She slipped you see. And all because of the cooking.'

The only trouble with eating when you're tired is that after the first blissful stimulus you get very sleepy.

Mal looked at me. 'Don't you want to hear who saved her?'

'You didn't!'

'She had a fur coat on. I was on the other side tying up when I saw her slide down the ice like a polar bear heading for the water.'

'I'll check up on this story when we get back to London Mal, so mind your language.'

'Take my word for it. I caught the 'em.'

'The what?'

'The hem,' he said. 'There was me, one foot locked on the rail, flat on my face in a rugby tackle with this fur coat and she screaming as loud as a fog horn, dangling half over. There was a Pole who jumped ship at Vancouver and he was mad about her because she listened to all his stories about his family and his troubles being a refugee and all that, see. He walked out on the ice like an acrobat. His feet never slipped an inch. He picked her up in his arms and carried her back on board and she had a dinner of mashed corned beef and diesel wrapped in black pastry like the rest of us.'

When I eventually stopped laughing, I fell asleep. Mal said, 'Eat up. It's getting light. I'll get some coffee.'

He was right. I watched a thin grey line that had appeared in the sky swell like an ooze of more water. I felt immovable with sleep. I must have dropped off again because I jumped when he put the cups down on the table. The coffee was as good as the fish soup.

A man came in at the door and shouted, 'Tanner!'

I was too tired to register anything much. And I'd forgotten the alteration in my name on the papers.

He shouted again and Mal said, 'What you waiting for, Mun? Cook wants you.'

I staggered to my feet.

'Go and get your own flying mixture,' he said, adding quietly, 'sir.'

Chapter
24

I DIDN'T WITNESS our exodus from Durban. I was down the galley cooking bacon as if we were doing breakfast in the Connaught: two kinds, crispy and plain. The other chap who skivvied with me was Daisy but I had no chance to say hello. The cook yelled at him as if he was deaf but he took it all with impassive courtesy, running from one hot plate to the other, born to please. Once the ship started moving the vibrations shook it like an elephant snoring. I thought that it was just a feature of starting up, but when a tanker gets going the vibrations never stop. Neither did the work for a full three hours.

When the cook noticed my left arm was in plaster which was not until after half an hour of panic activity, he stood and stared at me as if my very existence was an outrage personally inflicted on him. In retrospect, and bearing in mind the next few days, he was probably drunk, breakfast or no breakfast. I pretended I didn't understand. I said in immaculate cockney, 'Wassa trouble, Cookie? I can 'old the plates.'

I held one plate to demonstrate and when he saw I could just hold it he ground his teeth. According to him I was a complete fool to imagine that a filthy seaman who couldn't get a jacket over his arm was expected to serve the officers in the dining saloon. What though they were only Turks masquerading as the descendants of the finest race in the world with the worst cuisine. He, Frenchie (his name) had standards. The Goanese, both of them, would serve in the saloon. I could do the bloody chopping and frying. All of it. And I could carry the plates but not past the door. If the officers so much as saw me he, Frenchie, would find out and kill me with his bare hands.

I was a bit tired but I didn't fail to get the point. If it was his role in life to try to make my life hell he'd just have to get on with it. I had other fish to fry.

At one o'clock two men came to take over from Daisy and myself. I looked at them and looked at Frenchie. Someone not all that far away from where I was standing was a ruddy masochist. Neither of the two men knew how to cut a loaf of bread, whereas Frenchie had *Daube de Mouton Navarin* on the menu, and swore he'd slice his own heart out with the meat cleaver if it wasn't perfect.

I was off duty. I went up on deck shivering with cold as soon as the door of the lift closed behind me. After three hours in the galley I needed some air before going to my cabin for a rest. In front of me the seemingly endless expanse of the deck intercepted at wide intervals with slabs of mechanical equipment appeared deserted. I couldn't even see the water. I started to walk. It was difficult to identify the various mastlike structures except one which Mal had pointed out: Immarsat Radio satellite equipment, and unlike the rest of the ship, new. It meant that anything that happened on board could be communicated at speed. I put my bare hands into the pocket of my overalls, and hunched into the loose folds of my pullover. At least the sky was now blue.

I had never before set foot on a tanker, although the details of hundreds had passed through my hands on the floor of Lloyd's, including this one. I stood on the deck now making an inventory of myself and my surroundings. The people for whom I was working, on whose behalf I was making this absurd and probably fatal voyage, would be amazed if they could see where I was at this moment. And where were they? Roger had retreated inside his own head and slammed the door, Sylvie ditto to France, and as for Polly, who allied herself with Demetrios Chia and the killers of Thelamion, for the moment I couldn't imagine where people like her went when you were not watching them. I probably only needed some sleep but I felt as if I needed a life transplant.

I could see the water now alongside but resisted the temptation to stroll over to the rail. I wanted to walk to the prow where, on more normal ships, the bell was rung but on this no-one bothered to walk so far: to walk past number five tank head that was sealed with the stop-cock bolted down.

I was daydreaming as I tramped along thinking of Sylvie and Roger – wondering if things would ever be the same again. Roger and Sylvie might part, and then she and I could be together; but the idea gave me no pleasure at all. I wanted both of them, not trading one against the other. And for that matter, the sisterly element in my infatuation for Sylvie held a lot of charm. She was the ideal. If she walked into the drawing-room and came and kissed the side of my face while I was reading the Sunday papers, I was happy. But would she ever be able to do that again without embarrassment? Would the three of us ever be able to pick up where we left off? I trudged along, immersed in my thoughts, when a voice shouted, 'Tanner!'

I jumped and stumbled over a cable.

'What's wrong with ye man? Are ye deaf as well as crippled?'

'No sir,' I said. It was the First Officer who we'd met the previous evening on the watch, the powerful impact of his unwholesome racial mixture even more evident in daylight and in the open air. He seemed to have appeared from nowhere and to be in a chatty mood. He stood up ahead of me with his hands in the pockets of a warm jacket, his levantine hairstyle ruffled in the wind of our passage.

'It'll get warmer in a day or two,' he said. 'Is it London ye come from as I judge by ye're accent?' He gestured to me to walk alongside him and we continued towards the bows.

'Yes sir, Clapham sir.'

'How long ye been away?'

I hadn't worked that one out. What did my so-called discharge book say? I should have spent my waking time recalling details of that, not daydreaming about the situation at home.

'Off'n on sir. Don't remember really. Must be five year at least.'

'Married?'

'No. Not me sir.'

He seemed quite satisfied for the time being. We had reached the end of our walk. Like a couple of strangers on the seafront we stood by the flat rail and looked down fifty foot or so on to the water. The forward passage of the uncompromisingly square cut prow shifted the water massively ahead. It made a pattern like an earth mover on a building site: not the elegant arrowheaded furrow of a proper ship. I dug down into my jersey to get away fom the wind.

'I think I'll go back sir,' I said.

I felt, apart from anything else, that I must positively smell of deception. I didn't even know how to take leave of the superior officer who had buttonholed me on deck for a chat. How was it done?

He stayed leaning on the rail but twisted his head right round. I made to take a step away, paused, uncomfortable with his reaction. He said nothing for what seemed like at least a full minute, but looked at me searchingly as if the wildly disparate influences of his hybrid parentage gave him a lien on all things in this world that didn't fit, that were out of true. When he spoke, he didn't move his eyes away from my face. He said, 'Ye're no seaman. Don't deny it, man.'

He had all my attention. Except a fraction of it that was concentrated on Mal who had appeared very quietly and was coming up along the rail behind him.

'I dunno what you mean,' I said and waited.

'Police is it? In trouble are ye?'

It wasn't a bad idea. I said, 'P'raps.'

He kept his eyes fixed on me. He was thinking. And so was I. I said, 'Any objections? I handwashed the tanks didn't I? I do my bit. Best refuge from the cops since sliced bread.'

He kept me on the hook of his eye for another instant and then straightened his back and gave a sneering nod of his head. Mal had draped himself casually over the rail some five or six paces away and became invisible again.

'I'll be watching you Tanner. Remember that.'

'And I'll be bloody watching you mate,' I thought as I let him walk past me, 'you see if I don't.'

I waited in case he looked back but he didn't. After a careful few minutes I joined Mal by the rail.

'Nasty drop that,' he said, indicating the water.

'I think it's just as well you didn't throw him in though,' I said. 'It might have been premature.'

'Just as long as we haven't missed an opportunity we'll regret, Mun.'

'He thinks I'm on the run from the law.'

'He should know, shouldn't he?'

'Let's hope not,' I said. 'Come on. It's freezing out here. If nobody's going to object I'm off to my bed.'

We walked easily down the deck – a process that four hours later was hard to believe. If we had looked back we'd have seen the beginning of a cloud like a cliff of black rock growing up between the sky and the sea. Nature in a somewhat heavy-handed way was about to have a go at taking over our mission.

Chapter
25

FOR THREE HOURS I slept and then Mal and I met and went to the boardroom for a coffee and to meet Daisy, who was with his two fellow Goanese shipmates. They were charming men, all of them, beyond the mere fact of their oddly stylised courtesy and sometimes hilarious version of the English language. I'd have been delighted to meet them any time and now more than ever. The expertise they shared among themselves was extraordinary – from playing pipes and the sitar to wide-ranging knowledge of philosophy, sport, homeopathic medicine and, of course, electronics. They were in a state of humorous depression having discovered that the films taken on by the ship in Durban were all the same as the tapes offloaded at Rotterdam. But they would watch them nevertheless. They were off to the cinema at about the same time as Daisy and I had to rejoin Frenchie in the galley.

It was then that the beginning of the storm first struck. On the way to the lift the floor tipped me for the first time from one side of the gangway to the other, but I took no notice. I knew of course about the peculiar combination of dangerous characteristics sometimes created by the Mozambique Agulas current and bad weather off the South African coast. But my mind was on other things.

In the galley Frenchie already had all the battens up. Which was not to say that he had changed his intentions about the next menu. It was at first only difficult to chop and wash and generally manoeuvre around straps and boards holding all the equipment steady. At first. The change when it came was quite sudden.

I was breaking eggs into a bowl when something that felt like a gigantic hammer blow hit the ship and the laws of gravity suddenly went into reverse. The egg yoke went flying upwards, the bowl and the surface it was on dropped as if into a well and I ended up on the floor under a hail of kitchen equipment. I picked myself up double-fast because one of the huge locked fridges was straining against its mooring and I didn't want it on top of me. Daisy had blood pouring from his arm. I was about to ask if I could help him when I was hurled off my feet again. Frenchie cursed and swore at the lot of us until with another mighty heave all the lights went out and even his voice was drowned in the deafening cacophony of smashing equipment and roaring seas.

I started to try to crawl towards where I remembered the door to have been. In it there suddenly appeared an officer carrying a lamp. I hadn't seen him before and couldn't see him too well now but the amazing thing was that he remained standing. He staggered but didn't lose his balance as the ship leapt into another dive.

'Das Lal, Tanner, LeBrun.'

He shouted orders for us to go up to the Main Deck, which was to say not on deck of course but inside and using the stairs not attempting the lift. He hooked one lamp up. I tried to stand but couldn't remain on my feet. Daisy, with blood all down one side of his overalls, stood over me offering his other arm for my support.

'Thanks a lot,' I said. 'I'd better crawl,'

Like a party of hopeless drunks we managed to get out and up the stairs. On the Main Bridge Deck, apart from one Italian seaman having a passionate private conversation with the Virgin Mary, the men were surprisingly calm. I couldn't see Mal and presumed he was somewhere else being sick. I didn't feel sick myself but my arm ached murderously where I had cracked the plaster against the table leg. But if anything was capable of taking my mind off it, it was the incredible scene visible through the plate glass window on the open deck outside. I managed to get upright holding a bar and sat on a bolted down chair.

The ship, while still in the track of the Agulas current, had met the advancing storm, and freak conditions which had once cut a two hundred and fifty ton ULCC clean in half, were now upon us. No doubt she had had a weather alert. But the ship was well out to sea and into its course and there was no time, either from the point of view of the ship's vital secret deadline or the practicalities of navigation, to get out of the way of the storm.

There was a brilliant moon that went on and off like a floodlight with a faulty switch as black wedges of cloud either grappled or released it. By its light the storm and current combined could be seen in wild conflict, one minute sucking back chasms of water and the next hurling the piled up waves like solid mountains onto the deck. Tankers can't ride waves because of their weight but crash through them like piledrivers. In these conditions the technique didn't work. Three, perhaps five, times the huge mass, block of flats and all, dropped like a stone into space and we, sixty foot up in the superstructure, confronted eyeball to eyeball the shrieking crest of the surrounding waves. When they crashed down, the deck below, despite its height being half in ballast, disappeared from view, but each time eventually floundered back to the surface. Both masts on deck had been smashed off, including the essential top half of the Immarsat satellite radio mast. If Mal and I survived at all that could be useful to us. And in the intervals of bucketing chaos ghostly fireworks of spray in the half light shot thirty foot high.

At intervals officers shouted for individual men, mainly mechanical and electrical. Judging from the hasty remarks of one of the Indians who had been at work in the engine room there might not be much left for Mal and me to do. As far as going out on deck was concerned or trying to rescue any of the equipment, there wasn't a hope. No man however harnessed would last ten seconds. All one could do was watch.

Eventually the storm abated. Like a pack of wolves turning tail the winds howled at greater distances. Exhausted men began to make their way down to the lower decks. When the sea had calmed enough for me to be able to stand I was about to stagger after them when an officer arrived in the wardroom shouting, 'Messmen!'

I couldn't get through the door without passing him. He looked about eighteen and I could have strangled him when he said, 'Name?'

'Tanner, sir.'

He looked down a list he had in his hand. 'Coffee on the bridge, Tanner. Now.'

In any other circumstances I'd have ground his little ears together until they squeaked. As it was I slumped past him, hearing his voice call out behind me for other 'volunteers' from the room. I got into the lift not knowing if the blasted thing would work or not but it took me down to the kitchens. There, in the filthy chaos made by the storm, three seamen under the direction of a junior officer were exhaustedly struggling to clear the debris and set the place to rights. I made the coffee, every cup feeling like a lead weight, loaded a tray and staggered back up the lift. One of Frenchie's late recruits was with me. He looked Slav, huge hands wrapped around his tray, brow knotted in tiredness, probably like my own. He was going to the officers' wardroom, I to the bridge. I pressed the button with my elbow when he had got out and stood for a few seconds in solitary silence waiting for the lift to stop.

To map out again the geography of the bridge deck, the lift as I was standing was to the left of the chartroom and beyond that the bridge itself. As I stepped out I heard the sound of raised voices and an argument that didn't falter as I approached with the tray.

'Will ye speak English. I'm just as much involved in this as you are.'

My friend, the First Officer, sounding pretty heated was immediately soothed by the gravelly tones of the Captain. I strained my ears to hear. The tray was heavy.

'. . . time,' he was saying. 'We are on time. Now. First Engineer. Tell Anderson.'

I thought, 'Your Turkish seaman father didn't stop to

marry your Scots mother then.' I must have been half drunk with tiredness this time, not schnapps. I walked over to a table, put down the tray and said, 'Shall I pour coffee, sir?'

They had stopped talking now, waiting for me to go.

'Leave it,' said Kolnyses, 'Scoulos!' He gestured to the other man who started to walk over. Anderson's attention was fortunately not on me for once.

'Look here,' he broke out before I was clear of the room, 'If the plates are buckled . . .'

I didn't hear any more. The lift doors closed and I pressed the button to go straight down to the crew deck. This time no-one was going to keep me from my bed.

Dawn was breaking as I made my way along the enclosed walk between the hull and the row of rooms. There was not much debris here – nothing much to break. The light was dull and grey but as I turned to open my cabin door a splinter of pure sunlight pierced the clouds near the horizon. I watched it for a moment, but then turned and went off to my bed. Nothing seemed as beautiful as the idea of sleep.

I was off duty for the next eight hours and I slept right through it. When I woke about midday the first thing I noticed was that it was warm. I lay sheltered and silent in the half-light of the curtained room piecing my memory together. No more storm. Everything including the bunk that I was on vibrated with the steady rhythm of the ship's engines, but there was no other sound or indication of movement. My mind leapt anxiously to the date. It was the 11th of August. Four more days to go before the rendezvous in the Gulf.

I got up, had a shower, dressed. The plaster on my arm was cracked. I handled it carefully, tried to keep it out of the water and wondered what I'd be able to get for breakfast. As I was about to go out there was a knock on the door and Mal came in. Daisy was with him.

'Look what we got here,' he said. 'Another one-armed man.'

Daisy had got clean overalls on and a left arm padded from wrist to elbow with bandages.

'Excuse this intrusion,' he said, 'but I was worried about you. Mal said you were sleeping.'

'Thanks for trying to help me last night,' I said. 'How's your arm?'

'No problem, no problem. It is fine now.'

He smiled broadly. 'I asked da Sousa to strap my elbow so that I couldn't work in the kitchens for a while. He is a very obliging fellow.'

I preferred not to think of my own next stint with Frenchie. Together the three of us went off towards the messroom.

It was crowded in comparison with last time there, the atmosphere like a holiday camp as men, happy with the euphoria of survival, ate a variety of foods depending on what meal they were on. Since it was Frenchie's second in command who had prepared it I was happy that mine was breakfast. Bacon and eggs can survive as much rough treatment as the tanker apparently could.

Sun poured through the windows. The coffee was Greek this time or Turkish, depending on your politics. Two Italians, one of them the Virgin Mary's friend from the evening before, shared our table. They talked just like Italians should, about women and Italy all the time. When Mal suggested going for a swim they agreed with enthusiasm and we went off to the recreation area where, roughly behind the gymnasium and cinema a large pool in the open air had been refilled since the storm. There are seamen who work on tankers who never go ashore but live year in, year out, in the unreal unconfined confines of these huge ships. I could almost see the attraction of it. The grinding daily politics of ordinary existence was receding almost as fast as the African coast as our course cut further out to sea, beginning the long oblique line which led to the Gulf. I began to feel drowsy again lying in the sun. I saw my first albatross through a half mist of sleep and wondered if it was the real thing – the wing span, so beautiful, static and vast. I remember confused thoughts about a Chinese kite before nearly falling asleep but Mal had other ideas.

'I told Daisy we want to have a talk with him,' he said. 'Sit down Daisy. Mind his hand.'

'Violence is very bad.'

'I agree with you, Mun. But don't forget what Ghandi said, "there's an element of violence in allowing violence".'

191

Daisy looked doubtful. And ready, like any good Indian, to enter at a moment's notice into the minutiae of a philosophical argument. 'This was in relation to many thousands of Jews being led to their deaths. This great man merely pointed out that to agree with murder by apparent aquiesence was perhaps to reduce pacifism to another extreme. Extremes are bad. The middle path. This is what we believe in.'

'And if one man had had an opportunity to turn off the gas in one of those gas chambers he should have had a try?'

'Yes. Not with violence.'

'They'd have shot him as he walked over to the switch.'

'Alas, yes. But this brave man would have tried.'

'Right. Well, talking about gas, there's gas on board here.'

Daisy spread his hands. He thought Mal meant the product itself or its emissions. Every tanker seaman knows about that.

'No. There's one tank on this ship filled with a lethal nerve gas. Haven't you noticed that the number five centre tank is sealed.'

He nodded.

'It's a chemical warfare product from the USSR being carried illegally to the Gulf where it will be pumped out over the sea.'

Daisy's own reaction to this news was a model of the moderation he had just been advocating. He said quietly, 'How do you know this?'

'You know my job Daisy.'

He did.

'We're here to stop it.'

'How?'

Mal explained to him. I watched his face. In an odd way he and Mal were very alike. Also small and slight physically, Daisy's mild demeanour concealed a similar spark. There was no doubt at all that he would help us. He wasn't as confident as Mal was about his ability with the electronic mechanism of this particular ship. He was quite friendly with one of the electrical engineers. He'd go and chat with him during his watch.

'When it comes to actually doing the job Daisy?'

He answered at once. A sort of diffident enthusiasm seemed to have completely obliterated his pacifist commitment.

'Count on me,' he said. 'These villains shall not get away with it. We will defeat them utterly . . .'

I knew it had to be a quotation.

Chapter
26

WHILE DAISY GOT on with his homework we had another twenty-four hours of halcyon sailing towards Armageddon. The ship had moved back into a warmer climate and a couple of days' hot sun had already tanned my body unevenly over the scarcely formed scars. When I looked in the mirror in my room I realised I no longer outwardly resembled a tidy London broker: more a nineteenth century Dorset pigman who had had a particularly hard winter and then was left out to dry in a hot wind. My hair which had grown so raggedly after the hospital treatment had been cut by Sven, the ship's barber, in one of his sober intervals when he had not been quite sober enough. The plastercast was black with oil and dirt and reinforced with a motley criss-cross of adhesive bandages over the crack. If Anderson and Kolnyses looked, to the discriminating eye, like villains, I was a close runner up.

Except for one small job, Mal and I had had no work to do outside of our normal ship's duties. This one item was our radio communication system. Because the ship's radio satellite mast had been destroyed in the storm, modifications had been carried out on the bridge which Mal got wind of via Daisy. In order to be able to use our equipment when the time came and without detection from the bridge, a certain small mechanism similar to a bugging device had to be planted magnetically on their receiver. This involved going up on to the bridge which could only be done by a seaman on duty. As messmen, Daisy and I from time to time got calls from the bridge for coffee so we had the necessary access. Our plan was to go together and I would create a diversion by spilling the contents of the tray to give Daisy time to plant the device while the officer's attention was elsewhere.

We hoped we'd get a call during the third officer's watch because as well as coinciding with the last hours of our duty rosta, Scoulos was such an ass.

We'd had more than our fair share of Frenchie's tantrums in the kitchen that stint, owing to an accident that he'd had with some precious *pâté de foie gras* left out on the table to thaw, and eaten by the ship's cat. The very fact that this ship had a cat was something I had been unaware of for two days. Various members of the crew were so fond of the blasted thing they drew lots for whose turn it was to have it sleeping on their bed and it was already as fat as a pillow without eating poor old Frenchie's *pâté*. I think he would have poisoned it if he'd dared, but the crew would have lynched him.

When the moment came to take up the coffee I said, as I put down the blower, that there were four officers on the bridge whereas in fact there were only two. This passed as a good enough excuse to Frenchie, who was always drunk by that hour anyway, for a well loaded tray and two men. In fact when we walked on to the bridge deck Scoulos had only the second engineer with him – a bad choice but apparently only in there for company. I walked across the carpeted expanse with the tray, Daisy behind me. Scoulos was smoking a cigarette, his silly, handsome profile turned looking out to sea and incidentally towards the console line up, part of which was the radio. The engineer was standing facing the door.

As I said, I walked across the carpeted expanse with the tray. I rested the left side on my plaster cast and gripped with the right. The whole room was at least forty feet from side to side. I marked the spot with my eye where I planned to trip.

'Put it there.'

The engineer cut me short, pointing to a navigation chart table.

It was now or never. I made to turn, caught my right toe

behind my left heel, stumbled and perhaps overdid it. The contents of the tray flew through the air creating more than a slight diversion since a pint of coffee landed on the immaculate Scoulos. It was a good throw as I hadn't really been allowed to get close enough. He screamed like a girl, and they were both busy shouting at me for the next five minutes which gave Daisy all the time he needed. I wish I hadn't made quite such a mess because two of the cups smashed landing against the stem of the control desk and I was down on my knees with cloths and broken china, soon joined by Daisy, for longer than I'd have wanted.

Eventually we got away.

'Did you manage OK?' I said in the lift.

He was having a theatrical fit of laughter. 'Very good Len. Oh my gosh, the face of Scoulos.'

'Good wasn't it. And you had enough time to fix the clip?'

'Plenty. I could have rewired it.'

We dumped the tray and the remains as fast as we could. Frenchie had gone, the fridges and stores were all locked. We met nobody as we walked along to meet Mal. The ship could have been deserted in the vast waste of ocean with the rhythmic mechanical throbbing of its own heart. The lonely acres of the deck depressed us both or certainly cured Daisy of his extra high spirits.

Mal was in his cabin. 'We're here,' he said, pointing at a place on a chart, as soon as we closed the door. 'By the way, was it alright?'

We told him. He didn't crack a smile.

'What's wrong?'

'Nothing. Nothing Len. Nerves.'

'That'll be the day,' I said.

'We're getting near. Here's where we are.'

He indicated a point apparently another twelve hours sailing from the Gulf of Oman.

'How much leeway have we got? This is what I'm trying to work out.'

'Why?'

'We got to do our job in UMMS. That's night time. If we sail into our area in daylight and out of it again before dark it'll be very awkward.'

'Well, do we?'

'I don't think so. We should be able to pick our own time. What's the best time for getting everybody in their deepest sleep?'

'I don't know,' I said.

'You don't read the Bible, boyo. Three o'clock in the morning – that's when that bloodthirsty lot killed the other lot.'

'Times don't change,' I said.

'Three o'clock in the morning as long as time works out right, we go down. Unmanned machine space. Engineer's asleep. We got the switches all to ourselves. Right Daisy?'

'Very good Mal.'

'We all go down?'

'Yes. But you go to the duty engineer's room.'

'Oh yes.'

'When Daisy disconnects the alarm, just in case . . .' He looked solemnly at both of us, 'Just in case the duty engineer isn't asleep, notices a change of any kind in the engine sound, in case of error.'

'Who's the duty engineer who may be awake at three am?' I said suddenly suspicious.

'Giulio.'

'Giulio!' This must be how sales managers feel when they get the year's accounts and find they've halved the turnover. Or underwriters who lose all the syndicate's money on one ill-considered line. Or brokers who are about to get drowned in the Persian Gulf for nothing. I said inconsequentially, 'Giulio weighs twenty stone and plays patience all night.'

Mal nodded. He sat down on the end of the bed.

'What do I do with him if he does become suspicious?'

'Shoot him.'

I thought he was joking. But why should he be. 'Won't he think it pretty odd, me wandering in on a visit in the small hours?'

'Insomnia mun. He's a friendly chap. Ask him if he's got the cat. He's its biggest fan.'

'Carma was in talking with him five nights ago when you'd just joined. Little Parsee gentleman from Bombay.'

'Alright. Alright.'

'You go in at exactly three am when Daisy and I are in position. Stay with him for about ten minutes – that right, Daisy?'

Daisy nodded.

'Then make your excuses and go. We'll be clear by then. We must all get back to our cabins without being seen by anyone if at all possible. The captain and officers will know afterwards that there has been deliberate sabotage. What they won't know is who has done it.'

'They'll try and find out.'

'They won't have much time.'

That's what I thought as I went off to bed: not much time. Not much time for us.

Chapter
27

THE DAY WENT all too soon. Not a cloud in the sky. None of the expected repercussions from Scoulos. I walked down the deck once. They were gas-freeing No 3 tank again; more trouble with the suction valve. For half of my walk every step took me nearer to No 5 Centre Tank and then for the other half every step took me further away. I couldn't afford to appear to take too much notice of it. Anderson to date had lived up to his promise of keeping his eye on me.

Over on the rail the warm wind of our passage, the white of the water alongside, the halcyon expanse of quiet space should have been soothing but I was beyond it. Every nerve felt exposed to the unsheltered contact, as if laid outside the body's warm and lush cocoon even the beams of the sun grated and the air was like sandpaper. I reasoned with myself. But I saw only the thin wedge of land which had appeared on the forward port side, which was like a matchstick head in the morning, a thin line in the afternoon. Mal's timing would be perfect. It would be three am.

We turned in that evening after dinner and our stint with Frenchie. I tried to sleep and succeeded for an hour or so. When Mal knocked on my door, I dressed in the dark in my grey trousers, black seaboots and navy shirt. In the pocket of my trousers I put the small gun he gave me which had been packed with the radio kit and wireclippers. It was an awkward size. I had to put the silencer separately in my left pocket. Rather than use the lift which made a whining noise we went down the darkened stairs. The ship, of course, was not silent. The thud of the engines and the perpetual vibrations got louder as we reached the bottom. The lift descends into the engine room itself but the stairs land you up at a metal door much like the back exit from the cinema at night. We paused for a moment together and then slowly Mal opened the door about twenty inches and we slid in. The damage the storm had caused and the running repairs which had been kept up since might always mean the presence of someone on emergency work at night. There was no-one. The vast space, brightly lit, was unoccupied. I followed Mal and Daisy over to one of the electrical control panels.

'Keep looking around,' Daisy said to him. 'Don't forget someone might always come in.'

He took the pliers out of his pocket and I walked over to the door past the silent gaps between the machinery and him as he positioned himself before the board with its maze of wires and fuses.

'Right then. You know where the duty engineer's room is. Five minutes from now I'll cut the wire.'

I walked through the door that led from the engine room to the passage where the duty engineer's room was located. There was a light on in the passage. No-one stirred. Except me. I stood outside the door. Christ, was it the right one? There were two other doors. I was on the point of going back and double checking with Mal when I realised the doors were actually marked. I cursed myself inwardly, looked at my watch. I remembered almost too late that I had to assemble the silencer on the pistol. I took them both out and clipped the extension on to the barrel. I held the gun loosely in my left hand by the silencer so the length of it lay up against my wrist, and pulled the sleeve of my jersey right down over my fingers. If it became necessary I could reach it out with my right hand and use it.

I checked my watch again, assumed an expression of wakeful late night friendliness and knocked on the door. It wasn't locked and I walked in without waiting for an answer.

Giulio sure enough was playing patience and looked up with surprise. When he saw me he smiled in a friendly way and said. 'What you doing Len? No sleep tonight?'

He wore glasses and a huge white teeshirt crumpled loosely over the folds of his great chest and stomach as he leaned forwards in the chair.

'Nuffin much,' I said. 'Life's too restful. Can't sleep. 'Ave you got the cat?'

'Sit down,' he said. 'Lily's on the bed. I won her from Scatts at poker.' He smiled a happy smile and the cat carried on snoring. I wanted to look at my watch. I made a pretence at looking around in an interested sort of a way.

He said again with a remonstrating smile, 'Sit down. Why you no sit down?' A bell rang! I jumped out of my skin but he put a finger to his lips and picked up the phone with an urgent shake of his head at me.

'Yes sir. Everything OK sir. Yes sir.' He put it down. I was having apoplexy.

'Don you worry Len. You're not suppose to be here but don you worry. I won't mention it. This was the damn Scoulos from the bridge checking up.'

I had not so much sat down as collapsed.

'Wanna play?'

'No thanks mate,' I said.

'Come on. Come on. Is easy. We'll play two man jack.' He started peeling off the cards and laying down a pattern explaining it to me and talking in a mixture of learnt Cockney and Italian. The extraordinary thing about ships' crews according to Mal, and certainly this one bore it out, was that however mixed in race and however rudimentary their capacity, they communicate in English. Other languages of course are spoken in groups of particular nationality but the common language (although there frequently isn't one) is English. One ship going down the coast of Central America with a mixed Asiatic crew, not one of whom could read the Day Board, steamed for seven days through an impenetrable fog owing to complete lack of communication and the miracle was they hit absolutely nothing and emerged unharmed miles up a river near Managua.

'Now you.'

I turned some cards over. I managed a glimpse of Giulio's watch. It had already been five minutes.

'In Milan where my family lives – oh Len! You're missing one. Look!'

He completed a whole run. His glasses were getting steamed up. He took them off to wipe them.

'Your arm is hurting you tonight? You don use it.'

'Yep,' I said, 'a bit.'

'In Italy where I live,' he said, 'we have a very good doctors. Most famous of all in Milan is Firenze. Father and five sons is all doctors. Even the daughter, very beautiful. Play the jack now.'

'How do you know I've got one?'

'Expert. I am an expert.'

I looked at the back of the card carefully.

'Wha's 'er name?'

'You see it will come out now.' He laid down another five cards. I waited while he studied the two piles of cards lying face down. He was having trouble reading the scratches he'd made on the back of them. I smiled to myself at the idea of the fellow spending all night cheating himself at patience. At last he made his mind up and unleashed another successful run.

'What did you say?'

'Wha's 'er name,' I said, 'the doctor's daughter's?'

'Domeniça. Everybody knows. One year, must be two or three years ago, she nearly died. The very Pope himself gave the father special dispensation to operate on her for his great love of her and his brilliance as a surgeon. All the newspapers had pictures and the people who loved this man praying for her. She lived.'

'Sure,' I said.

'You know? You read about this? It was in the English papers?'

'I can't remember very clear,' I said.

'The throat.' He clutched his own throat just where a bunch of black hairs escaped from the rim of his teeshirt. 'Here. Inside.'

It was time for me to go.

At that moment the bell from the bridge rang again.

Giulio put down his cards, changed his mind, laid one on the pattern, couldn't resist laying another and then with a rush one more and picked up the receiver. He put it down after a brief conversation like before and looked at the cards with regret.

'What you saying Len blooding 'ell. That was going to work out. I got to go.'

'Wha's up?'

'This a ship! Always in a hurry a hurry. Tankers are all the same. But this one – something else!' He stood up.

'I'd better go,' I said.

Everthing was very still. No vibration noises. Suddenly he'd realised. He stood an instant, locked, listening, like a bird.

'Santa Maria in . . .' He slapped one huge hand flat on his heart as if feeling it, his face aghast.

'I'd better go,' I said again. 'Trouble?'

'Yes. Go quick. Mama mia!'

I got to the door. He followed me out and shot through into the engine room and I went as fast as I could the opposite way. I took my boots off and ran in my stocking feet down the passage round the maze to the stairs up like a rabbit who's heard the farmer's tread at the corner of the hedge. Two steps from the top I forced myself to stand motionless and listen. It was unnaturally silent. No engine noise. Then a distant bang. I ran for the promenades that lined the crew's cabins, flung open the door of mine and pitched myself on to the bed.

Chapter
28

DAISY MAY HAVE cut the essential alarm but there were others. The whole ship, five minutes after I reached my cabin, exploded in a cacophony of alarms. Every light came on including in my own cabin but they were quickly doused again presumably to save the alternators and the available distilled water. Trying to do what would be natural, I jumped out of bed but threw off some clothes rather than put some on. That way when the inevitable officer appeared in the door he saw a man half dressed and could assume which way round it was. The remainder of the night was spent running backwards and forwards simultaneously yelled at to do emergency work and threatened with incarceration; the same man wanting to both use and immobilise you. Every man on that ship from Kolnyses to myself, from the captain to the most inexperienced seaman running around like termites at their wit's end. One message came across loud and clear from the start. The officers knew that it was sabotage and just as soon as they could spare the time they'd comb through the men with drastic zeal and there'd be no nonsense about legality or tempering justice with mercy.

Dawn broke soon after the outbreak of the emergency. First light showed the coast of the Oman in a colourless slab some miles off the port side. Instead of the absolute silence of a totally disabled engine the framework of the ship vibrated with machine noise, weak and febrile like a trapped insect but still there.

'What's happened Mal?' I asked him as soon as I saw him in the melée. 'Why's the engine still running? Didn't the boiler blow.'

'Of course Mun. It's not the main engine. It must be the small auxiliary, the Donkey boiler. It won't be strong enough to stop the ship's momentum and keep us off those sandbanks.'

'No?' I wasn't so sure. It felt as if something was going wrong with our plan as well as those of Kolnyses.

The bosun was ordering us down the cat walk along the centre of the deck.

'They can't empty the water filled tanks,' Mal said. 'If the engine's not working there's no way of recycling inert gas into the empty spaces Mun. They're risking an explosion.'

'But if they lighten the ship and raise the hull in the water they may clear the sandbank. That's what they've got in mind.'

They weren't going to be worried about pollution either. The ship's momentum, which continued for several miles after the engine had cut off but with steadily diminishing control of steering, had slowed to almost nothing. But the feeble efforts of the auxiliary engine were not enough to reverse her against the tide. They were continuing to inch forward instead and trying to turn the ship away from shore. But with so little speed even that colossal draught couldn't get up enough leverage.

We reached the forward tanks. The placing of the water filled and empty tanks was carefully calculated when the cargo was mainly discharged in Durban to maintain a balanced load. We were now to empty two, one forward and one aft. I had no idea how the various stopcocks and winches worked, but if you're shouted at loud enough you soon realise that you're meant to turn a wheel anti-clockwise. They kept us busy. It became daylight. Slowly and beautifully the sun spread a paradisical light over the sea, like a huge flower gradually spreading its petals into a wider and wider arc. Also gradually around the hull of the ship a wider and wider trail of glutinous oil spread on the surface of the sea as some residue was washed out with the water. The radio controls of the officers sputtered in their hands as they exchanged instructions and information with the bridge. It was not broad daylight and still, in spite of the unremitting activity of the men, the inactivity of the engines made themselves felt in the flaccid near silence of the open waters.

When two tanks were empty they were closed just as they were. Mal had been ordered below. I volunteered to go to the galley although I was off duty. I wanted an excuse to get closer to the activity on the bridge to know the state of progress. I glanced in satisfaction at the satellite radio equipment as I passed it, still broken. Ordinary radio contact would never be fast enough for Kolnyses to call in a reserve ship on time. Down in the galley the atmosphere of panic was less.

'Where've you been Daisy?' I said as soon as I saw him. 'They've rushed Mal off to the other end of the ship and I still haven't had a chance to catch up.'

'Beautiful,' he said with deep satisfaction. 'Oh yes Len.'

'What did you and Mal do then?'

'Len, I disconnected the wire. That was OK. Then together we drilled a hole in the main condenser and the salt sea water should have gone through to pollute the pure distilled water inside the condenser.'

'And it did?'

'Yes,' shaking his head negatively in the time-honoured Indian style, and smiling broadly. 'Right on target.'

'So if we can just get about a mile nearer land either the ship will ground or Mal can make radio contact.'

At that moment the engine stopped completely and all the light in the galley went out.

'Watch out Daisy. Don't sound so excited man.'

'I'm sorry Len. I'm sorry,' he said.

The lights went on again almost immediately, powered by the emergency Diesel generator on deck not smashed in the storm.

'Don't the alternators have to have steam? If the engine's not working and the boiler's blown can they produce distilled water with the Donkey boiler?'

Daisy made a gesture of tearing his hair.

'Look here. I'm going up to the bridge.'

The second cook had neither Frenchie's talent nor his temper. He also seemed to think that I was a perfectly acceptable man to serve up the officers' food. At this time of day it consisted merely of getting food up to the officers' mess and laying it out on a heated tray. The mess was empty when I went in. No-one was having time to eat. I put fresh cloths on two of the tables and switched on the plate heater. There was a sudden rumbling thud from way below deck. I looked at my watch in quick alarm. But the engine had stalled again before I had had time to read the dial.

I left the messroom still empty and it was in the passageway outside that I came upon two officers frog-marching Giulio along under the supervision of Anderson. They had Giulio by his arms and as they pushed him through the door of the wardroom one of them kicked him, hard, in the thigh. I heard rather than saw him fall forward into the room. Anderson was watching me.

'Ye looked very shocked Tanner.'

I said nothing. He stood motionless by the door and then came back a couple of paces towards me. He was a bit shorter than me but not so short he couldn't look right into my eyes.

'Why do ye look so shocked Tanner?'

'Not me sir,' I said.

'Yer Nanny telt ye never to tell lies.'

'Wot yer mean sir?'

'Someone on this ship is not what they seem Tanner.'

'Ah said before sir, p'lice got no business with seamen.' I hoped to goodness I was sounding as obtuse as I intended. Giulio inside the room let out a yell. I quelled the flash of rage that leapt into my eyes. Anderson kept smiling but there was a poison in his eyes too, as if the irises were washed in acid.

'I feel there is something between you and me Tanner,' he said, slowly. 'Just now I haven't time but I'll turn my attention to it in a wee while. Don't ye try to run away.'

He thought it was a good joke and so in a way it was. I smiled at him as he went sideways through the door with his eyes still on me. Never let a snake see that you're worried. I'd started to walk down the passage when a door opened again and a voice shouted, 'Messman! Bring coffee to the wardroom.'

I said, 'Yes sir.'

It was Scoulos. I went back to the messroom, reloaded my tray with the coffee cups and carried them across to the wardroom. I marched over to a side table, put down the tray and began to pour out. There were four of them. Anderson, Scoulos and two others. And of course Giulio. The poor chap had a cut across his face and looked completely bewildered. He was explaining to them that he really couldn't be held responsible. Someone had obviously cut the wire of the alarm precisely in order to keep him out of it, and then the same person had sabotaged the engine. Scoulos looked impatiently over at me as I poured the coffee. Anderson asked Giulio, and I got the impression he wasn't asking for the first time, if he had seen anyone around during his period of duty.

But Giulio shook his head. He didn't look at me. I doubt if he would have said anything even if I'd not been there. Nobody. Not a soul. I handed round the coffee and left the room unobtrusively. No-one challenged me. Just before I closed the door I looked back and the four men all happened to be turned away from me while Giulio looked up. It gave me the opportunity I wanted. I smiled at him and made a gesture of thanks and good luck; and then I slipped out and away.

In the Galley Daisy had been joined by his friend Carma who had also sought refuge from the deck in a bit of overtime.

'Have you heard, Len?' he said as soon as I put the tray down. 'They say that it is sabotage; that the alarm was first cut and then the pump was drilled.'

'Who'd want to do that?'

'They do not know. But they are determined to find out. I am most concerned. My friend Giulio, who you know, is under suspicion. I will leave this ship at Dubai. These are violent men. Something is wrong.'

At that moment there was a low grating sound and unmistakably one could feel the ship's keel graze the bottom of the sea bed. Daisy stood absolutely rigid.

'What was that?'

'Touching bottom?' I said.

There was another gentle massive rubbing sound like a huge body scuffing slowly against something in the dark. And then the alarms broke out again.

'My God,' Daisy said running for the door. I followed after him and up to the deck. It was a case of back to the forward tanks and go through the same procedures to discharge water into the open sea. This time the forward and rear tanks were to be completely emptied. It had become very hot on deck. The oil that the ship had discharged along with the water now lay in patches all around under the hot sun. The coastline on the port side was about a mile away. No more. And yet no other ship or small boat was to be seen as yet. By my watch it was now half past nine. When the forward and rear tanks were empty the levels were checked and the keel was for the moment free. The order was given for the water jets to be turned on to wash the tanks, but at half pressure as the unavailability of inert gas from the engine meant the atmosphere wasn't stable enough to risk more. Hoses were linked again and the sludge was pumped out into the sea to join the rest. The ship had an unpleasant feel on the water. Although the surface was calm, glassy even with our contribution of oil, a sensation of almost secretive shifting and lurching irregularly made itself felt.

Until that is, with a sudden roar, the engine sprang back into life. The crew standing on deck shouted with delight, the hoses were uncoupled, the mixture of oil and water that surrounded us was churned up in a brown foam and very slowly incredibly we moved off. The three of us lined up with the rest of the men on the rails and watched aghast.

'How could it have happened?'

'We're not engineers mun. Daisy done very well with 'is electrics but they must have some damn clever bloke down there with the boiler.'

'How about the radio. Why can't we make contact yet?'

'We got to disable her, mun. The salvage vessel can't chase a perfectly healthy ship over the sea.'

'How could they get the boiler to flash again after it had blown?'

'They must have stopped it before it got that far: switched

off and used the auxiliary, had a plentiful back-up supply of distilled water, found the hole and mended it. Jowl, how do I know mun?'

Fortunately the ship was pointing the wrong way and willynilly moved towards land. There was a chance she'd beach herself still before enough leverage could be exerted on the water, or that the sand banks we'd scraped over already might catch her coming out on a higher curve. The crew lined the rails watching. At the moment it looked as if our projected course would hit the coast but the engine was now in reverse. With a sensation of bitter disappointment I watched the land recede.

'Don't smile so broadly mun. They got binoculars on the bridge.'

'Do you think we'll make it?'

We started out to sea, or rather to land.

'Touch and go.'

For full five minutes without a word said the massive bulk of the ship glided slowly backwards. There was a sudden splutter of unintelligible command on the officers' hand-held communication sets.

'Changing course,' Mal muttered. 'Turning into the Straits.'

'But I still can't see it.'

'Ship takes time mun. Too late to turn the handle to the left just when we're there. These things are steered a mile or two ahead of themselves like an upsidedown shadow.'

I liked his terminology; a mixture of cosmic measurement and driving a mini around London. Suddenly a loud grating echoed through the hull. Breathless we stood and waited. All along the rail the crew, unmoving in spite of the intense heat, craned forward, rigid with expectation. Under your feet you could literally feel the gigantic contact of sand and iron. Another shuffling sound under our feet wound up the collective concentration visibly along the line. Another. 'We're grounding,' I thought, 'bloody hell, we've done it.' I could feel myself breaking out into a sweat of relief. Too soon. It wasn't enough. There was another grinding shove and the ship plunged forward into what must have been a deeper

210

channel. The land swung round another cog. Not a sound could be heard except the steady roar of the engine. The men didn't stir. Another crackle of radio from the bridge. An officer raised his set to his mouth and spoke. The open space consumed the substance of his response.

'What did he say?'

'All Greek to me boyo.'

But it was over. The land straightened out along our side and the tension on board snapped in a collective yell of triumph. The tanker went forward towards the open sea and far behind, black on the glittering surface of the ocean, the guilty patches of oil that marked our passage swelled out in the sun.

'Hell!'

'Win one lose one.'

'They'll still lose seven and a half hours. They can't make that up. There must be something like fourteen hours more sailing before the Straits. It's eleven o'clock now. That's one am the 16th August. They'll be late; perhaps too late.'

All round us the deck had cleared except for one or two seamen and one of the navigation officers speaking to the bridge.

'It's cutting it very fine.'

I glanced at the forward tanks. We walked to Mal's cabin and I sat in the armchair while he had a shower and changed. I was worried. There was too much time. The captain and his men would have ample opportunity to comb through suspects. I told Mal about Giulio.

'We'd better keep out of the way then.'

'They know where to find us. I'm on duty,' I looked at my watch, 'now.'

I stood up.

'Anderson too.'

'What about him?'

I recounted our exchange outside the wardroom.

'As soon as you're off duty in the galley meet me here,' Mal said. 'No better still I'll come down to the galley. At what time? Two o'clock?'

I remembered also to pass on Daisy's information about

Carma. However, we both underestimated drastically the extent to which Kolnyses and his men were determined to discover the identity of the opposition on board. Although we had made precautionary plans to stick together as much as possible, Mal, as he explained later, discovered almost as soon as he went into the crew's mess how much the atmosphere on board had changed. It was not that it had ever been a comfortable or friendly ship where relations between officers and men were concerned. But relations between the men had been relaxed before. Now each seaman was being treated like a criminal, called in rotation for questioning by the officers. Mal immediately went over to a group of men he had been working with. The group included Claudio Ponza the Italian who prayed so much. They were anxiously discussing Giulio whose disappearance was all too easily explained. A junior officer came into the room at intervals and shouted a name. Each man had to go up to the officers' wardroom. They were scared. Seamen are meant to have a strong psychic nature and although most of the crew weren't seamen in much of the true professional sense, in this quality at least they seemed not to be lacking. They were aware of the villainous character of the officers, and of the fact that whatever lay behind the sabotage of the engines, more lay behind the frantic reaction of Kolynses and his men. Speculation was rife on what that might be, but the favoured opinion was that one of the least popular officers had done it from drunkeness or for reasons of his own.

For my part, the galley was much the same as it had always been. Frenchie didn't care a damn about anything that went on on board except food and his own private drinking. His temper had very sightly improved towards myself since he had discovered my rudimentary interest in French cuisine, and towards Daisy since I'd explained to him that if he continued to be too abusive I'd smash his private drinks supply.

There was the usual stampede to produce the food and no time for conversation on other matters. The time passed quickly and Mal made his appearance before I had finished my chores. Frenchie was in an affable mood and made him sit down. He seemed not particularly to have noticed all the fracas on board. Perhaps even the alarms could not penetrate his drunken sleep when he was away from the kitchen and his uselessness for any other function had been recognised by the officers. I'd guarantee that if there was a man who could positively not cope with turning a stopcock or linking a hose that man was Frenchie.

Daisy and I ate our lunch at the butcher's block in the centre space where Mal and Frenchie drank to keep us company and Lily foraged for scraps. It was a calm interlude. Frenchie talked about Dijon and the All Blacks – his favourite subjects after food – and Daisy interjected anxious comments about Carma and the ship's officers. It was a calm interlude alright and like all calms should be, it was well and truly followed by a storm.

The first was a message from the bridge. They were looking for Mal. Was he in the galley?

'What have you done?' Frenchie asked when he hooked up the speaker and from its tipped up position swung his chair back level with the table.

'Nothing,' Mal said. 'They're questioning everyone.' He stood up.

'I will come with you,' said Daisy.

'You can't Mun. They're having men in one by one.'

'You come too Len,' Daisy carried on taking no notice. 'Three is better than one. They have no right to interrogate us like criminals.'

I looked at Mal. Perhaps it was a good idea.

'Carma can come as well and Sven.' A deputation might hamper them. Anything for time.

'We'd better hurry up.'

I swallowed the last of my wine as it happened to be a Leoville Lascasse and followed them to the lift. The most likely place to find other members of the crew at this time was in the recreation room adjoining the mess. There, sure enough, in a still anxious speculating group most of the men were gathered together. Daisy spoke to them like a born rabble rouser. Carma, Sven, Claudio, da Silva, another Goanese, Daisy, Mal and I finally went up in the lift to the captain's suite and knocked on the door. I was still wondering how much of a good idea this was. I looked at my watch. Anything that killed time was good – might it not have been better to let Kolnyses work his way through us all one by one. At the same time, Daisy was unstoppable. He was obviously a thwarted strike leader or future politician. His extraordinary version of English, combining such a sophisticated vocabulary with naive grammar rolled off his tongue in grand phrases that at first took Kolnyses aback and rendered him speechless. But the spell was broken by Anderson, bursting through the door in mid-sentence.

He stopped. 'What's this then?'

Daisy, in a dignified and gentle posture reminiscent of Ghandi, turned his head to Kolnyses to let him have the floor. And he took it. With full-blooded relish the lying bastard said that the ship was carrying a very valuable supply of high technology medical equipment. It had been ordered by the Sheik of Kuwait in an effort to save the lives of a number of people desperately ill with Legionnaires' disease or 'some of the such which' as my mother used to say. And for probably religious reasons the dissident member of the crew was determined to delay the ship until it would be too late.

Pretty good, wouldn't you say! Did he think of it just off the cuff or have it lined up ready? Daisy was pulled up in mid-gallop.

Sven said, 'But this is very wrong. I would not do such a thing.' He turned round slowly on his feet as he said it as if addressing the four points of the compass.

'And what do you think, Mr Turner?' I didn't spot the reversion to my name. I tried to frown a bit and look reflective. Anderson, every time he spoke to me, flexed the skin around his eyes in a way that caused a long fold to form under his lower lid.

'D'ye think an Englishman – a Lloyd's broker perhaps – would have such an incentive?'

I wasted no time on surprise or speculation. I bent my left elbow behind my head and swung the cast sideways catching Anderson a crashing blow on the left ear. Simultaneously with my right hand I opened the door. Also at the same time Scoulos fired a largish hand gun of a type I'd never seen before and wondered where he'd kept it.

Daisy said, 'My God!'

And I was standing on the outside of the door with Mal who had somehow acquired Scoulos' gun.

'Run!' he said.

'Where?' I followed after him. He raced down the stairs. 'The deck. The deck.'

I grabbed hold of him for a breathless second. 'Listen Mal. We're got to hide somewhere. Empty tank.'

'Last resort boyo. Don't like brain damage. Follow me.'

We were not exactly alone. The crash of our pursuers' steps made the stairs echo again in every fibre of their metal treads. I raced along behind Mal not knowing where he was aiming for. I thought we were on the lower deck but I could have miscounted. I wish I'd had time to inform the men about the advanced medical technology.

'Hang on Len.'

We'd reached a rectangular metal frame – a hole in the wall, goodness knows where. Mal crooked his hands over the upper lid of it, swung his legs and disappeared. I said a prayer and did the same in so far as my left fingers could clutch something for a fleeting second only. It would have been helpful if I'd known what to expect. I imagined some sort of floor, or drop, but it was a laundry shoot. At the bottom I didn't try to regain my balance or stand up but lay instinctively as still as a corpse, making no sound. My instinct was right. We had got just enough ahead of the chase. There was a rattle of feet above and then they stopped. I still didn't move. After a moment they went on. For now, they had missed the hole in the wall. After another motionless pause I gathered myself together and regained my balance although still sitting at an angle on the slide.

Mal said, 'You got real talent Mun. I didn't have time to tell you but you knew how to do that.'

'Thanks,' I said.

'I'm going to smoke a cigarette.'

To my amazement this man who'd never smoked in front of me and to my knowledge didn't possess the equipment took out a cigarette and box of matches and lit up. In the brief flare our cosy corner, a little mousehole for sheets and boiler suits, glowed and went black again. It was extremely dark.

'When people ask me if I smoke,' Mal said in a whisper, 'I'm tempted sometimes to tell them that I do. But only in moments like these. When I know one is coming up I put a packet of fags in my pocket.'

I realised why individuals in war are sometimes happy. It brings genius out in ordinary people. Without a doubt I had grown very fond of my peculiar friend and if he chose to smoke me out in the laundry hole I was really quite happy to put up with it. In the end it took Kolnyses and his men four hours to find us. But they were persistent. I fell asleep. I woke with that odd timing which so often stirs a sleeper moments before some vital contact would have roused him anyway. I looked at the phosphorescent dial of my watch, straining my eyes to focus in the dark. It was nine thirty.

'Mal.'

His voice answered. Whether he had been already awake or not I didn't know. The quietest of whispers was his reply. Voices and steps outside the metal door enclosing us marked the arrival of our pursuers I had no doubt that Mal had the gun ready. Unfortunately I had no weapon except my plaster-cast. I was totally unprepared for the light. When eventually they flung open the door I saw, after hours of pitch darkness, forms in fractured swingsong of voices and events which rendered me virtually harmless. Not so Mal. He must have realised and prepared himself. The explosion as he pulled the trigger was deafening inside our little metal box. By my knees Scoulos folded up like a silly little upholstered deckchair. Even in death he provoked nothing but a hurried comment of dismissal. Not right. Not right. I knew I would come back to it. For now there was nothing to do but run for my life, with Mal behind me shouting in a whisper.

'Up Len. The tank.'

The sudden noise on metal as the chase latched on to our heels was deafening. I raced up the stairs. We emerged from an opening I'd never noticed halfway down the deck on the starboard side. Following Mal's example I dodged from cover to cover. Mal shouted, 'Number three.' He was making for the emptied tank with the faulty suction valve – gas free. He dived past me and swirled the right hand wheel, painted red and just gleaming in the dim lights on deck. I should have remembered. Also, all systems, except the Bons, the Nazis and the Japanese, count clockwise. The tank opened too slowly. We were hidden from observation and from the superstructure by the broken mast of an unused crane system. Mal lay almost flat. There were also very few deck lights.

'Anyone come yet?'

We were well ahead; perhaps because of Scoulos, they had lost us. We disappeared inside and spun the internal wheel system. I was ten or twelve rungs of the ladder down. Mal above me.

After ten minutes I whispered to Mal, 'I can't hold this position. My other arm is breaking.'

'Try turning round and sitting on the rung. Careful mind.'

I thought of it but darkness didn't eliminate my memory of the ninety foot drop. I came out in a cold sweat. Just in time to take my mind off it the deck above reverberated with the heavy tread of several men running. The penetrating crackle of a deck to bridge radio handset, and the one word 'Lights' could be heard and then presumably the deck was floodlit. But they'd missed us for the moment. The idea of the tank didn't occur to anyone yet. Silently we made our way down the ladder. At first I distrusted the solid floor when I came to it; ran my foot over the ground in a radius trying to remember if there had been any platforms or halfway stages. We'd never be able to sit it out for any length of time. The roof of my mouth already felt as if it was coated with oil.

Before there was time to say anything about it there was a deafening clatter as someone spun the wheel on deck to open the tank plate. Mal and I both felt our way cautiously away from the ladder base. With the first crack of light I darted behind a strutt. Mal had also disappeared. As soon as the opening was wide enough Anderson's voice shouted on deck. 'Why is this tank gas free?'

No-one seemed to know. Anderson shouted down the handset.

'The pump failed,' Mal whispered to me. I jumped. I had no idea he was just behind me. 'The pump of the gas system and the valve. I had nothing to do with it.'

The air from the open plate could be felt now. I breathed in with relief. The confused noises from on deck were hard to decipher. The shaft of light from the open plate was painted in a strip down the darkness. Before reaching the bottom it seemed to fade. Just as I was peering at it and listening, the lights inside the tank went on. I drew right back.

We both froze. The opening was so far above we would not have been able to hear at all were it not for the soundbox quality of the empty metal cavern.

A voice boomed shouting down into the tank, 'If ye'r in there Tanner you can come up now. I'll give ye two minutes and then the gas is goin on.'

'They can't,' Mal whispered. 'Don't worry Mun.'

'Tanner! Mister Turner!'

His voice sounded unearthly in the colossal enclosure. We didn't stir. Our advantage lay partly in the fact that they didn't know if we were down there or not and partly in the fact that they couldn't risk our still being alive and fighting on the other side when the ship was attacked at the Straits. Nor, when I thought of it, however remote the chance of any of the crew surviving, was our survival without risk to the ultimate success of the whole enterprise. I was thinking of every reason why Anderson should come down after us. Perhaps just hatred was enough.

Another voice shouted. 'Bo'sun saw them go through the hatch behind the starboard winch.'

Anderson said, 'You go with him and Critas, come with me.'

At last there was a thud of boots on the rungs of the ladder. Mal whispered almost without breath. 'That's it my beauty. You come down here.'

He tapped the back of my sleeve. I looked for the first time round the girder at the two bodies clinging high up on the ladder, and then to where Mal had disappeared into deeper shadow. Soundlessly I also stepped back and kept my eyes on Anderson who could not help signalling his intentions to try and look round by pausing and getting a double hold. When he turned back again I followed Mal further into the shadows.

As the two men reached the bottom we held back out of sight. Anderson with one hand still grasping a rung motioned his companion to silence and stood stock still, raking the suspicious spaces with a catlike attention. The other man hung obediently on the ladder. After a few seconds Anderson removed his arm and climbed down. Every sound echoed in the metal cave. Inches from Anderson's feet I noticed for the first time a dull sheen that I'd forgotten. He moved away from it unaware. With a sudden rush of alarm I looked urgently at the nearer surfaces, trying to memorise where the putrescent tinge of coloured light marked the poisonous residues of gas.

'I see ye Tanner!'

Before I could complete a spontaneous reaction of leaping to deeper cover, Mal seized my arm. His grip was steady and hard as steel. Anderson started to walk stealthily away from us at an angle towards the first transverse metal support. Mal let go my arm.

Critas stood undecided. He drew a knife out of his left pocket. Of course. To fire a gun would explode the whole tank.

'Let's get a run at ye Tanner. And yer friend.'

Anderson stood still again. It was like watching a homing device, half-human in this inhuman place, guided by the smell of malice to its target. One more step and he'd see us. I edged a pace back.

Critas said, 'They're not here.' His voice sounded pathetically young, almost with the scratchy resonnance of early adolescence. Anderson turned to him and Mal said, 'Now!'

He leapt out and the next moment was through the access opening in the transept, myself so close behind him that I was grazed on the face by one of his boots. Critas threw his knife but it hit the rim and by a miracle didn't cause an explosion. It could have made a spark and blown the whole place up but it didn't. My foot slid as I regained my balance.

'Get away Len, get away!' Mal actually grabbed a handful of sleeve and dragged me with him away from the lethal residue that I had just stepped in. But this section of the tank was full of it. As soon as we reached the furthest point away from the access hole and its dangerous fumes I could stop to view the floor and glint after glint of the evil sludge showed a jigsaw of deadly patches. There was a shout from the tank opening way above and Anderson called back.

'Down here. They're down here.'

More men, spiderlike on the thread of the ladder, started the long climb down. If it had been possible to use guns they would have had us easily. Fortunately, since the sparks from discharging a gun would blow up the tank and everyone in it, and the ship, and possibly release the contents of the deadly sealed tank prematurely before the captain and his crew had got away, they were ruled out. I looked at my watch. It was near midnight. If we had not succeeded in fouling the plans for attack by our delays the attack on the ship by the terrorists would be launched any minute now.

'We've got to get out Mal,' I said.

'You're telling me Mun.'

'They're in the second section.'

The voice came from the ladder. I looked quickly up again. While my attention was distracted, Critas had come through the access hole. He was standing in the oil marking us with his knife. I made to run but Mal put his hand on my arm and said, 'No need.'

Critas had bent his arm back like a darts thrower but he didn't release the weapon. For an instant he froze on the brink of death in a strangely classical pose, then moved his forearm in a little arc that was curiously pathetic. The blade fell from his slack hand about three feet away from him, his legs collapsed, his head drooped forward and he slid down on to the floor.

Anderson's voice shouted from the other section, 'Critas!'

'He won't hear you where he's gone to,' Mal shouted back. 'I hope you boys are watching the gas and not being careless like Critas.'

There was an outburst in Greek.

'Shut up!' Anderson shouted.

One man half-way down the ladder started to climb back up. Another unnoticed by us had launched out on one of the wings. I saw him poised high above our heads a second before he threw his knife. He also saw that I saw him. It made him change the tension of his body just as he flicked his arm

220

forward and the combination of the two destroyed his balance. To watch him fall was awe-inspiring. His body turned over in the air some distance below the bridge of the ladder and then slowly opened out. It seemed to take a long time to come to rest as the saying is. His screams still echoed for an instant after he was dead.

'Len,' Mal had run zig-zag to the next transept. I followed him. After the recent uproar a silence had fallen, or almost silence, in the vibrating space. They must have been deciding what to do next. It was then the voice of Kolnyses shouted from the deck.

'Anderson. Get up here.'

A deafening outbreak of shouts of men, running feet and gunfire on deck drowned his words. The raiding party had arrived.

'We mustn't let Anderson get up that ladder before we do,' Mal said. There was more thunder of running feet on deck.

'Hold your horses Mun.'

Three men started to scramble up the ladder. The first six feet or so were masked from us by the partition buttress. The fourth was Anderson. While I was still wondering how to tackle the situation, Mal crouched slightly on his fragile body in a beautiful line of tension and threw out his arm. I knew he had one of the knives. I didn't know he could throw it. The men had their heads down concentrating on the rungs. Anderson, I think, sensed what was coming to him and began to look round but too late. Mal's aim was perfect and true. Like a darts champion he hit a bull's eye. The knife stuck hard in Anderson's throat. He grasped it, grasped the ladder, staggered round, dropped. I stared horrified and fascinated.

'Come on,' Mal said urgently, 'Hold your breath.' He ran towards where the body of Critas lay on the ground. We stepped over him, through the hole and out the other side and started to race up the ladder. About halfway up there was another louder outburst of shouting and running over our heads and then the deafening sound of machine gun fire. The first man stopped and called back, but the hesitation was only momentary. It wasn't exactly safe being suspended in a well of volatile gases watching sparks fly across the opening above your head. And the first three men above were as aware of it as Mal and I. As the first man stepped out an explosion made the deck shake. Frantically the other two followed him, with Mal and I on their heels. There was no danger now of a reception committee under Kolnyses. There was altogether a different scenario to worry about.

Chapter
29

As MAL WHIRLED the closing wheel on the tankhead I surveyed the surrounding scene. On the water nearby burned a huge fire. I realised with a sinking heart that it was the *Chios*. In the combined darkness of night and glare of violence it was hard to make out where we were by the normal methods: by knowledge and guesswork we knew we were in the Straits. As my eyes became more accustomed I picked out flares and small lights that could only be shore lights.

All this took less than five seconds. Just as Mal straightened up about five men in the loose grey combat gear and paraphernalia of the Israeli military, but also wearing huge gas masks, came charging in a surreal group down the deck shouting, for good measure, in Yiddish, 'Get back! Get back! *Lechu achora! Lechu achora!*'

As they swept Mal and me along to the bows, another of their outfit way back at No 3 tank threw something and ran.

'Those are the other two empty tanks,' Mal said.

An explosion, muffled at first and then piercing, ripped that section of the deck apart flinging torn shreds of burning metal high up in the air. The contaminated tank remained intact and the ship hardly quivered on the water. It's not that easy to sink a tanker.

'Did you make radio contact?' I shouted at Mal, 'Before.'

'Yes.'

'Where are they?'

'My God!' he suddenly shouted 'Time release.'

'What's that?'

'They'll have put the contaminated tank on time release. The bridge. For God's sake Mun, follow me.'

There was a burst of shooting but not particularly at us. It was hard to run along the deck – the mess was incredible. And the ship was still a quarter of a mile long. Mal flung himself up the stairs and I after him. The sound of another explosion pounded behind us but we didn't pause to look.

The Bridge was deserted. No Captain on that one. In the ghostly shadows riding above the doomed fabric of the ship the machinery glimmered. Mal ran across the floor with the certainty of someone who knew exactly what he was making for. A facade of clocks with levers had a cosy facia like an old car. Mal bent over it.

'Alright. No panic. Ten minutes to go.' He checked a switch and moved a lever. The light on one of the clocks changed from red to green.

'God forgive me,' Mal said.

'What for?'

'I nearly forgot it Mun. Forgot it. Come on.' As we reached the deck again parts of it were on fire. By its light the sea around us was more brilliantly illuminated. On this side of the ship, looking away from the other burning ULCC, there was much going on that was worthy of our attention. In the first place, Kolnyses and his employees were just descending in the lifeboat helped by one of the invaders, his machine gun slung over his shoulder to leave both hands free. And in the second, about a hundred yards away but drawing closer, a large well-lit stocky vessel flying an Omani flag was preparing to come alongside. At that moment Kolnyses had just seen it. In the confusion and the din his reactions could only be read like the events in a shadow play but they were satisfying to watch.

'It's a salvage vessel!' Mal yelled.

Kolnyses was screaming something to the soldiers so loudly that although we couldn't hear his words the ring of his voice was an identifiable component of the surrounding noise. The soldier shook his head violently and waved his arm then ran.

'Quick,' Mal said.

The combat group had already cleared from the deck, running with urgent force towards the stern of the port side. I raced after Mal, dodging the still-burning metal. The deck was now sunk in at both ends, like the floor of an old house with broken joists, but miraculously the sealed tank containing gas, insulated from its neighbouring tanks, like they all are, had not been damaged. As the soldiers neared the superstructure they fired bursts from their machine guns at random, presumably with the idea of keeping everyone still alive at a distance. Another explosion, less violent but no doubt fatal, burst through the deck behind us. It threw me nearly off my feet. When I regained my balance Mal was just in front of me. Another soldier in front of him already disembarking and halfway down the side of the ship, with his head on a level with the deck, managed to balance on the ropes well enough to lift his rifle and fire at Mal, at the same time shouting, *'Iiurkod! Imshi bsurah!'*

I remember the words precisely.

Palestinian Arabic, not Hebrew. It was slim evidence though, and later no-one took much notice. Mal was caught in a hail of bullets. The last of the soldiers disappeared over the side. The ship's deck lurched, shifting into its wounds. Mal stood. I waited, horrified, for his body to slump forward. It didn't. With something – I must say, an expression of some surprise – he turned, a broad smile on his face. 'Missed!' he said.

I couldn't speak.

'That mast,' he said 'Look. I must have been in exact line.'

It was only about six inches in diameter – one of the nondescript bits of metal standing up on deck.

He was already racing back to the other side. As we ran the sound of gunfire rang out again but this time from the water on the starboard side. The salvage tug had been joined by another. They were trying to get a line on the ULCC but they were hampered by the absence of crew on our decks and by also being fired on by Kolnyses and one of the other men from the lifeboat.

'Get Daisy,' Mal shouted. 'Run Len. They're probably near

the Bridge somewhere. And Sven and a few others. Quick!'

I ran. I came on the crew at last huddled in a group. Giulio's friend was in tears. I shouted to them, 'Come and help. A salvage tug is trying to tow us out. Come and help. Where's Daisy?'

One of the Goanese – I think it was Carma – turned, and as he stepped aside I could see. He said in a dignified almost puzzled tone, 'Our poor friend is dead.'

I shouted at once, 'Come! Come now. Please. On deck!'

They seemed dazed but a few of them responded. Not Daisy though. As they stumbled out I stood by him a moment and took his hand. Carma happened to look back. An expression I couldn't read – it looked almost like relief but I must have been mistaken – passed over his face. I had to go. I laid poor Daisy's hand on his chest. One couldn't touch him without getting covered in his blood.

I ran after the men shouting, 'Starboard bows', as the sound of more shots rang out. Someone had holed the lifeboat. It was sinking slowly. Kolnyses and friends up to their knees in water had several choices of temporary refuge: the salvage tugs, the crippled *Aenaftis*, or a small MTB just coming up alongside with great military neatness and speed. Kolnyses must have been wishing rather passionately that he had not fired on the salvage tugs. There could be no doubt about his role in this fiasco now. As a captain found abandoning ship whilst most of his crew were still aboard he was never going to be an international hero. But as a captain who fired on salvage tugs he was something else.

The other members of our crew who were not watching the drama being enacted below were busy on the bows securing lines from the salvage tugs. As soon as they were established the salvage vessel started very slowly to make way. As the lines tightened the ship at first held rigid in the water as if deliberately resisting. Then very slowly, with an ungainly corpselike drag, she followed reluctantly out into the open sea.

Chapter 30

'THERE'LL BE A lot of disappointed criminals around the world tonight, Mal.'

'My heart bleeds for them Mun.'

I pressed the button on the armrest and let the seat drop further back.

'Watch your glass, Len. I don't want champagne all over my best suit.'

I laughed. He was still wearing the filthy clothes off the ship. Probably the most disreputable couple they'd ever had flying first class from the Middle East to London.

'Poor old Milton was so worried you'd skip,' I said. 'You're lucky he let you have a bath with the door locked.'

I could just see the poet diagonally across the gangway, knocking back his favourite food. He had turned up like the proverbial bad penny in the Oman trying to pretend to the Brendons that he wasn't disappointed.

'What's he going to do with us when we get back to London, that's what I want to know?'

'Nothing,' I said. 'I'm going to be too busy with Lloyd's and Roger to hang about with him. I hope he's got that straight.'

Mal kept his eyes shut, but I could feel him looking at me through the lids.

'And if you think,' I commented in response, 'that I'm

going to allow myself to be frogmarched off by him or anyone else in that useless mob you're mistaken.' But I was the one who was mistaken.

We were taken from Heathrow airport to what was called a 'safe flat'. Safe from whom? There were beds and a change of clothes – our own from Seeb – and decent bathrooms. Even a good dinner and vintage wine. But no phone. And two heavies who behaved like butlers and had trouble not letting their muscles burst the seams of their jackets.

For the time being I had reserves of satisfaction which could tide me over until morning, and for Mal it was the same. But when day dawned again I woke with my mind full of urgency to test out the current climate in the City and by the time James came strolling in at ten thirty I was in no mood for more delay or any more mystery tours.

'FO,' he said shortly, in reply to my questions.

'What does that stand for?' I said. 'Advice to yourself by any chance?' I knew of course that he had meant the Foreign Office.

'Tell him, Mr Harris,' he said. 'You know the form. Let's not give ourselves hangovers fighting the tantrums of some bloody amateur before breakfast.'

I had to laugh. In different circumstances I'd have liked the bastard.

'How long will it take?'

'If it was me, six months and then some. But the nobs are more reasonable. After debriefing you can probably go.'

'We were never briefed in the first place,' I retorted.

'Well you're going to be debriefed anyway, whether you like it or not,' he said with a malicious smile. 'So out. And on the way I'll tell you what I want in return for my cooperation.'

Was that what he called it! We went down and into the waiting car. The driver didn't need any instructions. James pulled down a chair and sat facing us. He composed himself, his eyes taut with their own unique gleam of friendly aggression.

'I just want one thing from you,' he said, and turned to flick open the connecting glass with the driver. I couldn't hear what he said. He turned back.

'Think hard before you answer. What was the actual nationality of the terrorists who attacked the ship? And your word that you will not repeat the substance of our confidential discussion in Piraeus.'

'That's two things.'

'Don't get too damn clever,' he snapped. 'Mr Harris?'

'The nationality of the attackers was Palestinian.'

'How do you know?'

'Their contact with Kasteros before the event.'

'Meaningless. That was another venture. Clothes?'

Mal described them.

'Israeli combat gear. Right!' He paused. 'Language?'

'Arabic.'

'Oh really! You say so. Why do other members of the crew say they heard them shout "get back" in Yiddish,' he said.

'Deliberate, sir,' Mal said. 'I myself heard them shout in Arabic among themselves. And there's the one picked up by the MTB. Ask him.'

'Unfortunately,' James took a packet of cigarettes out of his pocket and carefully lit one.

'Don't bother,' I cut in. 'I can guess. You accidentally dropped him in the sea and he accidentally sunk to the bottom.'

'Speeding up aren't you,' he acknowledged, 'I like a man who learns.'

'Do you mean that, sir?' Mal said, after a momentary pause.

'More or less.'

'Dead?'

'Deadish,' James snarled apologetically. 'These accidents happen. Very disappointing all round.'

'Very.'

There was a pause.

'Who are we seeing at the Foreign Office, sir?'

'Sir Michael Benheim.'

'Indeed.'

Mal's tone sounded as inoffensive as ever provided you were psychologically deaf.

'Sir Michael doesn't like us as you know, Mr Harris.' His tone held a just-discernible nuance of respect. 'We don't want to damage the partnership of Shipping I S and SIS, though, do we?'

Mal said nothing. I could see signs of that making James Milton uneasy.

'Disclosures about our discussions in Piraeus could be badly received.'

'I see, sir.'

'I'm not asking for any favours, but if you want our help in future . . .' Mal smiled in a manner that brought his to a stop. He balanced on the edge of his own last word, motionless, for a full minute then flicked open the window and threw the remains of his cigarette out into the Mall.

'Have it you're own way,' he said. 'But don't say I didn't warn you.'

We had arrived. We got out and walked in silence into the buildings, and in silence followed James through the various checks, across a small inner courtyard, to a suite of rooms impressively panelled and furnished. And empty.

'I leave you here,' James said. 'Sir Michael will join you in a minute, but for me, it's goodbye.' He held out his hand smiling. 'Can't say I'm sorry.'

'I shouldn't think you ever do,' I said.

He laughed. 'Touché. Maybe you'll be on my side next time.'

'There won't be a next time,' I retorted.

He shook hands with Mal, then paused momentarily in the doorway and said, 'I shouldn't be too sure!'

'Len,' Mal said with mocking gloom as he watched the door close, 'I'm very much afraid that he likes you.'

It was mid-afternoon by the time the Foreign Office had finished with us. With every detail written down and signed and some poor weary chap called Cutthorpe onto his second typing ribbon, we were finally free to leave with their blessing.

'I shouldn't be surprised if we get an MBE in the next Honours,' Mal said solemnly, as we stood outside trying to get a taxi.

'What on earth for?'

'Saving the world, Mun.'

'You may laugh,' I said, 'but I bet they won't even give us a tax rebate on our expenses. Come on. Let's get to the City. Here's a taxi.'

In the end he insisted on being dropped off at Fenchurch Street and I arrived alone at Collingham Ward Kaye. The building was still there. The revolving door was still there. I walked in.

'Afternoon Roberts.'

'Good afternoon, Mr Leo.' He picked up his phone as I walked towards the lift. I didn't ask if Collingham was in; if he was still sleeping in his office. When the lift door opened, Jasper Wentworth was standing waiting for me. I saw a brief expression of shock cross his face. I'd forgotten that I hadn't been able to shave because of a burn on my jaw, that I was deeply tanned and that my jacket hung loose over my left arm.

'Sorry about the way I look,' I said.

'Dear boy.' His voice sounded choked. 'We've been waiting for you. Come in. Come in.'

I followed him towards the familiar door. 'Is Roger here?'

'He certainly is. But don't let me spoil the surprise. Come in.'

The door was open. A desk was littered with newspapers. I hadn't seen one for days. I'd forgotten about the press.

'You know the Chairman of Lloyd's.'

I shook hands with him. I couldn't understand why he was there.

'And Ian Crosswell.'

'How do you do.'

'And . . .'

My brother stood up. He had lost weight, looked smaller, as if he had had a serious physical illness. In a really crowded room I might not have recognised him. In the relatively crowded circumstances of this reception committee the problem was different.

'Roger.'

I held out my hand, not knowing if he'd take it. For a moment he hesitated. It didn't occur to me that my own appearance could have anything to do with his reaction. But he made a visible effort, blinked his eyes, and took my hand in both of his.

'Leo.'

I grinned speechlessly at him. For the life of me I couldn't think what to say.

'Sylvie and I,' he began and then stalled again.

But he was alright. I knew it at once. The wear and tear only showed on his body, where it belonged; in his eyes I could see once more the man I knew so well.

'Suspicious bastard!' I said. He threw back his head and laughed. At the sound of his voice the tension in the room broke, and Jasper Wentworth called out, 'Champagne!' in the tones of a referee at some arcane contest registering a goal. My God, we've got some celebrating to do here. Take your glasses. Take your glasses.' Mal would have been glad to hear what followed. Apparently saving the world was nothing to saving Lloyd's and if foreigners think English men are inhibited they should see them just after they've been saved two hundred and fifty million pounds. It was none of that mealy-mouthed pay-off that his lot get given on TV for bailing out what they call MI6.

And as he raised his glass Roger looked at me and said, 'Welcome home, Leo. Welcome home.'